The Tamar Black Saga - Book Four

BY NICOLA RHODES

IBSN: 978-0-9561495-3-4

In the same series

Djinnx'd
Reality Bites
Tempus Fugitive
The Day Before Tomorrow
Faerie Tale
Anything But Ordinary
Rise of the Nephilim
Pantheon

Tomorrow is a fresh start, a new beginning.

Tomorrow, I'll make the change.

Tomorrow, I'll go on a diet.

Tomorrow, I'll find a new lover.

Tomorrow, I'll move to the South of France.

Tomorrow, I'll write my thesis.

Tomorrow, I'll find a new job.

Tomorrow, I'll find enlightenment.

Tomorrow, things will be better.

Tomorrow, all our dreams will come true.

All the things we would do, if only we could get into Tomorrow.

So, what will we do with today?

And I saw when the Lamb opened one of the seals, and I heard, as it were the noise of thunder, one of the four beasts saying, Come and see.

And I saw, and behold a white horse: and he that sat on him had a bow; and a crown was given unto him: and he went forth conquering, and to conquer.

And when he had opened the second seal, I heard the second beast say, Come and see.

And there went out another horse that was red: and power was given to him that sat thereon to take peace from the earth, and that they should kill one another: and there was given unto him a great sword.

And when he had opened the third seal, I heard the third beast say, Come and see. And I beheld, and lo a black horse; and he that sat on him had a pair of balances in his hand.

And I heard a voice in the midst of the four beasts say, A measure of wheat for a penny, and three measures of barley for a penny; and see thou hurt not the oil and the wine.

And when he had opened the fourth seal, I heard the voice of the fourth beast say, Come and see.

And I looked, and behold a pale horse: and his name that sat on him was Death, and Hell followed with him. And power was given unto them over the fourth part of the earth, to kill with sword, and with hunger, and with death, and with the beasts of the earth.

REV. VI. 1 – 8

Who can comprehend the motives of Heaven?
Lao Zi, Spring and Autumn Period.

~ Prologue ~

MANY HUNDREDS OF thousands of millions of billions of …
Look – it was a long time ago, okay? When this lump of rock
we call home was still a sphere of molten fire, and there was no
sentient life in the galaxy, mainly because the parking here is
so lousy.

The gods were arguing. Well, all right, they were not gods,
not as we understand the term; they were more like filing
clerks. They kept the files of the universe in order, adding new
and deleting or archiving old, as appropriate, keeping
everything in its proper place, in this universe and others.

'Sentient life?' said one in a contemptuous tone. 'There is
no sentient life in this sector, Crispin, that's why I took this
job.'

'Ah, but there *will* be Talbot,' said Crispin. 'All the data
predicts it. It will evolve on that planet there.' And he pointed
to the fiery and rather small planet on the screen.

There was laughter. 'There?' said Talbot. 'Please? A
greeble bug couldn't survive on *that*!'

'The planet ...'

'If you can *call* it that,' he was interrupted.

'The planet is cooling, and anyway, you can't argue with the
data – look.' He changed the screen to a complicated table of
numbers and letters. The others looked.

'He's right you know,' said one eventually.

'Damn,' said the one named Talbot, 'is it too late for me to ask for a transfer? Sentient life is such a lot of work. I didn't sign up for this.'

'Neither did I,' said another gloomily.

'I take it we will have both real and unreal life?' said a young one enthusiastically. There's always one – the office junior, who is too clever for his own good, the whizz-kid.

'Yes,' said the second one, 'very good, Matlus. First the real life, will appear, and then the unreal,'

'Wicked!' said Matlus.

'Why is that?' said the one who is a bit slow, and never went on the firm's executive courses (there's always one of these too).

'Sentient life is imaginative Dolus,' explained Matlus. 'So it always creates unreal life, by its unreasoning belief in it, see?'

'No.'

'Crispin? How soon can we expect this life?' asked Matlus.

Crispin referred to the data. 'Couple of billion years, give or take. We should get busy.'

 'Get busy doing what?' asked Talbot.

'Sentient life needs certain things,' explained Crispin. 'Certain moral codes and emotional support, passions and purposes, things like hope, and love and even hate. Things like that.'

'Why?' asked Dolus.

Crispin lost his temper. 'You should know all this stuff. I bet Matlus does. Get him to explain it to you.'

'Teacher's pet,' muttered Dolus.

'I'd be happy to,' said Matlus, smugly.

'Ah! Mrs. Bennt,' said Crispin, as a fat housekeeper, waddled in.'

'You wanted to see me sir?'

'Yes, indeed Mrs. Bennt, we have a lot to do. Do you have the box?'

~ Chapter One ~

DEATH STALKED THE dark streets, hungry and restless. This was because Mrs. Death had thrown him out again, after another row about whose turn it was to wash the dog, or was it take out the rubbish bags? Why had he ever got married?

He headed for the pub.

After several pints of old peculiar, he heard a strange tune playing in his ears. He reached inside his robes. *Damn mobile phones.*

War was coming! – slowly. His horse was, after all, over 2000 years old.

He was in a bad mood. Well he always was, what with being War and all. But today he was in a worse than usual mood, trudging along this dusty highway when he would far rather have been at home watching the football. Still, duty was duty, and he had had the call, so he had to go. He moseyed along muttering under his breath. '2000 years, they couldn't have waited until the World Cup was over! Huh, s'not like I don't have anything better to do.' And so on.

Famine was widespread – he took up two sofas now, and was getting bigger. The boss was going to be furious. Not that he was not doing his job, taking food out of the mouths of mortals the world over, but he was not supposed to be eating it all himself.

And now that the call had come in, how was he ever going to get on his horse? There was nothing else for it; he would just have to lose some weight. It was not as if he did not have a working knowledge of the concept, he was the one who had invented dieting, after all. But the irony, the cruel irony of it – Famine – on a diet.

Pestilence took the stage; the crowd roared. This was the life, sex drugs and rock and roll. That was the way to spread disease these days, and he loved it. He loved it so much that he had formed his own band, the better to facilitate his work. Then he had got sucked in, the bright lights, the adulation, the girls. But soon it would all be over, he had had the call, he was a little sad about that, but at least he would go out with a bang. But first – one last show. He strummed his guitar, gripped his mike and roared over the screaming crowd 'Hello Bug Tussle!'

~Chapter Two ~

THE PHONE WAS ringing. Denny gave it a black look and turned to Tamar. 'It's for you,' he asserted sourly.

Tamar sighed. He was probably right, but she felt that she should at least make a token protest. 'How do you know?' she said.

'Call me psychic,' he quipped. 'I just got this funny feeling in my balls,' he continued, 'like they were being squeezed in a vice, and I thought, who wants to do that to me? And the answer just came to me in a flash. It's ...'

'Okay, okay, very funny,' snapped Tamar, cutting him off. 'You can shut up now.' She glared at him. 'I'll answer it, shall I?' She picked up the phone, which, in violation of all natural probability, seemed to be ringing more insistently the longer it was ignored.

'Hello'

'Oh, hi Mum.' She gave the triumphant Denny an acerbic look, and he retired to the living room and switched on the TV quietly, though, so that he could still hear the conversation, or at least one half of it.

'Yes Mum, everything's fine ...'
'Well, I've been a bit busy...'
'No, of course we aren't fighting ...'
'He's at work, I ...'

'Because I fell in love with...'

'Well I think it's a good reason – Mum, look if you're just going to ... (sigh) okay, okay. How's Dad?'

'No, I'm not pregnant yet. I've only been married for...'

'No, he's not; he's fine, more than fine actually. Do you want the lurid details?'

'That ought to shut her up,' thought Denny. But of course, it did not.

'No he is not infertile; I'm still on the pill, if you must know.'

'Because I'm not ready for a baby yet. I have a career to think about, I'm trying for my Law degree. I don't have time for...'

'No, it is not because I think Denny would make a bad father. Why can't you just... Mum? Mum?'

She glanced up to see that Denny had put his finger on the cradle, cutting off the call. He gently took the receiver out of her hand and replaced it. She stifled her recriminations when she saw his face; it was as white as a sheet.

'Come on,' he said hoarsely, and led her into the living room.

Tamar switched off the television; she and Denny looked at each other in despair. He took her hand and squeezed it with a wan smile.

'So, that's it,' she said. 'We're at war. I can't believe it'

Denny did not say: 'It'll be all right.' Because it clearly would not. He did not tell her not to worry, because she would anyway, and rightly so. All he said was: 'I'll be drafted, I suppose.'

'Will you?' she asked 'I thought World War Three would be a nuclear war.'

'No, not if they can help it,' said Denny. 'Weren't you listening? Besides, they wouldn't be so stupid – would they?' he sounded a little uncertain. 'No, they wouldn't! – Surely? They'd be just as afraid as anyone.'

'Huh, if by "they", you mean the world leaders,' she said. 'Why should *they* worry? They've all got cosy little shelters to run to. They'll be all right.'

This was inarguable.

Denny sighed. The Prime Minister, when making the announcement – in suitably sombre tones – had, by dint of cunning words and phrases, seemed to explain the situation quite clearly. But when Denny went over it in his head, he realised that he could make neither head nor tail of it really. He suspected that the PM could not either. It was perfectly clear from the announcement that the world was at war again, but everything else was vastly more confused.

Tamar looked out of the flat window down at the dirty streets. They seemed so peaceful; it was hard to believe what she had just heard. Everything looked just the same. She had expected to see people running about in panic, army recruiters stalking up the street to take the young men away – to take *Denny* away. She felt her throat constrict. No, not Denny, it just was not possible. They had only been married a year, although they had known each other since school, and had been sweethearts since the age of nineteen. She was not ready to lose him so soon. And Denny was not exactly the military type. It occurred to her – although she pushed the thought away – that he might die. What would she do without him?

Everybody who knew them had been surprised at their romance. She so beautiful and he so – well … not.

She herself had been surprised, in a way, when this love had sprung up out of friendship and engulfed her. People had said that it would never last, that they were too different and that she was a vain and selfish bitch anyway, who would leave him for someone rich and handsome within six months. But she knew that she could not live without him and that he felt the same. They had been in love for seven years now, and Tamar knew that she would rather have him than all the money in the world. This was just as well, since he did not have any money. They would be together forever, she had once thought. Suddenly forever did not seem as certain as it once had.

Denny sensed her thoughts and turned to her. 'They won't come round to the house,' he said. 'It'll be a letter, probably.

'Or a phone call,' he added after a moment's thought. 'And even then, I'll have to pass a physical test.' He laughed. 'And I mean, just look at me. They're more likely to draft *you*.' It was a hollow reassurance, and they both knew it. Denny might look unimpressive, but there was nothing actually *wrong* with him. Even his eyesight was perfect (although people who saw them together had their doubts about *hers*). She knew also, that he would not try to dodge. Denny hated fighting and the idea of war sickened him, but he was no coward.

'They'll make you cut your hair,' she said, just for something to say. She pushed his long fair fringe out of his eyes.

'Just as long as they don't try to make me wash my socks.'

'Ha, even I couldn't manage that.' It was the closest they could come to a normal conversation. They were trying desperately to act normally, as if this terrible thing were not hanging over their lives. It was a weak attempt at comfort.

Tamar allowed herself to be comforted though. She crawled onto his lap, and he put his arms around her. They sat together like this for a long time, feeling helpless, as the shadows lengthened. Then, abruptly, startling them, the phone rang.

~ Chapter Three ~

IT WAS AS DENNY had predicted. Within six months of the announcement, the general forces of the army had been decimated, and the draft was in full swing. There was no sign of an all-out nuclear exchange being on the cards. Apparently, Denny's surmise had been correct, and nobody was willing to go that far – 'Yet,' as Tamar said darkly. Denny had had his papers and he was going to China, having passed the physical with no problems. He faced his fate stoically, and Tamar felt that, for his sake, she could do no less.

She was to remove to the countryside the day after he left. London was no longer safe. It was being bombed every night.

She stood on the platform, tears in her eyes that she could no longer hold back, and a sense of unreality, that must have mirrored that of her forebears who had watched their own loved ones leaving to fight, and sometimes die, in the last war. It was this comparison, as much as anything that made it seem so unreal. She had, learned, as we all did, about WWII at school, and had since seen documentaries on the "Hitler" channel (officially known as the History channel) but nobody had ever thought it could happen again. At least, not in such a similar way. There were differences of course, but not significant ones. All the atomic paranoia of the fifties and sixties, the nuclear paranoia of the eighties, and now WWIII was here, and saw troops going off in trains to fight as infantry or in tanks or planes. Just like before. No wonder she could not quite believe it, it went against everything she had been taught to expect.

The train pulled away, and Tamar was left on the platform feeling lost. The other women on the platform seemed to share her feelings, some of them had children, who ran about unheeded while their mothers just stared at the disappearing train as if in a trance, unbelieving and frightened of a future that had never seemed so uncertain.

Tamar went home slowly to pack her things; her own train would be early in the morning. Civilians were now only able to travel by rail between the hours of four and six a.m. This meant that it would take three days of travelling to get to her friend's home in the country. Staying, no doubt, in "inns of dubious reputation" known to the rest of us as Bed and Breakfasts. Tamar sometimes had a curiously old fashioned way of expressing herself.

Tamar had been popular at school – in that superficial way that attractive, well off people often are. But real friends, the kind that last, had been rare. However, she had stayed in touch with Ophelia Ostley, a dainty fluffy sort of person, who had less reason than most to be jealous of Tamar and who had married into the peerage and, therefore, now enjoyed a sense of superiority over her old friend (who had only married that strange Sanger boy) which completely mitigated any envy she might otherwise have felt, and which she enjoyed immensely. Therefore, they had continued to correspond, and Tamar and an uncomfortable Denny, had been invited to stay at the family pile every year, the better to facilitate the gloating aspect of their relationship.

It was to the home of Ophelia – now Ophelia Ffawlkes Buffington Smythe – that Tamar now proposed to go.

'Of course you *must* come, Darling.' (Always said with a capital D nowadays – Ophelia had not been so aristocratic back at Hill Road Comprehensive) 'Dear Tristan won't mind a bit, I assure you.'

Tamar knew this last bit, and she knew why. It had probably been his suggestion that she come in the first place.

Dear Tristan was a tall, thin aristocratic type – good-looking, Tamar supposed, if you like that type of thing. He had limp, floppy hair and a limp, floppy personality. Tamar felt she had no reason to envy Ophelia.

It was the last place that she wanted to go, but after Ophelia's invitation had arrived ('You *must* come. You really can't stay in London with all those nasty bombs Darling. It's not nice.' For Ophelia, the world was divided into 'nice' and 'not nice'.)

Denny had insisted that she accept. He would feel happier, he said, knowing she was safe.

"Safe" was a relative term, Tamar thought. Safe from the bombing certainly, but not safe from Tristan Ffawlkes Buffington Smythe's wandering hands. (It was not just his hands that wandered. A tall, thin, sparse personage; he seemed to be permanently on the move, restless and twitchy – afflicted with what Denny referred to as the "look arounds".)

Oh well, she had not been known at school as "The Bitch Queen of Hell", for nothing. If *she* could not handle one chinless wonder, however amorous, who could? She wondered if Ophelia knew what she had married. Some people would put up with any humiliation for the sake of money.

~ Chapter Four ~

DENNY WAS FRIGHTENED, more frightened than he had ever been, but not as frightened as the young, dark haired boy – and he *was* a boy – seated next to him. Denny still had enough self-possession to hide his feelings, but the lad beside him was gnawing on his fingernails and looked as if he were about to cry. They were all in the same boat, Denny realised. Being sent to a strange county to fight people with whom they had no personal quarrel, for reasons that they did not understand. What was it to them if Russia had invaded China? And China was now their ally by virtue of being the enemy of America, who had declared war on most of Europe. The edict of a mad President who believed that America was destined to rule the world. This much Denny understood, but not the reasons why. There were American troops now charging through Europe, as once the Nazis had done. Germany was now Britain's ally; all beach towel infractions now forgiven. And Russia, although not allied to America, had taken the initiative from them, and invaded their old enemy of China instead of joining forces with the rest of Europe against America. It was all incomprehensible to Denny. And he was not the only one.

* * *

Captain Jack Stiles stood before the General looking bemused. This was not terribly surprising since he was drunk again. The General was haranguing him about his conduct, but Stiles did not care. For him, the only way to get through the horror of this war was to look at it through the hazy glow at the bottom of a bottle of whisky. It still made no sense, but at least this way it made at least as much sense as anything else did.

The General was threatening to throw him out of the army.

'No such luck,' thought Stiles. It was an idle threat, he knew. They were just too short of troops; and he did not care if he got demoted, he was not a proud man. And it was for this very reason that he made such a good Captain – when he was sober. They could not afford to lose him – unfortunately.

'Report to the camp surgeon,' barked the General, giving up and dismissing him.

'Yesshir,' slurred Stiles and lurched out of the General's tent.

'And try to sober up, man. Before the new troops arrive,' the General shouted after him.

The General put his head in his hands after Stiles had departed. He looked at the orders that had set Stiles off again on this latest binge. He knew how the man felt. He did not understand it either.

Stiles wandered outside into the dreary sunshine. 'More troops?' he thought, 'more cannon fodder.' And did anyone know what the bloody hell this war was about anyway?

~ Chapter Five ~

'THE APOCALYPSE, Dolus, get that through your head will you, that's what this war is all about. Well, it's what it's *supposed* to be about anyway.'

'Supposed to be? Surely it is, or it isn't.'

'Hah! You'd think so wouldn't you?'

'What's the problem then?' drawled Talbot.

'Well, it's just not bloody happening, is it? In your private ear, I'd say there's been a cock up somewhere. I just hope I don't get the blame, that's all.'

'Any reason why you should?'

'Well, if they're not destroying the world as *per spec*, then that can only mean one thing, can't it?' he paused.

Talbot just looked blank.

'It was my responsibility, I suppose, back then,' he mused. 'But I did my bit,' he wailed. 'It's not my fault if it's all gone wrong now.'

Talbot continued to look blank, Crispin was exasperated. Matlus, had he still been here, would have got the point immediately.

'The *box*, Talbot,' he snapped. 'What's happened to the bloody box?'

Talbot took the point. 'You think it's gone missing?'

'How else do you explain it?' asked Crispin wearily. 'The box was always an integral part of the plan.'

Talbot thought about this and then went pale. 'Oh *system failure*,' he said. 'Do you think it's too late for me to request that transfer?'

Dolus looked up from his crossword. 'What box?' he said

~ Chapter Six ~

A GIRL CAME SWIFTLY out of the gloom, with a click of high heels – a tinsel blonde, heavily made up, but pretty. She looked about twenty five. Even in her outdoor clothes, she was very shapely. A man opened the car door for her, and she climbed in.

'I thought you were never coming,' she complained.

'Don't see why,' said he, 'I'm not late.' The car moved off silently, now filled with a cloying scent.

'Maybe I was early,' she shrugged, anxious not to offend. 'I'm nervous I suppose, I've never done anything like this before.' She sounded slightly breathless. Spoke quickly.

The man jerked his head irritably. 'Shut up Cindy,' he told her. 'We've got work to do.'

Cindy subsided immediately. She was not in the least submissive by nature, but this man frightened her, he knew her secret; that was why she was here.

The car pulled up sharply outside what even Cindy knew was a doss house. Another man – a youth – was lounging casually – too casually – against a lamppost. On seeing the car, he strolled over and climbed in the back.

'Hey Tom,' said the driver.

'This her?' asked the youth excitedly.

The man grunted assent. 'Put that cig out, Tommy boy,' he added, 'ain't you got no manners?'

'Sorry Mack,' said the youth.

Cindy closed her eyes and prayed to Hecaté to get her out of this. If only he had not got a video of her she would be okay. After all, without that proof, who would believe him? Although admittedly, never the brightest star in the firmament, she still could not believe that she had been so stupid. Now all she could hope for was that she was good enough to keep him happy; she was so out of practice, and if he carried out his threat … Perhaps people no longer believed in witches, but Cindy knew her history. She believed in witch-hunts.

* * *

Tamar felt lonely in the big old house. Most of the servants, whose company she generally preferred to that of the master and mistress of the house, were gone. Tristan Ffawlkes Buffington Smythe III was best avoided, and Ophelia, who had never been the best company, was now intolerable without Denny as a buffer. Worse, she was expecting, and could talk about nothing else but "baby" and how proud she was to be bearing the next scion of the great house of Buffington Smythe, until Tamar felt like she could scream. Never sensitive to the feelings of others, Ophelia never realised that Tamar wanted to be alone with her anxieties. And probably would not have cared if she had.

Tristan was better, at least he was sympathetic, and it was he who anxiously scanned the mail every day for a letter for Tamar. And it was he who, with great jubilation, brought her the first one after a week of waiting.

She recognised the handwriting immediately, as you might expect, and hugged it to her, tears of relief shining in her eyes.

'An't you going to read it then?' asked Tristan.

'Oh, I will, but I don't care what it says,' she told him. 'I just care that he's alive to write it.'

Tristan nodded and left her to read it alone, sensing, as his wife could not, that that was what Tamar wanted. He bustled Ophelia from the room with a rather overdone carelessness, and a remark about taking care of herself in her condition, and didn't she feel like a lie down, as she was looking a little wan.

Tamar gave him a grateful smile and resolved to try to be nicer to him in future. Not as nice as he would like her to be, obviously, but nicer than previously. After all, it could not be easy being married to Ophelia. She was later to be glad that she had made this resolve.

For now, however, there was Denny's letter.

Oct 25th
Dear Tam,
Just landed in ████████ *I am with the* ██ *th everything is okay, please don't worry. Captain Stiles is our captain, and he is a decent bloke. I feel like I know him from somewhere. I am billeted with a good bunch, but some of them are very young to be here I think. My bunk mate is Karl Morris who is only 17 but is built like a brick out house. I have shown him your picture, and he wasn't half jealous ha ha.*

Tomorrow we are setting out for ████████ *which is where the front line is, but don't worry Captain Stiles says nothing much is happening at the moment. I'm only telling you, because the mail is slower from the front lines and I don't want you to worry if you don't get a letter next week, although I will write. Captain Stiles is a right laugh. He says General* ██████ *is a right* ██████ *but he seems okay to me, just a bit pompous, you know. Speaking of pompous how's Tristan whatsisface? He'd better be behaving himself. Why isn't he up here with us lot anyway, did he tell you? All right for some eh?*

I have to go now, make sure and write to me soon. I love you. And God knows I miss you. Captain Stiles says it'll all be over by Christmas. Well, he says it had better be. Do you recognise the name? I'm sure I know him from somewhere. I love you.

Always, Denny x

* * *

Denny was on sentry duty with Karl. It was freezing cold, and Denny was tired. The push to the front had been postponed for reasons unknown. But Denny suspected that the reason was Captain Stiles, who had exploded impressively when the orders had been confirmed. So impressively, in fact, that the whole camp had heard him. Denny grinned at the memory. He had ranted on at some length about incompetent Generals and raw recruits. Denny appreciated it. Here, at least, was one officer who cared about the lives of his men.

The Captain had been found, later that night, wandering around drunk as a rat and singing loudly about the army and how he didn't want no more of it. 'The Generals in the army are all a bunch of bas-tards – I don't want no more of ar-my life. Gee mom I wanna go home.'

Denny sighed, it wasn't funny really, wasn't it how they all felt? And the Captain had been here from the beginning.

The other recruits had been reluctant to handle him in this state, and so it had been Denny who had propelled him into his tent and put him to bed. He did not feel like the Cap was a stranger for some reason, like the others did. Every time he saw him, he felt a strange sense of *Déjà vu*, which he had played down in his letter to Tamar, knowing her scorn for all such chimera. Anyway, Denny was used to handing drunks, his father had been one, but not like the Cap who was a friendly drunk. Indeed the Cap loved the whole world (except, apparently, the Brass) when he was in his cups; it was impossible not to like the guy. He had probably got drunk on purpose to delay the move to the front lines.

Denny did not like sentry duty; too much time to think, and thinking, in a place like this, could drive you mad. So far, he had avoided it, mostly by taking care of Karl who was prone to thinking. But now Karl had fallen asleep, and Denny did not consider it worthwhile to wake him unless something happened, so he had nothing to do but think.

Captain Stiles stumbled out of his tent to Denny's simultaneous relief and alarm. He shook Karl urgently, but the Cap was upon them.

He treated Denny to a toothy grin. 'Naw, don't wake him,' he said. 'He's a growing lad, he needs his sleep,' and he put a finger to his lips. 'I won't tell.'

He settled down next to Denny and lit a huge cigar, which Denny surmised to be the property of the General.

They sat in a companionable silence for a while. But the Cap kept looking at Denny and opening his mouth then shutting it again. Sometimes he would begin a sentence then stop. Clearly, he had something on his mind.

Denny decided to help him out. 'Do, you know something Cap?' he said, 'I have the strangest feeling we've met somewhere before.'

~ Chapter Seven ~

CAPTAIN STILES HATED the army, and he hated it even more when the new recruits had turned up. There they stood pale and weary in a ragged line straight off the wagon. Waiting for their orders. Good god, he thought, some of them were little more than *children*.

Like that one at the end there, despite his prodigious size, he was baby faced and clearly in over his head. But the one next to him, the skinny undersized one who seemed to be the only thing holding the big one up, although not literally of course, he was officer material if ever Stiles had seen it. A former high-ranking policeman at Scotland Yard, Stiles had an unerring eye for men, and this one interested him. A small, skinny man himself, he knew that a large man just makes a larger corpse and Private Sanger's almost uncanny self possession in the face of the horrors before him as compared with Private Morris's clear terror, made him living proof of the archaism "size matters not." He found his eye repeatedly drawn to this young man. He was only average height but seemed taller because he was so thin. Sharp featured with hollowed cheeks, he was not at all handsome, but he was striking. (Stiles sensed rather than saw that he was older than his companion. He was one of those men who would look young for the rest of his life. Which was in Stiles's opinion, something of a mixed blessing) He stood so still in contrast to the nervous fidgeting of the others, looking calmly around him. A listener and a watcher this one. He looked no older than his companion until you watched his eyes. It was in the eyes, Stiles decided, the difference between a young man and a boy, not the physique. Thus, before he had ever spoken a word to him, Captain Stiles had marked Denny Sanger out for promotion to Corporal.

Captain Stiles was not prone to fancy, and he put his "feeling" about Private Sanger, down to his experience of men in general and in no way did he think that it might be because he instinctively felt that he "knew" the man and his character.

But when Denny said that he thought they might have met before, he realised that that indeed was the feeling that he had been trying to put his finger on for the last three days. However. 'I don't think we've ever met,' he evaded.

Denny sighed. 'No, I suppose not,' he said.

'Mind you,' said Stiles, 'You're a London lad, aren't you?'

'Yes, sir.'

'Don't suppose you've ever been arrested, have you Sanger?'

Denny shook his head.

'No I didn't think so,' said Stiles. 'I only ask because I used to be in the police force.'

Denny gave a violent start. 'I'm sorry sir, but now I'm *certain* that I know you from somewhere.'

'Well, I have the same feeling,' Stiles admitted. 'But I don't suppose it matters.'

Denny thought it *did* matter, although, if he had been pushed, he could not have said why. Therefore, he dropped it.

'You wanted to speak to me sir?' he ventured.

'Yes,' Stiles cleared his throat. 'The thing is, I reckon we'll be pushing on to the front tomorrow – day after at the latest.'

Denny bowed his head in agreement.

'That Damn General won't be told – anyway, I can't delay any longer,'

Denny smiled at this.

'So, ahem, anyway, I'm going to need a good right-hand man up there, and I reckon that's you – Corporal.'

'Er, that's "Private", Cap.'

'I know what I said.'

* * *

Tamar had taken to watching Television as a way to avoid conversation. Since the set was in the old servant's quarters, and both the Buffington Smythe's considered Television a pastime that was beneath them, she found that she got quite a lot of peace that way. Unless Tristan ran her to earth and delivered his "Television is the opiate of the masses" speech and tried to tempt her to a stroll round the garden.

She quite agreed with him in a way, but she was finding the TV soothing. It demanded nothing from her, and, in its banality, she could lose herself for hours on end and almost – not quite – but almost, forget her troubles. Besides, there was the aforementioned bonus of avoiding conversation. Ophelia never came in here. She thought that "vibrations" from the TV set were harmful to your health.

Sometimes Tristan would wander in like a pallid ghost and sit with her in silence watching old programs that neither of them had seen before. (Repeats and war updates were all that was ever shown these days.)

Perhaps, she thought, he liked the peace and quiet too.

* * *

The house that Mack was planning to rob was, like most large houses these days, fairly deserted, all the staff having gone, either to war or to be back with their families. But there would be some people there, and that was where Cindy came in. She was to make them invisible.

Until he had discovered her, Mack had contented himself with small jobs, looting and petty theft, but he had seen the advantage of the war at once. He knew that these big houses – once impenetrable fortresses – would now be half empty and vulnerable. He just had not had a plan – until now.

He had been watching her for some time; she was undeniably good looking and pretty well off. That was enough to interest him initially and then he had started watching the house. When he had seen her literally vanish for the first time, he had not been able to believe his eyes. He had set up the surveillance at first, with no idea of blackmail; he just wanted proof that he was not seeing things. Only when he had the taped evidence in his hands, did he realise what he might be able to do with such an accomplice.

Cindy was a witch, not a very good one mind you, but still a witch. And invisibility was easy anyway. You just had to move onto the astral plane where you could not be seen.

She had explained to him that you could not touch things on the physical plane whilst you were on the astral plane, but you could take things with you onto the astral plane – your clothes for instance and yes other people and jewels and suchlike if you wanted to. So that they could get into the house unseen but once inside, they would be exposed until, they had finished the job and were ready to leave. Also, if the house had guard dogs these might be a problem as animals were more sensitive than humans and might sense their presence even while on the astral plane. This had happened to Cindy, she told him, hoping that he would give up the idea. But she had to admit that the dogs would not be able to see them or to touch them, and if they roused the house, Mack said, she would just have to hide them on the astral plane, that was what she was there for. Besides, they would reconnoitre first and find out if there *were* dogs.

It was foolproof he said. Cindy was not so sure. Besides, it was wrong!

'Hecaté forgive me,' she said to herself.

Witches traditionally have a bad press, but actually, they live by a code of honour as strict as any you may find. Magic power is not meant to be abused, and novice witches take an oath never to do so. Some break it of course, but most find that they do not want to. Their power is earned by long years of training (Cindy was actually forty, she just *looked* twenty five) and with the training comes discipline.

They pulled up at the gates of the large house. Cindy had not told Mack about the teleporting that she could do. If he knew that, she surmised he would have her teleporting them all over the county to rob places.

'Get out,' said Mack, 'round the back – now, do your thing.'

Cindy reluctantly obliged.

'Here,' said Mack, 'I can still see you, what are you trying to pull?'

Cindy sighed. And was about to explain when an obliging tramp came round the corner and walked straight through Tommy. She held out her hands. 'See?'

Mack nodded. 'Okay, let's go,' he turned to Tommy who had gone as white as a sheet. 'Come on you,' he barked, 'we haven't got all night.'

This was not strictly true, as Cindy knew, since there is no time on the astral plane. But she did not feel inclined to mention it. She wanted this over with.

~ Chapter Eight ~

IT WAS RAINING HEAVILY. Although technically, the temperature had gone up, Denny felt colder than ever; he had never felt so miserable in his whole life, and tomorrow they were to engage the enemy. He sat under a makeshift shelter trying to write to Tamar, but it was hard to find the words. Tomorrow he might be dead, and there was no point whitewashing it. He could not say as much in his letter, but neither did he feel like filling it up with pointless trivia about the weather and Harper's BO or Morris's aspirations as a painter (a house painter, not the other kind – he wanted to go into the family business.) It seemed a modest enough ambition, and yet, to Morris, it was the height of wonderful and completely out of his reach. It made Denny sad.

He gazed out across the grey, rain drenched fields designated "The Neutral Zone" by Woodley, a big Star Trek fan. Out there, somewhere, was the enemy. Was there a young man there looking back at him feeling the same way as he was? Probably. And they would have their own Morris and Wood and others. Men just like them. And these were the men who he would have to kill, and who would try to kill him, it was ridiculous. They would not want to be here anymore than he did. Except for the odd few fools, they had a few of them over here as well – all gung ho and macho bravado. Denny despised them, whichever side they were on.

He drew on his cigarette (he had taken up smoking recently – taking care of his health seemed pretty pointless now) and sucked in the cold air between his teeth.

He threw the cigarette down and began to write. He was still writing as the streaky dawn drew across the sky.

* * *

Tamar threw the letter to the floor. 'He writes as if he's going to die,' she said.

Tristan looked sympathetically at her. 'Well, he *is* in a war,' he said. 'Doesn't mean that he *will* die, just that it's on his mind, dontcher know? Men in combat and all that'

Ophelia floated past and cocked her head to listen.

'We're *all* in a war,' said Tamar. 'It's no safer here, any more than it is over there, but *I'm* not giving up.'

'Oh Tamar Darling,' tinkled Ophelia, 'you always did have a head full of magic,' she said this without having the least idea what she was talking about – which was her usual way of going on.

Tamar bristled. This was a colloquialism that her (Ophelia's) mother had been fond of. It meant that Tamar was "not quite with it", or was being unrealistic – "away with the fairies", so to speak. It was an insult if you like, even though it was partly true.

But now, Tamar wondered about this. It had never occurred to her before, but people had always used these strange, magical-related expressions to describe her.

For example, her beauty had always been described, not as "radiant" or "luminous" or anything other than always "enchanting". Almost every time, that was the word used. She was an "enchantress". Admirers spoke of her "casting spells" on them, or "weaving enchantments on their hearts'.

When she thought about it now, she realised that modern men were not usually given to overblown expressions of this type.

Jealous girls had referred to her, not as a "bitch", but more commonly, a "witch".

And there were other examples of this strange circumstance. The most peculiar being her French teacher's habit of calling her a "genie". She was trying to express the idea that she considered Tamar a genius of course, but her grasp of English had not been as impressive as Tamar's grasp of French. And Ophelia's mother had always said that she had "a head full of magic". Never ever did she say: "oh she's off on another planet.' Or even, simply: 'She's a daydreamer'. It was weird now she came to think about it; it was weirder still that she had never noticed it before.

It was almost as if the universe was trying to tell her something.

She left the letter behind when she left the room and Tristan picked it up curiously. He read:

Dear Tam

I wonder how many of the enemy feel just like I do about ▮▮▮▮ ▮▮▮▮ *we* ▮▮▮ *and I think about how they probably don't want to any more than I do. After all, they're just men like us really, probably just like us. I bet they'd much rather be at home, just like I would. I don't want to kill anyone. I bet they don't either. But I will, and they will too, because we have to. Nobody asked us if we wanted to. It's ridiculous, if we all just said no, what could they do about it? But we won't because we know the other side won't say that and so it's them or us, I suppose. How did it get like this?*

It's almost dawn. I have to go, I hope this letter reaches you.

Promise to go on, Tam, don't give up whatever happens. I put my hope in you now. After all, if it's not for you, then what am I doing this for? You are the reason, the beginning and the end. If you survive this, then that is all I ask for. As for me, just keep me in your heart. I know you will.
I love you always

Denny X

Tristan sighed to himself as he put the letter down. 'Oh to love like that!'

* * *

When Morris was blown to bits beside him, something changed in Denny forever. He learned, in that moment, how to hate and how to kill without remorse. The enemy had come upon them just before dawn and taken them by surprise.

Now Denny lay in the trench, spitting and swearing bloody murder, wreathed in smoke from the machine gun and totally unafraid, as bullets hammered into the sandbags around him, watching the lines of grey figures approach out of the early morning mist. Hundreds and hundreds of them. Not men any longer, they were just "The Enemy".

Through the mist in his head, Denny could vaguely hear his comrades shouting: 'Load!' 'Cock – Range?' 'Reload.' 'Fire! Fire!' All was desperate panic and confusion. The Captain had been right; these boys just weren't ready for this. Denny shivered. With a cold fury, he shot, and not five yards from him, a man fell and another and another. Beside him, Private Jones fell with a cry, Denny continued to shoot.

Then somebody lobbed a shell into the trench; everybody dived out of the way as the ground around them sprayed upward like water. Everybody seemed to be screaming. There was fire everywhere. Denny was flung backwards by the force of the explosion. He was lucky – he was still alive. He just had time to let this thought register, before everything went black.

* * *

Tamar had been sat in the same position for five hours now, ever since she had opened the letter from the Army Liaison Office.

When she had read the opening words, a pit had opened up beneath her feet, and she had slid into it, down and down. She felt it close over her head and understood that she would never come out again, not as long as she lived.

Denny was dead. How was she ever going to live without him?

How indeed? It had to be faced; it is not for any of us to say how long we shall live. Too late, she realised that she had put too much of herself into him, that she could no more live without him without agony, than she could cast aside her right arm. Too late for even the bitter solace of telling him this. That he did not know, would never know now, for she had never shown him that he meant as much to her as she had to him.

Had – had! Oh God! The black years of emptiness that stretched before her, she could not face them – she could not!

She had feared to show him the truth in case she lost him. Had feared even to face it within her. What a fool she had been! To think that she could protect her heart by denying it. And now she must pay for her folly, as for a crime.

After a while – she never knew just how long – she hardened her will. She would go on. It was what he had wanted. She was heartbroken, but she was also free. Nothing else could ever hurt her again. She was steel – rock – impenetrable. Now she was finished with love (or love was finished with her) she would try ambition.

She made her way to Tristan's room.

~ Chapter Nine ~

INVASION! IN HER mind's eye, she saw them. The faceless hordes storming across the county, lines of tanks crawling before them. They had marched across Europe and across her nightmares. Now they would march across her home. Followed by the SAS. Knocks on the door. People dragged away. Firing squads. For the unthinkable had happened. They were here, and more were coming every day. Britain was now an occupied county.

Tamar was packing up what little she had; they would be leaving tomorrow. There were troops heading this way. Ophelia was in a flap, as was to be expected, she wanted to pack up everything they owned and Tristan could not seem to make her see sense. She could not bear the idea of those dirty soldiers touching her beautiful things. It wasn't "nice" Darling. Tamar wanted to slap her, but Tristan was feeling guilty about his affair with Tamar and was being especially gentle with his wife. And Tamar judged that it was too soon to start acting up with him, so she kept out of it, even when Ophelia suggested that they could make more room in the car by leaving some of Tamar's things behind.

She said nothing, just narrowed her eyes. Tristan was becoming more and more enamoured every day. It would be Tamar's turn soon enough.

'Then everything will be paid for,' she thought. Every gloating remark, every selfish impulse, every insult. Everything.

* * *

The first robbery had gone according to plan, to Cindy's mingled relief and dismay.

Mack was now moving his operation further down the country. The big country houses would be better, he said. More pickings and less security. And cheaper living. This was what appealed to him about crime. The easy rewards, the quick money and free spending. Clothes, comfort, girls. Mack was a hedonist, not a master criminal.

Now they were doing a job a week, living high and to hell with the future.

Tonight they were planning a big one. A large, isolated county house, Mack told them. Belonged to some peer. A big payoff. They should be able to live off this one for a couple of months at least …

* * *

It was just before dawn when Tamar awoke with the feeling that there was something wrong. Downstairs she could hear noises, the faint, but unmistakable sounds of people moving about. 'Soldiers?' No, whoever it was, they were trying to be quiet, more likely it was burglars.

Tamar slipped her robe on and went downstairs. Nobody could move as silently as Tamar when she wanted to; thus she took the intruders by surprise.

There were two of them, a man and a woman with bright blonde hair, who stood wringing her hands while the man calmly emptied the safe.

Tamar thought swiftly and matched her actions to her thoughts. She picked up a heavy lamp and brought it down on the man's head with a crack. The woman screamed. The man, although dazed, got to his feet (It's a lot harder to knock someone out than Hollywood would have you believe) and glared menacingly at Tamar. He raised his fist, but Tamar was quicker, she spun low and kicked his legs from under him, then kicked him in the head where he lay on the rug. He subsided. The scream that the woman had let out had evidently alerted an accomplice of some sort, who had come in by the open patio doors, for Tamar found herself grabbed from behind by strong arms. Her arms were pinned to her side. Instead of struggling futilely, she allowed herself to go limp. The man loosened his grip almost imperceptibly, upon which, Tamar threw her head back violently, breaking the man's nose. As he raised his arm instinctively to his face, he freed Tamar's right arm, and she slammed her fist into his crotch, and he doubled over, as you might expect. She spun fast and kicked again, she hit him in the ribs; it made a horrible sound like a butcher chopping meat. Then she rained blows on him anywhere she could reach face, ribs, whatever. The man was on his knees now, covering his head with his hands. Only when he fell sideways silently, did Tamar stop shocked and confused. How had she done that, when had she learned to fight that way? She had no time to wonder, she turned and glared at the woman who looked – it could not be relieved? It must be the light in here. The dawn was breaking fully now, and, through the deep window space, the room was lit by a dreary half-light. Tamar and the woman stared at each other in shock now, each for their own reasons, which were very different.

Eventually the woman spoke. 'They made me do it,' she said. 'Please don't hurt me.'

Tamar nodded. 'Who are you?'

'My name's Cindy.'

Tamar nodded again. 'I – I know,' she muttered. *How* did she know?

She rallied. 'All right, all right,' she said 'I'm not going to hurt you.' She glanced out of the window at a sound from the garden. 'They might though,' she added gesturing outside.

Cindy followed her gaze. The garden was full of soldiers.

* * *

Denny opened his eyes and looked straight into the eyes of Captain Stiles, who smiled at him. There it was again, that feeling of a memory half grasped, slipping away; it was terribly frustrating. He had to get to the bottom of this.

'Nice to have you back son,' Stiles said.

Denny blinked, the captain was adorned about the head with a sparkling white bandage and Denny himself was lying in a fairly comfortable bed. He put it together. He checked his extremities; they all seemed to be intact although he was badly burned here and there. He reached up to his face.

'Don't worry son,' laughed the captain, 'you're still beautiful.'

'Blimey, they really *can* do miracles these days,' grinned Denny.

'It's a good job I was here, you know,' said Stiles 'I had a hell of a job getting you transferred. You seem to have lost your dog tags. Very careless, soldier.'

Denny groaned. 'Morris had them. It was stupid really. He thought they might bring him luck. I guess it didn't work. – What?'

Stiles was frowning at him in consternation. 'Morris had *your* dog tags on?' he asked.

'Yes sir. Look I know it was a stupid thing …'

'And Morris is dead?'

'Yes sir, I …'

'Wearing *your* dog tags?' He waited for Denny to work it out.

Denny's face fell suddenly. 'Oh, no!'

Denny struggled to a sitting position. 'How long have I been here sir?'

'Long enough,'

'I have to write to her sir, I have to let her know I'm alive.'

Stiles sighed; this was not going to be easy. He had hoped to put off telling him until he was stronger, but now there was nothing else for it.

'She'll never get the letter son, Britain's been invaded.'

Denny's answer was automatic. 'So, what else is new?' Then his face fell. This was no time for flippancy.

Stiles glanced at Denny's stricken face and hurried on. 'She may not have got the first letter, even. It's possible.'

'But not very likely,' said Denny.

He looked down at his injuries. They were serious enough for a discharge. 'Will I be going home sir?'

Stiles shook his head gently. 'Home isn't there anymore, son,' he explained

* * *

It was as Tamar had feared. The soldiers, having wasted no time taking over the house, rounded up the men (there was only Tristan and the two intruders) and shot them. Tamar had covered her eyes when Tristan had been shot. Ophelia had become predictably hysterical, but Cindy had seemed indifferent when the other two men were shot.

She mentally shrugged. 'Oh, well, out of the frying pan ...'

Then the women were herded off down to the cellars while the soldiers made free with Tristan's stock of wine and spirits.

* * *

The doctor peered at Denny in an officious manner. 'How are we feeling today?' he asked.

'Why do doctors always have to talk to you as if there were two of you?' wondered Denny. (Although in Denny's case, he was not far off the truth.)

'Weird,' said Denny. 'I keep feeling as if I'm not who I think I am.'

'Probably the concussion,' said the doctor crisply. 'I wouldn't worry about it son.' He had heard it all before. He thought Denny was bucking for a section eight discharge (for insanity).

'Or maybe it's incipient schizophrenia,' joked Denny. The doctor gave him a black look.

'Or maybe not,' said Denny hurriedly, wondering what he had said.

The truth was he had been having slightly schizophrenic thoughts. Ever since his bang on the head, he had been having odd memory flashbacks of things that he knew had not happened to him. Yet they felt real, like memories, not dreams. It was as if the concussion had placed a dark stain on his consciousness, and opened a door in his brain, a door to another place. A place from which he was being visited by messengers whose words just escaped him. By a glimpse of a world that he could never quite grasp.

And just to confuse matters further, Tamar seemed to be in most of the memories that he saw. A different Tamar, different and yet the same. There were also other familiar faces, Stiles, for example (and this only compounded his feelings of *déjà vu,* and the *déjà vu* made him certain that the memories were somehow real). And he saw other faces – faces that he did not know, and yet he did.

He looked at his face in a pocket mirror, his familiar face. 'Maybe it *was* the concussion,' he thought. But that didn't mean anything. He still felt sure that he wasn't who he thought he was.

* * *

Ophelia had gone quiet – unnaturally so. She sat in the corner and rocked back and forth. Tamar ignored her. She was also silent, thinking – about what had happened of course, and also about Cindy. She had always scoffed at the idea of *déjà vu* and all that sort of thing, but it was such a strong feeling that she could not shake it off, and then there was the curious incident of knowing Cindy's name before she had been told, although she could not be certain of this, but she thought …

Cindy herself was calm now that the violence seemed to be over – for now. She intended to be out of here before it started again. As soon as these two women were asleep, she would teleport out of here. The soldiers' arrival had been fortuitous in a way – for her at least – Now the only person who had known her secret was dead. She intended to make sure that no one ever found it out again.

Tamar troubled her though. There was something … something! Cindy could not put her finger on it, but it bothered her. She put it down to guilt; she knew in her heart that she should take these women with her to safety. She felt as if Tamar somehow knew what she was planning, which was clearly ridiculous. It was her conscience that was making her imagine these things.

Tamar was also planning an escape although in a far less dramatic way and involving far more work, not to mention, peril. To her credit, she had no intention of leaving anyone behind, although she was sorely tempted to leave Ophelia, who was now muttering to herself and clearly on the point of beginning the gibbering. She would definitely be more of a hindrance than a help. But Tamar could not help that. She would have to come. And Cindy? Well Tamar did not intend to let her out of her sight if she could help it. Cindy had not been entirely wrong when she had thought that Tamar knew what she was planning. While having no idea what Cindy was actually planning, Tamar's considerable intuition told her that Cindy was definitely up to *something*.

Which was why, several hours later, when Ophelia had finally fallen into an exhausted slumber, Tamar was only pretending to sleep. Cindy was also pretending to sleep. The two women were actually watching each other like cats, Cindy ready to dash, Tamar, to pounce. The tension was palpable.

Eventually Tamar sat up. 'Okay,' she said, 'this is ridiculous.' She grabbed a terrified Cindy by the shoulders and starting shaking her. 'All right,' she said. 'Who Are You?'

Cindy had been impressed by Tamar's handling of her former cohorts. Now, she decided, was not the time for prevarication. 'I – I 'm a witch,' she admitted as clearly as her wildly nodding head would allow.

Tamar dropped her arms. 'O – kay,' she said slowly, as if thinking this over. A thought occurred to her. 'So ...' she said, 'who am I?'

~ Chapter Ten ~

WHERE DOES THE truth lie? Where does it hide? In people's heads? In their hearts? Perhaps it all depends on what truth it is you are looking for.

Tamar and Denny knew the truth about themselves, but only one truth. There was another truth, just as true, one that they had forgotten. That they had been made to forget. Where was that truth? Where was it hidden? And if that was the truth, was the truth that they knew, really a lie? And was it really forgotten, or was it just hidden?

Now that Tamar and Denny were looking for the truth, it surely could not remain hidden much longer.

* * *

Cindy was nonplussed, which was, by the way, a common state of affairs, but this time she really had some excuse.

On the other hand, she had an inkling, just a feeling, of what Tamar was getting at. So, she answered. 'I have no idea what you are, but perhaps Hecaté will know.'

'Who?'

'Hecaté, the goddess of witches.'

'On speaking terms with her are you?' asked Tamar sarcastically. She could hardly believe she was having this conversation.

'All witches can call on Hecaté for help,' Cindy told her. 'She's very accessible.

'Oh.'

'First I think we should get out of here.'

'How?' said Tamar with some of her old asperity, 'by magic?'

'Of course.'

Tamar digested this. It was not easy. 'What about Ophelia?' she said. 'She'll have a nervous breakdown.'

'What do you mean, she *will*? She already has.'

'So …?'

'So, we'll take her with us. Drop her off at a hospital somewhere. She'll be okay, better than here anyway.'

'Okay good. And where are *we* going to go?'

'We'll go to my place. I need to get some things anyway. To summon Hecaté.'

* * *

Denny was planning to go AWOL. As much as he needed to get back to Tamar, he also needed some answers, and home was the place to get them. Captain Stiles might have been another source, but unless he was a most consummate actor, it was fairly evident that he knew as little about what was going on as Denny himself.

He laid his plans carefully and slipped out of the hospital in the early hours of the morning. That would give him a good four hours before his absence was noticed, and, by the time it had been reported and verified and the MP's had been notified, he would have another hour at least maybe two. Denny grinned. Thank God for good old army efficiency. With papers made up for him using Karl Morris's tags he hoped to get as far as the air field. From there it would be easy. And, since they would be looking for Corporal Sanger, even if he was stopped, so what? He was Private Morris, and he could prove it.

This was getting ridiculous, he thought. Just how many people could one man be in a lifetime? He was already two of him.

* * *

Tamar took to the teleporting like a Djinn to a bottle, so to speak. It felt disturbingly familiar. Also, it was fun.

With Ophelia safely deposited in hospital, Tamar felt like she could breathe easier. She wondered vaguely what the soldiers would think when they found their captives mysteriously flown, but she had other things on her mind.

Cindy's house was a surprise. She had expected something a little more austere or perhaps even gothic. Certainly not the abundance of pink roses and chintz that met her eye. Cindy was, after all, by her own admission, a witch. And she favoured black for clothing as most witches do. (Cindy also liked black because it showed off her bright hair nicely.) But as far as interior décor was concerned, she apparently preferred the feminine approach. Her living room was the only thing that might have given away her true age – it was firmly stuck in the 1980s.

Cindy had that look on her face, that look of modest pride, which some women have when they are showing you their baby. Tamar was evidently expected to gush and say: 'Oooh, how lovely.' But Tamar never said anything that she did not mean (which is not the same as saying what you do not mean– sometimes silence is golden). Instead, she got right to the point. You might think that under the circumstances, Cindy would have been in control of the situation, since it was *her* goddess that they were summoning, and her idea to summon her. Not to mention that she knew how to do it, and Tamar did not. But this was not the case. Tamar had never found herself in a situation that she was not in command of, and this was no different.

'So, let's get started then.' It was a command, not a request.

'Well, I ought to do it in private really,' Cindy demurred.

'Why?' said Tamar flatly.

'Well ...'

'We're summoning this god person for *my* benefit aren't we?'

'Yes, I ...'

'So, I ought to be in on it, oughtn't I?'

'It's just that I ...'

'Anyway, two heads are better than one.'

'I really think ...'

'I should be there. Why are you being so secretive, what have you got to hide?'

'Nothing, I just ...'

'I want to see you do it. Anyone would think you were making the whole thing up, the way you're going on. Come on, let's get on with it.' She propelled Cindy into the kitchen. 'In here, is it?'

Cindy made a last ditch attempt to assert some authority. 'Look, it really ...'

'Now!' insisted Tamar.

'I knew I'd see it your way,' sighed Cindy. 'No, not in there, we'll try scrying first, it's quicker.

'Mirror mirror on the wall, who is the fairest of them all?' intoned Tamar sarcastically.

The embarrassed look on Cindy's face strongly indicated that this was, in fact, what the mirror was usually used for, as Tamar would have seen, had she been able to see her from this angle.

She continued to gaze into the mirror with an expression of acute concentration on her face. From Tamar's point of view, she did not actually appear to be doing anything. Then the mirror went cloudy.

The scrying had a peculiar effect on Tamar. For one thing, the actual business was bringing on the *déjà vu* in the worst way. And then there was the fact that she only half believed it. And when Hecaté actually appeared in the mirror Tamar was overcome with a mass of conflicting feelings. She did not believe it, and yet she *had* to. She was overawed and, at the same time, frankly sceptical. And worst of all, the appearance of Hecaté brought on the worst *déjà vu* of all. She had seen her before; she knew she had. And yet, she also knew that she could not have. She was sure she would remember something like that. But memory had become a treacherous thing.

Hecaté's opening line was encouraging. She looked Cindy squarely in the eye, and said: 'You took your time did you not?' She glanced at Tamar and added. 'Both of you.'

She answered their gaping looks with a tinkling laugh. 'What did you expect?' she said. 'I *am* a goddess, you know.'

'So, you know then?' asked Tamar.

'Oh yes, pretty much everything. That is, I can see what has happened, but not *how* it has happened. But it does not matter I suppose ...'

'What *has* happened?' interrupted Tamar. Cindy trembled, but Hecaté just smiled – austerely – remotely. 'Ah, but you already know, do you not? Look inside yourself. These are answers that you have to find for yourself. If I tell you, you will never be sure whether they are your true memories, or those that I have given back to you.'

'Can it really matter?' asked Tamar.

'It matters very much,' Hecaté told her. 'Why should you believe anything I say? You would never be sure. And you will need to be sure.'

Tamar shook her head. 'I don't understand.'

'Think of it like this,' said Hecaté. 'Suppose you had had a terrible accident and lost your memory. You cannot remember anything, not even your own name. Somebody – a person you were close to, but whom you cannot remember, *tells* you your name. So, you now know your name, but you have not remembered it for yourself. You only have this person's word for it. Understand?'

Tamar nodded.

'And you do not even know this person. As far as you are concerned, he could be anybody. Until you regain your memory, you have no idea if this person is telling the truth or not. And anything he tells you about yourself has to be taken on faith, because you have no memory of it. It is not real to you. But it *becomes* real. You assimilate it into your mind until it almost feels as if it *is* a memory. But it is not. Then your memory begins to return, how then do you differentiate between the real memories, the ones from your own consciousness and those that you have been given?'

'I can't,' Tamar supplied the answer.

'Exactly. And thus you will never be certain how much of your memory is actual memory and how much is information that you have been supplied with.'

'*Have* I had an accident?'

'In a way, although I would characterise it as more of an attack really. It was certainly done deliberately.

'Can't you tell me *anything*?'

'Oh, yes, you would not have summoned me if I could not help you at all.'

'Okay, what *can* you tell me?'

'That you are not who you think you are, but you know that, do you not? The world has been changed. Once you find the truth within yourself, you will know how to put the world back as it was.'

'How do you know all this?'

'I am not mortal. I have been unaffected by the change in the world. I still have my memories of the world as it was. I can see both the new world, in my memory, and the old.'

Hecaté sighed and looked wistfully at Tamar. 'And I know it is within you also.' she said. You are a far more powerful being than I.'

Then her manner changed suddenly. She looked at Tamar with pity and love as she said: 'He is not dead. There was a mistake. He knows of it, and he is on his way back to you.'

Tamar's head spun. But it never occurred to her to doubt that it was the truth. As soon as the words were spoken, she knew, realised that in some deep part of her soul she had always known. If he had really died, would she not also be dead by now?

Then another thought struck her. 'What do you mean, I'm far more powerful than you?'

She glared into the mirror. At her own reflection. Hecaté had gone

'Who was she talking about?' asked Cindy.

* * *

News from home was so hard to get now that the Americans were in occupation, but Denny had ascertained that many of the country's large estates had been taken over. So there was at least a chance that the Buffington-Smythe home was now in the hands of the enemy. This was worrying. In any case, that was where he intended to head for, but, under these circumstances, it might be prudent to change his identity again. His American accent needed very little improvement, the American culture being such a large part of the British one these days. Denny had seen every single episode of "Friends". And, after all that he had already been through to get this far, stealing an American uniform should not be too difficult.

He was currently in France, having blagged a ride on a troop transport from Italy. He had reached Italy in much the same way, only by plane. Troops were being moved about all over the place at the moment. It made Denny very aware of the scale of this war.

But getting to England from here would not be easy. There were no troops headed for England except American ones. Well, he intended to become an American sooner or later anyway – why not make it sooner?

~Chapter Eleven ~

SECOND LIEUTENANT Jamie Adams was not a happy man. This was not the army he had joined. He had been shocked at the callous way his commanding officer had shot those three English guys. And, like most of the participants, he did not understand this war. What had the English ever done to America? He liked the English; he had nothing against them. But he hated the English weather being a Californian by birth, with the typical Californian looks, tanned and fair-haired, with blue eyes. Although his tan was fading, in the endless rain of European weather, and he was beginning to look washed out

And he wandered through the house (and it was *the* house) feeling like a trespasser. So, he had many reasons for wishing in his secret heart that he was not here.

He was also concerned about the women in the cellar. Some of these guys had had enough booze as was good for them; most of them were good lads, but you always got a few bad apples, and the women's good looks had not escaped attention. He went down to the cellar and made sure that it was locked. It was, so he never thought to check that the women were still there. Then he pocketed the key. They would be safe for the night now, he thought. Tomorrow they would be moved to a prisoner camp, and their fate would no longer be his concern.

But as long as it was, he intended to see that nothing happened to them. Not on his watch.

As he made his way back up the stone steps, a silvery gleam just above his head caught his eye. He stepped back to get a better look. There was a small alcove set into the stone wall at an inconvenient level. Had it not contained something shiny, no one would ever have noticed it. That, he thought, was probably the idea. A hiding place. Intrigued, he reached up, although he was a tall man, his hand only just brushed the lip of the alcove.

'A dammed *good* hiding place,' he thought.

He thought for a moment and reached for the rifle slung on his back. Raising it above his head, he poked about with it in the alcove until he managed to dislodge the shiny thing. It fell with a clatter on the step. He picked it up curiously. It was some type of large dagger in an intricately patterned sheath. The sheath was dull as if it had developed a patina over silver. It was the handle that was shiny. He drew it out and looked at it. The blade was also a dull silver grey colour. In the dim light, it did not look particularly interesting. Jamie shrugged and sheathed it again then slung it in his pack. He would take another look at it later maybe, in a better light.

By the time he had ascended the stairs, he had forgotten about it.

* * *

'Where are we going?' It was pouring with rain and freezing cold. Cindy's hair was plastered to her head, her jeans were stuck to her legs, and she was frozen to the marrow and utterly miserable. The last thing she wanted was to be helping Tamar lever off a manhole cover in the middle of the night. She had a feeling that this was likely to lead to being cold, wet, miserable *and* smelly.

'Down there,' said Tamar, confirming Cindy's worst fears.

'I knew it,' she said. 'Why?'

'I want to see something.'

'In the sewer?'

The manhole cover came off with a clang. 'Come on, at least we'll be out of the rain.' Tamar started to climb down the rusty iron ladder.

Cindy gave a sigh and a shrug and followed her down. She had long ago given up any pretence at being in control of this situation in the face of Tamar's overwhelming personality.

She made heavy weather of the descent and arrived at the bottom panting, which is difficult to do when you are trying to hold your breath. Tamar sniffed the air. Unbelievable, thought Cindy, trying *not* to smell the air, that was the trick here, surely?

'This way,' Tamar decided and set off, with Cindy stumbling beside her.

After they had walked about 20 yards, Tamar stopped and shone her torch at her feet. Cindy looked. To her surprise, there seemed to be another type of cover here, made of wooden slats, which led further down. Tamar levered it up and peered down. 'I think this is it,' she said.

Down this hole there was no proper ladder, just a series of footholds driven randomly into the sides of the hole. Bits of rock and wood distributed unevenly and not always very securely. Tamar shinned down easily, and waited patiently for Cindy to slip, stumble and slide down after her.

The stench hit them as they reached the bottom; it was a foul rank smell, a revolting miasma that rose up, as if from the depths of charnel house. It bypassed the nostrils and immediately started to melt the brain. It was the smell of rotting flesh and old blood.

The smell in the upper level now seemed almost refreshing by comparison. One missed the beguiling nosegay of human refuse.

On the higher level, Cindy had wrinkled her nose and tried not to breathe too deeply. Down here, she gasped and retched. She wondered what the hell she was doing here.

Tamar was down here because of a particularly strong memory that kept coming back to her. 'I have to see if it's real,' she said. 'Hecaté told me that the answer lies within myself. I want to see if she was right.'

Up ahead there were faint lights moving about. These turned out to be people. Tamar sighed; she had been hoping that she had been wrong.

These people looked curiously at her and Cindy as they approached. Apart from the fact that they were living under the sewers, most of them seemed like ordinary people. There were even a few children running about. Cindy was shocked beyond the capacity for rational thought. These families had built themselves little homes, well rude shelters, divisions between each dwelling, shored up with bits of planking and the odd sheet of corrugated roofing. Across the row of residences, which really did rather crudely resemble a street, were retractable metal gates, which the people now pulled across their homes closing themselves in. It looked to Cindy rather like a row of prison cells.

'What are they *doing* down here?' she hissed to Tamar.

Tamar shrugged. 'They live here.'

'Why?'

'Because they don't have anywhere else to live.'

'How can they stand it?'

'They're used to it I suppose. Lots of people live worse lives. They say a body can get used to anything, even being hanged.'

'Why have they locked themselves in like that? Are they afraid of us?'

Tamar hesitated before answering. 'No. Not us, I don't think.'

'What is that terrible smell?'

'Sssh.'

They rounded a corner into complete darkness; even Tamar was moving cautiously now. Then something loomed up before them, something truly horrible. It had a leprous look about it. Vaguely human shaped, but of such exceeding thinness that it seemed to have been grown in a lighter atmosphere. The face was white and the eyes were red. Its hair and clothes were matted with the filth of innumerable years. It had not seen them.

Tamar never hesitated for a second, without missing a beat she grabbed Cindy, dragged her into a recess, and put her hand over her mouth.

The creature seemed to be able to smell them; at least it stopped and sniffed the air waving its head about, like the light from a searchlight, as it did so.

'What the hell is that?' Cindy wondered.

But Tamar knew. 'Vampire,' she hissed. 'Feral, not like ordinary ones, they're more like animals. They live down here, and they are extremely vicious, although not too bright. Don't move.'

'*Ordinary* ones?' Cindy thought incredulously. '*Ordinary* vampires? Oh my God, I'm going insane, that actually sounded like it made sense.' She shook her head in disbelief.

The feral vampire moved off, and Tamar and Cindy breathed again. Only not too deeply.

'How do you know all this?' asked Cindy.

'Good question,' thought Tamar. 'How the hell *do* I know all this?' She decided that it would be better if she stopped asking herself that question.

'There are demons down here too,' she said instead of answering. 'It didn't use to be too bad, but now they're overrunning the place. God only knows where they're all coming from. Those people we saw, it's not safe for them down here anymore, but where else are they going to go?'

'Why didn't you tell me any of this before we came down here?'

'Don't be silly,' snapped Tamar. 'I didn't *know* it until I came down here.'

She remembered now, though. She and Denny had come down here a few times. She could not quite remember why. And there was something else too; now that she was down here, she was certain they had discovered something else down here, something of vast importance, but what it was she simply couldn't remember. But it might have something to do with why the world had changed. She had followed her errant memories in obedience to Hecaté's instruction, in the hope that she would begin to find out the truth about herself, and it had led her here. But what the hell did it all mean?

She was pondering these matters when the vampires attacked. A pack of six. Tamar immediately understood. The vampire that they had seen had been a scout, she remembered now. She also remembered how to fight.

Just as she had back at the house against the burglars, she acted on instinct, if she let herself think about what she was doing, it would all fall apart.

If she closed down the rational, thinking part of her brain and just let her subconscious take over, it would be okay. That part of her knew how to fight vampires, but the rational part of her brain would try to tell her that she could not do it. She allowed her subconscious instincts to take over, and they thoroughly enjoyed themselves. And the more she fought, the more she remembered. This was why they had been here, to fight. Denny too; to help the people who lived down here. But she still, even when the last vampire fell, could not remember what it was that they had discovered down here that was so damned important.

* * *

Captain Stiles was having the most amazing dream that he had ever had. It featured the most beautiful woman he had ever seen, and yet she was haranguing him like a fishwife. 'Jack,' she said, 'you are not listening to me. You never do listen to me.' Jack inclined his head to indicate that he was listening. She made a face at him. 'Do not give me that look Jack Stiles,' she said, 'I know that look. You seek to humour me, well! I have had enough of this.' She paused, as if to let this sink in.

Stiles manufactured a look of alert interest and put it on his face.

'Yes dear,' he said automatically. It was a prescribed response, but in this case, he did not know where it had come from.   He pulled himself together.   'That was totally inappropriate,' he thought. Yet it had come out quite naturally.

'Denny Sanger has not gone AWOL,' she told him. 'Ah, I thought that might get your attention.' Stiles stared at her in bewilderment. 'Wha …?

'Look Jack, will you get it through your thick head once and for all. I am *not* a dream. I am trying to help you – I want you back,' she added quietly and to Stiles complete mystification. 'You said that Sanger …?' he prompted.

'He has been taken prisoner by enemy forces. You must go after him. You should go alone,'

'Go AWOL, you mean?' Stiles sounded unsure.

'Yes, by the time you can get anyone to believe you, it will be too late.'

'That should get him moving,' she thought.

She vanished.

She reappeared. 'You know Jack,' she said, 'I wish you would take better care of yourself. You need to eat properly. A man your age needs to take care of his heart. You need the four basic food groups.' She vanished again.

'I've got your four basic food groups,' said Stiles with an air of chagrin. He counted off on his fingers to the empty air. 'Beans, bacon, whisky and lard.'

* * *

Denny was lurking in the corner of a dark inn, of a kind that is only still found in rural France, in his current incarnation as a French labourer. The inn was in Calais, quite near to the coast, a favourable tactical position for the American forces headed for England.   This being the case, the room was full of American soldiers having a good time and waiting for their sailing orders. He felt like the Scarlet Pimpernel. 'Well, they certainly are seeking me here and there,' he thought in some amusement.

Denny's target was sitting alone at the bar. He was perfect, already drinking heavily and not a bad match for build, perhaps a little taller than Denny, but not too much, it would be okay. If he tucked his pants into his boots, no one would notice. And best of all, as mentioned before – he was alone. Denny just hoped that the soldier's French was no better than his own. He waited until the soldier had ordered another drink; then he made his move.

He tapped the soldier on the shoulder then moved swiftly to the other side of him so that by the time the soldier had located him, he was feeling disoriented.

Denny slid into the seat next to him. 'Ah bonjour Monsieur,' he began, with an inane grin on his face.

The soldier swore at him.

'Ah, Ah non, non, Monsieur,' said Denny wagging a rebuking finger at the soldier. At this point, his high school French gave out, but it looked as if it really would not matter. The soldier was not in any condition to notice if Denny had talked to him in Greek.

'So,' he said plastering a look of weasely cunning onto his face. 'The night is dark for those who walk alone, Heh?' This was a sufficiently strange comment for the soldier to turn and stare at Denny who was mugging furiously at him, twitching his head and winking broadly. Through the fug of alcohol, the soldier seemed to dimly understand what Denny was getting at. 'One of those flamin' traitors eh?' he slurred.

'*Please* Monsieur, I facilitate. I am, how you say, liaison between our two peoples, I help you, and you help me, everybody have a nicer war, eh? I was told you would be interested in what I have to say.'

'You got some information?'

Denny inclined his head and put a finger to his lips. 'I may have,'

'What is it then?' said the soldier sceptically.

Denny shook his head. 'Not here,' he said, looking about him with exaggerated caution. 'I need to ask you for the countersign. All must be done properly, Monsieur. So silly, but it is the way these things are done eh? All cloaks and daggers heh?'

There was a silence. Eventually the soldier said. 'Countersign?'

Denny immediately back-pedalled. 'Ah Monsieur, I think we have been talking at cross-purposes, but it is no matter. I shall now leave you in peace to finish Monsieur Gilbert's excellent wine. So sorry, so sorry...' he was backing away nervously, looking about him with the look of a man who has been trapped into saying more than he intended and was now very worried about it. Now he just had to hope that the soldier was brighter than he looked. But not *too* bright, obviously.

The soldier caught up with events just in time and grabbed Denny's arm. 'Hey,' he said. 'Just hold on a minute. Whatever it is you have to say, you can tell me. I'm an American officer.'

'I?' said Denny with overdone innocence. 'I, Monsieur? I assure you, I have nothing to tell. Nothing at all.' He allowed his eyes to dart about the room like a trapped animal seeking a way out. 'And now, Monsieur, I really must be ...'

'Oh no you don't,' said the soldier, narrowing his eyes. 'You tell me what it's all about, see. I can pay you, if that's what's bothering you.'

'Please Monsieur. I just come in here for quiet drink, nothing more.' He managed to slip away and headed for the door. Now the soldier was, as Denny had intended, almost frantic to know what Denny was concealing.

Denny was lounging against a handy tree. By the light of the upstairs window of the inn, he watched the soldier approach with a greedy look on his face. He was thinking, no doubt, of promotion.

Denny grinned to himself. 'Gotcha!' he thought
* * *

Denny had managed, by dint of some cunning talk, some stolen papers and his purloined uniform, to join up with the 2064th heading for the grim shores of old Blighty. Now it was time to go on the run again. He had deserted now from so many regiments by now that it was a wonder he had not been court martialed by every army on the globe. 'Join the armies, see the world,' he thought with grim irony. So, he was in Dover, only seventy odd miles to go. Considering how far he had already come, it should be a piece of cake. But this part, he knew, was going to be the hardest stretch of all.

He was sneaking out of the camp when he heard a sound that made his heart sink. 'Hi, who goes there?'

Denny turned and saw the Private on sentry duty pointing his rifle straight at him. He was clearly headed out of camp; there was no way out of it.

'Second Lieutenant Chip Bentley,' he said. 'Just going for a walk, Private.'

The private came up to him and peered closely at his face. 'Sir?' he said. 'Sorry sir, I didn't recognise you. I'm sorry sir, but I can't let you leave the camp. The colonel would have my guts for garters, sir. Against regulations see?'

Denny unslung his rifle and hesitated. He was not sure it was in him to kill a man who was not actively trying to kill him. And yet, he thought. Technically any armed American soldier was trying to kill him, wasn't he? Weren't his side at war with this lot? And wasn't it supposed to be his job to kill American soldiers?

'Sod this,' he thought. What had this man ever done to him?

The Private was looking at him perplexedly. 'Sir?'

'Over there,' Denny pointed with his rifle behind the man, who turned to look.

Denny brought the rifle down on the man's head, just behind the ear, as the Cap had taught him (a man who had a surprising repertoire of dirty fight moves for such a peace lover). The soldier went down like a sack of potatoes.

'Thanks Cap,' breathed Denny under his breath.

He then had the most unexpected good fortune. Right there completely unguarded at the edge of the compound was one army jeep – regulation – fully fuelled – escapees for the use of.

Denny hopped in. As he drove away, he was singing in his peculiarly melodious voice – "California Dreaming".

* * *

'All the leaves are brown … And the sky is Gra-a-ay,' warbled SL Jamie Adams mournfully and tunelessly. He had passed homesickness three stops ago and was now at that point where he was making everybody around him feel sick as well, although not necessarily home sick, just sick of him.

'I'd be safe and warm – if I was in E-E-L. A-A-A-A. Ca-a-a-alifornia Dreeemin…'

Who can say what subtle influences are brought to bear on the new owner of a relic that was once an integral part of another's life. What indefinable, tenuous connections might be brought about by the possession of said relic, between the new owner and the old?

It was not that Jamie hated the army. But he had joined up to defend his county not to push civilians around. Where was the honour and glory in that? And what had the Limeys ever done to threaten America anyway? Part of him – the career soldier part – knew that it was not his job to reason why. Soldiers took orders; that was it. But the human part of him tended to want to know the reasons and even had a treacherous habit of sometimes, in his secret heart, questioning the wisdom of the orders, although he had never been known to go as far as actual disobedience – yet.

* * *

Next, Tamar wanted to go back to her flat in London, just to pick up a few things, she said, but Cindy was not falling for that one again. Over the last few days, Tamar had wanted to go to various places "just to have a look", or "just to see something", or even "just to do a bit of shopping". Even though, to be honest, she could not see the danger of going to an empty flat, or the point of it to be frank, nevertheless, she decided to put her foot down. She was not going anywhere without an explanation this time.

Tamar sighed; one of her more serious shortcomings was her lack of patience with intellects less sharp than her own.

'Isn't it obvious what I'm doing?' she said.

'No, not really.'

'I'm trying to sort out one set of memories from another. I have plenty of memories of that flat. It's been my home for three years. But some of the memories don't fit. At least I don't think so, it's so hard to tell, so I want to go back home and just see … see … if anything comes to me. You see?'

'I – I – think so.'

'It's so hard to know what's real anymore,' said Tamar with a sigh. 'What about you,' she added suddenly, 'don't you feel like this, like there's something you've forgotten about?'

'Constantly,' said Cindy.

'I mean, you're in some of my memories. I know that we must have known each other before. Don't you feel it too?'

'I try not to think about it,' said Cindy, which was as good as an admission.

'Well don't,' said Tamar, because if I'm right, then you're not who you think you are either.'

'Who is?' said Cindy gloomily.

'Why don't you want to know?'

'Because – well, what if the world has changed for the better.'

'Better!   How can *this*,' Tamar swept an arm around the room in an encompassing gesture. 'Possibly be better?'

'Well, you don't know. Neither of us knows, maybe we're happier now than we were then. We have no idea what the world was like before it changed, just fragments no real picture.'

'Oh I see, better the devil you know, is that it?'

'I suppose so.'

'Oh, don't be such a coward. Somebody messed with our lives, and I, for one, want to know who – and why?'

'Besides, what if it's better the *other* way?' she added thoughtfully.

* * *

As Denny drove through the county of his birth, he was afflicted with the strangest feeling that he had landed on an alien planet. The Americans, like the Martians in the "War of the Worlds", appeared to have transplanted a mysterious vegetation that had covered the land with stars and stripes. Every doorway, front porch and gateway, every pillar and portico, every tree and lamppost was festooned with fluttering banners. It made the whole world look like the Land of Oz, once dreary black and white, now in fabulous Technicolor. It made Denny depressed. He had once quite liked Americans – well, everybody needs somebody to look down on, but right now, he felt as if he would hate them all forever. Somewhere in the back of his mind, he was reminded that from somebody's point of view, that was probably the idea.

He had been having these thoughts for a while now, intermittently. The idea of a great cosmic conspiracy was growing on his mind. It certainly would explain a lot of things. And he was even having what he thought of as delusions of grandeur. That is, he thought that maybe it all had something to do with him personally – or at least, if not him, then certainly Tamar, and himself by association.

He put a lot of this down to his unwillingness to believe that ordinary human beings were capable of making purposeless war all by themselves, just because that was what they were like. He *wanted* it to be a conspiracy, a menacing shadowy plot in which humans were just the innocent pawns. A view that he knew was naïve in the extreme. But still the feeling persisted.

And yet, the Americans in particular, had swept across nations with frightening efficiency. And Denny supposed that they ought to be good at war if any nation was. They had certainly made enough films about it.

Of course, to be fair, they had also made a lot of TV shows about adolescent angst but it did not mean that they had the monopoly on it.

~Chapter Twelve ~

HOME! IT LOOKED just the same as she remembered it, until she realised that her memory of late had not been terribly reliable. Perhaps home did not really look like this at all. Had never looked like this. No sooner had she thought this then the room seemed to change before her very eyes, just for a fraction of a second. It became far bigger for one thing. Behind her, she heard Cindy gasp.

She turned. 'You saw that too?'

Cindy could only nod.

'The room changed, didn't it?' Tamar persisted.

Cindy agreed to it.

'Then it was real, it wasn't just a memory.' She looked around her as if she expected it to happen again. The room remained resolutely the same.

Disappointed but undeterred, Tamar continued in the same vein. 'Then this means that the world is coming back – the other world, the way it was before, doesn't it?'

She picked up a photograph of her and Denny; this had been taken about a week after they had first got together – at least she thought it had. Perhaps it had not; perhaps this photograph was not really here at all. She remembered it being taken, in one of those silly little passport photo booths. They had been nineteen, at college together. She remembered the night they had finally got together. Caught up in her incipient nostalgia, the world started to go wibbly round the edges. 'Uh oh,' she thought with that tiny unchangeable part of her that would always be sarcastic. 'Flashback time.'

She had been dating a medical student at the time, wealthy and handsome of course. Although she still hung around with Denny. When they had walked into the swanky restaurant, she had been shocked to spot Denny sat forlornly alone at a table for six. What was he doing here?

She had thought quickly. When her date had gone to check her coat she made a swift phone call from the lobby the result of which was that, as a medical student, he was paged by the hospital, to assist the house doctor.

He apologised profusely and hurried away leaving her with her taxi fare and a promise to call her later. She was very understanding about it.

As soon as he had gone, she made her way over to the table where Denny was sitting and sat beside him without waiting to be asked. 'Stood up?' she asked. 'Where's your Indian friend?'

Denny's brow furrowed. 'Who?'

'You know, Jon somebody. The one they call "Dances with trousers down".'

Denny managed a weak smile. 'Oh, him. He's probably dancing – with his trousers down, at the "Slug and Lettuce",' he said. 'I'm waiting for my parents and Miles. They visit once in a while. They're always late. Well, it's just me after all.'

Tamar pursed her lips. She had never met Denny's family – he tended to keep people away from them, if he wanted to keep them as friends – but she had heard enough about them.

'So, why do *you* bother to turn up on time?' she asked.

'Hah, well you just know that the one time I turn up late, they'll be on time, and I'd never hear the end of it,' he said. 'It's just not worth it.'

'Why a table for six?' asked Tamar puzzled.

'Five really,' said Denny. 'Miles always brings his latest girlfriend with him. To rub my nose in it, I suppose. I always feel a bit sorry for them. My mother always disapproves of them, you see. She always manages to make sure I know that I could never get a girl half as nice, while at the same time indicating that she still isn't nearly good enough for him. I'm used to it, but I always think it's a bit rough on them.'

Tamar's lips pursed again. Then her eyes twinkled. She called the waiter over and ordered a drink.

'What about Mr. Perfect?' asked Denny, as he always called the medical student boyfriend, although Tamar never knew whether he was being sarcastic or not.

'Oh, he got paged,' she said airily. Then she stood up to greet a couple who were headed for their table. The woman could not have been anyone but Denny's mother. Not with that expression on her face.

'I'm sorry ...' the woman began to express her doubt at Tamar's presence.

Tamar cut her off. 'It's quite all right,' she said sweetly. 'We haven't been waiting long.'

The woman's mouth fell open. She had been put at an immediate disadvantage. Tamar had contrived to indicate that she had been rude and had then forgiven her. Denny gave her a look of pure gratitude.

Wrong footed, Denny's mother sat down without another word, and now she seemed uncouth, as it was left to Denny's father to begin the introductions.

Miles, a younger edition of his bluff and brawny father had brought a fluffy blonde who introduced herself as 'Lindi – with an i.'

'Of course you are,' said Tamar, saccharine sweet. She took Denny's hand and squeezed it, then laid her head briefly on his shoulder, so that there would be no lingering doubts in anyone's mind about their relationship.

Tamar, beautiful and intelligent, and witty to the point of being scathing, dominated the evening. As she had begun, so she intended to continue. She would bring them all down a peg or two. She managed to indicate that Lindi with an i, whom she really rather liked, was far too good for the likes of Miles, while her own dazzling presence was enough to show that, she would not quite be good enough for Denny. She made them all feel dull and stupid by her own sparkling repartee. Denny, she was pleased to note, was the only one who seemed able to follow her conversation. Denny seemed more like himself as the evening progressed. He was coming out of his shell in a fashion that had his parents and his brother staggered. Tamar had always known that beneath his shy exterior Denny was witty and intelligent, but it was apparent that, among his domineering family, this side of him had been ruthlessly suppressed.

Later there had been dancing. Tamar had been appropriated by Miles, who had flirted and been put back in his box in no uncertain terms. Then by Denny's father, who had been treated to a display of quiet outrage, at his want of fatherly feelings when he had tried to indicate that surely, she was not serious about Denny, and surely, a girl like her could have any man she wanted. She hoped that her remarks would get back to Denny's mother, who she was sure had put him up to it.

Then she had danced with Denny, and destiny had happened. It had started innocently enough really. Miles and Lindi were ostentatiously sucking out each other's fillings, and Denny's parents were watching them (Tamar and Denny) like a pair of starved rats after a flake of cheese. Tamar knew what they were waiting for. She snuggled closer and brought her mouth close to Denny's ear. He jumped and reddened, and the moment was lost for now. 'Thanks for doing this,' he said.

She smiled 'It was fun,' she said.

'Well, that's not something I ever expected anyone to say about an evening with my parents,' he grinned. She brought her face closer to his.

'You don't have to …' he began.

'Oh I think so,' she said. 'They're watching us.'

'You've done enough.'

'Not quite,' she reached her hand up behind his neck and kissed him on the mouth. 'How was that?' she murmured.

'Amazing.'

Tamar grinned to herself. 'What?'

'Oh, er, yeah, very convincing, yeah.'

She did it again, just for luck. 'I think I want to go home now,' she said.

'Whatever you want,' said Denny. 'I'll get your coat,' he hesitated.

'It's my blue one,' she told him, palming him the cloakroom ticket.

He had walked her back up to her room, and she marched in leaving the door open for him to follow. He hesitated then followed her in leaving the door open. Tamar opened the window, knowing that sooner or later it would cause the door to slam without her having to make the effort to go and close it. She had thrown her coat on the bed, and now she was shivering in the draught from the open window, which she was stood right in front of. Denny came and stood behind her and draped his coat over her shoulders.

'Do you believe in magic?' she asked him suddenly.

'What, like witches or goblins, that kind of thing?' he said, surprised.

'Well *do* you?'

'I dunno, I suppose everyone would *like* to believe in that kind of thing.'

'Well, destiny then, fate?'

'Yes, I believe in that,' said Denny.

The door slammed shut.

Tamar turned and enfolded herself in his arms. 'Stay,' she said

'What about Mr. Perfect?' said Denny.

'Oh I think he's already here,' said Tamar, without cringing at all. Love can do that to a person.

'Seriously,' said Denny. 'What about Christopher or whatever his name is?'

'Oh, I think that's over,'

'Then I guess I'm staying.'

And that had been the beginning.

'Tamar.'

Tamar came out of her reverie to the sight of Cindy's concerned face.

'Are you all right? You were miles away.'

'I'm okay.' Had any of that really happened? It was one of her favourite memories. 'What if I lose it, if the world goes back? What if I forget?'

She pulled herself together. 'I think I've seen enough' she said, 'Let's go,' and she suited the action to the word in the most dramatic manner. She vanished.

* * *

Denny was having a similar experience at the old house. As he drove up the approach, the house suddenly seemed to change before his very eyes then change back. He blinked. He had been having some strange feelings of *déjà vu* lately but nothing quite as concrete as this. For the house that had briefly appeared to him, had seemed far more, familiar than the one that now loomed over him in the grey light of a December morning. And yet it was as unreal a looking place as you were ever likely to see, it had had turrets for God's sake. They were gone now, but he had seen them as clearly as he could now see the anxious looking soldier heading towards him. It had not been as if he had had an hallucination, it was more like he had been wearing a blindfold that had slipped for a moment to give him a glimpse of something he was not supposed to see and had then been replaced. Brought back to reality (or unreality as the case may be) he slowed the jeep and wondered what he was going to say about his presence here. Too late, he realised that he had forgotten all about his cover story.

The soldier with the bright blond hair walked up to the jeep and saluted Denny. Denny saluted back, while trying to think quickly.

'Second Lieutenant Jamie Adams,' said the soldier. 'We were beginning to think you were never coming.'

Ah, here was an opening, if he could only find out who he was supposed to be.

He climbed out of the jeep slowly and extended his hand. 'Second Lieutenant Chip Bentley,' he said, remembering to use an American accent.

The soldier nodded. 'The prisoners are in the cellar,' he said. 'And I must say, I'll be glad to have them off my hands, I don't like the responsibility and that's a fact.' He walked as he talked. 'It's hard enough to keep the lads in order without women about. You know what I mean?'

Denny's heart soared. Not only did it appear that Tamar and her friend were here, safe and alive. But better than that, he had been taken for the prisoner of war transport officer. Not only would he not be prevented from taking them, he was actually *expected* to take them away. It really could not be better.

'Nobody's been near them, you have my word on that, except the lad who takes them food and he's only about ten years old. He never says a word, scared to death I guess, poor thing. It's been rough on him.'

Denny found himself liking this man, and he would always be grateful to him for protecting Tamar as best he could under difficult circumstances. He did not know who "the lad" might be, but he guessed that he was probably one of the myriad servants that Tristan had always kept about the place. Well, he would take him away too, and if the soldiers did not like it, they could stuff it. He did not wonder why the soldier did not mention Tristan; he knew what was likely to have happened to him – poor Ophelia.

'Do you want to see the CO?' asked the soldier.

'I don't see why?' drawled Denny, keeping his voice as casual as possible, though his heart was beating like a piston hammer. 'I'm already late enough, without a lot of red tape holding me up even more. You know what these Colonels are like.' Denny was taking a chance with this line. But surely,

Colonels were alike in every army, and their subordinates likely to react to them in the same way.

'I sure do,' the soldier laughed.

And Denny breathed a sigh of relief.

'It's probably just as well,' the soldier told Denny. 'I think the old coot's still asleep,'

Denny laughed as well, this time.

They made their way down to the cellar. Just as they reached the bottom step Denny saw his surroundings change again, from a dusty but well-ordered wine cellar to a huge dungeon with rows of cells lining each side and back again. The soldier did not seem to notice anything. Still it was dark down here, and it had only lasted a second.

'In here,' said the soldier drawing out a large rusty key and opening a small door in the back of the cellar. He went in first; Denny followed him. The room was small and bare. There was no place to hide. Not even a shadowy corner, it was brightly lit from a small grate above their heads, too small, it need not be said, to admit a full-grown woman through it. So where the hell were the prisoners?

'Where the hell are they?' said the soldier in honest astonishment. 'They were here. They were right here?'

'So, where have they gone?' asked Denny, forgetting, in his panic, to use his American accent. The soldier turned in surprise. 'Hey...?' he said. He never got any further. Realising that he was busted, Denny swung round and kicked the soldier's legs from beneath him, he never knew how he did it. The keys skittered across the floor. Denny grabbed them and locked the door. He knocked the soldier backwards as he came after Denny for the keys. He never knew where he got the strength, but it held. After a short tussle, the American lay on the floor panting and nursing a bloody nose.

Denny slowly and deliberately pocketed the key and stared down at the man on the floor with a gaze that could have cut diamonds. It said: 'You're not going anywhere pal.'

Jamie believed it.

'All right you Yank bastard,' said Denny. 'Where the hell is my wife?'

* * *

Of course, she reappeared again immediately, but Cindy was in no doubt as to what she had seen.

'You teleported,' she pointed an accusing finger at Tamar.

'Only for a second,' said Tamar strangely diffident. 'It's gone now.'

'You must be a witch.'

Tamar shook her head. 'No, I don't think so. I don't think that's it.'

'But you *must* be.'

'No, remember? Hecaté said that I was more powerful than her. Are *you* more powerful than she is?'

'Of course not, she's a deity.' Cindy looked puzzled. 'She *did* say that, didn't she? What's more powerful than a God?'

Tamar sighed. 'I wish I knew,' she said gloomily.

~ Chapter Thirteen ~

UPPER MANAGEMENT were in an uproar. In all the preceding millennia, there had never been a cock up like this one, and no one had the least idea of what to do about it.

Crispin had been right about one thing. In the manner of all sentient beings everywhere (whatever their calling) they were looking for a scapegoat. And he was it. But finding somebody to blame was not helping the situation. It was ridiculous, six thousand years of planning all gone to hell because of one detail that had somehow been overlooked. The war of the apocalypse had begun well enough, only to be stalled in its tracks. Satan had been overthrown, as predicted – although not quite as anyone had expected – and was now having a lovely holiday. The Horsemen had ridden out and were now waiting around like so many pensioners at a bus stop. Death was still busy of course, and War was keeping his hand in, stirring up minor revolutions just to keep things entertaining. (To War, even the smallest coup was as much fun as the major world war that he had started.) Pestilence and Famine were, of course, a part of human existence just as they had always been. Perhaps at the moment they were a spreading themselves a little more voraciously than previously. But all this was beside the point, it was all nothing compared to the main event, which was they had ridden out for.

There was even a rumour on the thirteenth floor that peace talks had broken out in several areas. It was looking very much as if the apocalypse might have to be cancelled – or at least postponed. The humans should have been arming their nuclear weapons by now, but there was no sign of this happening. It would never happen either, as long as humans still had hope. Until all hope was lost from men's hearts, they would never destroy the world.

Clive, a minor file clerk on level C was watching the situation with great interest. He was himself looking for the missing box, although he had not yet decided what he would do with it if he found it. It was unheard of for a file clerk to break out in this erratic fashion, although Clive had done it before. And thinking as an individual can become habit forming, one might almost suspect that he had a mind of his own.

He knew very well why the dim-wits upstairs wanted it so badly, but Clive had ambitions of his own

Thus, he wanted to find the box for himself, and his unique experiences of human beings meant that he was capable of thinking in ways that his colleagues were completely unable to comprehend. He was fairly confident that he could find it before they did, unless they had the most unbelievable good luck.

For example, he knew that an immutable law of the universe is the one that states that wherever the thing you have lost is, it is always in the last place that you look. By utilising quantum, surely he could eliminate the "looking for it" part and just get straight to the "finding it" part. Another immutable law tends to be that if you have an important box (or case or file-folder) it is usually on top of the wardrobe. Sometimes it is in the *foot* of the wardrobe or in the cupboard under the stairs. Or, occasionally, in the chest of drawers in the spare room. Having decided on this, and realising that these would be the first places he would look, he could eliminate these possibilities. What did that leave, apart from the attic, or down the back of the sofa? No, that was loose change – whatever *that* was.

They, that is, the dim-wits upstairs, were currently trying to trace the box back through history. The last known possessor of the box had been Zeus, but he no longer existed, and anyway, it would be just like him to leave it lying about somewhere.

'The fools!' thought Clive. That was not the way to find it, he knew. Nor was trying to find it by magic. They had tried that too, throwing various locator spells into the ether. He understood the theory behind it. After all, the only thing that could shield a magical object, strangely enough, was Tupperware – and what were the chances? On the other hand, what they had failed to realise, was that the box itself was not magical in any way. It was just a box. And hope is not magic, although it *is* an item of faith, and Clive could see where they might get confused.

He realised that he himself was stumped, but he was not giving up. He was better than his cohorts at human thinking, but not as good as a real human. *That* was what he needed. And as luck would have it, he had, in the past, had actual contact with real human beings, another unheard of innovation of his own – talking to the people – and these were not just any people, they were distinctly heroic types. There was just one problem …

Clive did not know how it had been done and, therefore, he had no idea how to fix it. Oh he could see it clearly enough, and it was damned clever, he thought, and dammed inconvenient – particularly for the people involved he supposed, but he was only thinking about himself at the moment. He realised that there was nothing he could do this time; they would have to sort it out for themselves. All he could do was watch in frustration. Watch and hope. But maybe he could help a little.

* * *

'Where the hell is my wife?' Denny snarled.

The soldier was crouched on the floor trying to escape the wrath of this madman who had locked them in.

'I don't know, honestly. No one could have come down here I swear, I had the only key.' He brightened. 'They must have escaped.'

'How?' said Denny scornfully, but he calmed down a little, the man was so obviously telling the truth.

The soldier shrugged.

Denny sat down on an upturned box. 'What about that lad you mentioned, could he have taken them the key, dropped it through the grate perhaps?'

'And then they very considerately put the key back in my pocket before they left?'

'Hmmm, well they might have done, so that you wouldn't suspect anything. To delay the search for them. Have you got a better explanation?'

The soldier did not and besides, even if he had, he judged it wiser to say nothing at this point. Denny sank into a brown study.

After a while, the soldier ventured the opinion that perhaps someone might wonder where he was and come looking for him.

'Will they?' asked Denny sceptically.

'No, I suppose not,' the soldier admitted.

'What did you say your name was again?' asked Denny.

'Jamie.'

'I'm Denny,' he held his hand out. Jamie shook it gingerly.

'Well,' said Denny, 'we can't stay here forever, I guess I'm going to have to head back to London.' He paused and grinned. 'I'm afraid I'll have to have you along you know.'

'Why?' asked Jamie, although he knew. 'Look, you can leave me here, I won't squeal, I swear. They'll never know you were here.'

Denny shook his head. 'You know I can't risk it,' he said. 'It's not as if I *want* to take you with me, and I'm sorry, really I am. But ...' he shrugged his shoulders expressively.

'But I'll be AWOL,' said Jamie.

'Captured by the enemy,' corrected Denny. 'There might even be a medal in it for you – eventually.'

'Uh huh,' said Jamie pessimistically

'It'll be okay,' said Denny. 'I went AWOL, came here all the way from China. Had the most amazing luck – up until now anyway. I suppose it had to run out sometime.'

As they passed the chapel near to the house, they heard from within the sound of voices raised in song, a strange sound in these days, and it reminded them both that it was almost Christmas. They raised their heads for a moment to listen, the words were unfamiliar to Jamie, but the tune was mournfully beautiful. Even though these were rough and ready county folk, with reedy voices, when their voices were joined together in harmony, swelling in the still morning air, they sounded quite enchanting, and it was possible for a moment, to forget the war and believe in a better world.

'What's that they're singing?' asked Jamie.

'*Donare Nobis Pachem,*' replied Denny austerely. 'Give us peace.'

Jamie nodded. 'Amen to that,' he said.

'I thought you were a career soldier,' said Denny.

'I am, but I joined up to defend my country, not to … not for *this*.' He shrugged to demonstrate that he could not find the words.

Denny nodded. 'I knew I was going to like this bloke,' he thought.

* * *

They were sleeping under the stars. Well, they were actually going to sleep in the jeep, because of the weather, which was too cold even for Denny. Though at least it had stopped raining, but only in order to start snowing. But they were cooking under the stars at least.

Denny had brought some supplies from the house, and was currently trying to get a tin of soup open with the can opener on his army issue multiplex knife.

They were camping out because Jamie was officially AWOL and, anyway, Denny did not want to attract any more attention than was necessary. Besides, this way they could use most of their spare cash for petrol, or "gas", as it was now called up and down the country.

Jamie was disconsolate. He was wondering what he was really doing here, certain that had he really held out against this, Denny would not have forced him physically. Now that he was over his fit of temper, he seemed perfectly genial. Jamie was generally a good judge of people and Denny did not seem like a bully to him. So why had he gone along with him?

Denny cursed as his hand slipped and he sucked at a cut finger. 'Jesus Christ! – Shit!' He went back to his operation. There was a loud snap and a piece of metal flew upwards and struck Denny's face.

Ignoring the blood pouring down his cheek, Denny merely looked ruefully at the stricken can opener. 'Broken,' he said laconically. 'Have you got a knife?'

* * *

'Here it is,' said Cindy. 'Things more powerful than gods: Demons – that is, certain types of demon, not your common or garden variety obviously, angels, again not all of them, and the Djinn. Except they don't have free will, so their power is limited by what their masters wish for, but technically – phenomenal cosmic power.'

'The gin,' said Tamar, what's that?'

'What are *they*?' corrected Cindy. 'Mortals call them genies.'

'Mmmm?'

'But I don't think that can be it. Do you remember being trapped in a jar or a bottle or something like that?'

Tamar thought about it. '*Yes!*'

'Oh.' There really did not seem to be anything else to say.

'Then, maybe that's what happened,' Cindy continued after a minute. 'Maybe it was a wish that changed the world. I suppose it's possible. Says here that the Djinn can do practically anything, as long as their master wishes for it.'

'You mean that it was *me*? That *I* did this.'

'Well technically you could have, but only if someone wished for it. Morally I suppose it wasn't you. A Djinn is a slave you see.'

'Then surely the most powerful being in this equation is the *master* of the Djinn – a human being I suppose.'

Cindy checked the book, one of Denny's – it had his name in it – that they had found in the flat (Tamar had been flabbergasted – 'I never dreamed that he read this sort of thing,' she said)

'Yes, you're right,' Cindy told her. 'Only humans can be the masters of the Djinn – how did you know that?'

Tamar pulled a wry face in answer. 'What do you think?'

Cindy looked blank for a moment. 'Oh, oh, yes of course, you remembered it.'

There was a silence while they both processed what this meant. It was Cindy who put it into words. 'So, you *were* a Djinn then.'

'I think I'd rather have been a Djinn than a demon,' said Tamar defensively. This conclusion had made her rather unhappy. She had no desire to be anyone's slave again – and if the world was restored …

'Well actually it says here that a Djinn is a type of …'

'Shut up,' snapped Tamar 'Just – shut up, I want to think. I *need* to think, something doesn't fit here. If I was a Djinn, why do I remember things as if I was a human as well? And I know that – well I seem to remember anyway – that Denny and I lived together, wouldn't that have meant that *he* was my master? If I *was* a Djinn, which we haven't proved yet. And why, if he was my master, would he make such a wish? Why would anyone if it comes to that, it doesn't make any sense.' She was doing her thinking out loud, as you can see, but Cindy quite naturally assumed that these remarks were addressed to her.

'Maybe to free you,' she said, startling Tamar who had forgotten that she was there.

'We-ell,' she answered cautiously after a moment's thought to sort this one out. 'That *does* sound like Denny I suppose, but surely it wouldn't be necessary to change the whole world like that. And if it was, then he wouldn't do it. No it still doesn't make sense.'

'Maybe Denny wasn't your master then. I mean maybe he was, and then someone else was – if you see what I mean?'

'It still doesn't make sense. Like I said, why would anyone who had a Djinn want to free it?' Besides I told you, I can remember – *being – human*!'

'Maybe, that wasn't the point of the wish at all,' said Cindy. 'If there *was* a wish,' she added hurriedly. 'Maybe the point was to change the world. – However it was done,' she finished, Tamar was glaring at her.

'Now that makes sense,' said Tamar. 'That's what we thought all along. Wish I knew who it was. '

'I wonder why they did it,' said Cindy.

'Well, that's the point, isn't it?' said Tamar. 'However it was done – Why?

'That's what we still don't know.'

* * *

Jack Stiles (we can no longer refer to him as Captain, since he was now AWOL) had no idea why he was doing this. So, one of his men had been captured – what did he think that *he* could do about it? And then again, sure, Sanger was a good bloke, but he, Stiles, had only known him for a few weeks – this, he was less certain about. But that woman he had met, or dreamt or whatever, had been very definite about it. And that was another thing, why did he feel obliged to listen to her? She had spoken to him as a wife might do, and, as such, he had taken her, and had simply gone along with her wishes without thinking about it, just as many husbands do for the sake of a quiet life. But, now that he had had time to think about it, he wondered … Stiles shrugged, he had made a decision; he would not wonder about it anymore. He knew he was going to do this, so what was the point of making a lot of heavy weather about it? He might as well just get on with it, and not torment his mind with a lot of questions that he did not have the answers to. He had enough to worry about as it was, like where the hell he was supposed to be going, and how he was going to get there, and what he was going to do when he did. Oh well, he was sure that it would all work out for the best in the end.

Actually, he was not sure of this at all. But Stiles had been a copper first and then an army man, and he was accustomed to believing that somehow the orders would make sense in the end. That was the surface Stiles. The real Stiles, the one deep down, knew that this was actually a load of shit, but habit, especially habits of thought, are hard to break.

He had been trudging along aimlessly for several hours without any clear idea of where he was headed for, and it was now getting dark. Time to find a place for the night, it was snowing, and he needed to find some shelter. He spotted a lonely looking house about a half hour's walk away. Even at this distance, it looked empty. It was a fairly large house, yet there was no car in front and no lights on, despite the dusk. Probably the owners had packed up and left; he was still quite close to the front lines. It would do anyway. He hitched up his pack and headed for it.

* * *

If you asked somebody where they would hide a box that contained something of vital importance, the sensible man would tell you that he was not going to tell you where he would hide it. And if he will not tell you where he has hidden it, has he, in fact, hidden it at all. And if it's not hidden, is there even a box at all? After all, it was a rhetorical box that you asked about in the first place, wasn't it …?

'But we *know* there's a box Talbot,' said Crispin impatiently. 'Don't be so silly. If you want to get all metaphorical, do it on your own time. In the meantime, why don't you make yourself useful? If we *don't* find it, it's *my* head on the chopping block, and trust me, I can take all of you down with me.'

'But surely hope resides in the hearts of men,' said Talbot.

'Oh, well, if you want to believe all that hippie claptrap...' said Crispin.

~Chapter Fourteen ~

DENNY WEIGHED THE knife in his hand. It was heavy, but it did not feel so to him. It felt as if it were a part of him almost – as if it were growing out of his hand. He drew the blade from its sheath and looked at it. There were swirling patterns in the metal, moving in and out of each other with a horrible liquidity, never still for an instant. The metal looked as if it were alive. Yet, when Denny gingerly touched the blade, it felt solid enough, cold and hard just like any other blade. It was only when he looked at it that he got the strange feeling that it was writhing under his hand.

He sheathed it again and looked curiously at Jamie. 'Where did you get this?' he asked.

Jamie told him, and added, 'why do you care? It's just an old knife.'

'It's called an Athame,' Denny told him and wondered how he knew. He put it into his pack. Jamie never even thought to feel resentful about this; it had never felt like it belonged to him anyway.

Supper, it seemed, was to be abandoned. Jamie was a little resentful about *this*. You were supposed to *feed* prisoners of war! It was in the Geneva Convention or something; he was sure of it.

Denny packed up their stuff and extinguished the fire without saying a word. They went back to the jeep to sleep.

It was the early hours of the morning and Jamie was fast asleep, but Denny could not sleep. Eventually he succumbed to his wakefulness – knowing that the more he tried to fight it, the worse it would get – and climbed out of the jeep. He knew what the problem was – it was the Athame, it was preying on his mind. He sat down a few yards from the jeep and opened his pack.

It belonged to him somehow, he could feel it. He withdrew the alarming blade and stared at it, hoping that it would jog his memory. But although the usual memories of another life were seeping through his mind, he could not get anything specific about the Athame. The vague feeling that it belonged to him was coming from the blade itself and not his mind. This was quite contrary to the usual manner of inanimate objects that stir feelings of familiarity, where the memory is usually quite specific, and it is the feeling behind it that is vague. It was almost as if the damn thing was alive. Or, at least, had a mind – a consciousness – of its own.

Denny gazed at it in frustration. This thing had answers; he knew it did, if only he could remember …

In his head, he heard a voice from the past – which past? – saying. 'If you want to know something – ask.' It was something that Mrs. Allen, a teacher of his, had been fond of saying, and yet he was sure that it was not her voice.

Denny put the blade back in the sheath and laid it down, sighing. If only he knew the question.

* * *

'So,' said Tamar, 'if it wasn't a wish that did it, and I don't think it was, because I remember … well anyway, putting that idea aside for now, and just to cover all the options –   what else could have changed the past like that and altered all our memories?' She looked interrogatively at Cindy, who looked back at her in slight panic.

'Oh come on,' snapped Tamar. 'You must have *some* ideas. Just off the top of your head now. Throw some ideas at me.'

Tamar was understandably desperate to prove that she was not a Djinn – Anything but that – and she was willing to cling to any other ideas that presented themselves.

'I can't,' Cindy protested. 'Look I just don't *know* what could have done it, if not a Djinn. Maybe a god. No, not even a god has that kind of power.'

'Look it doesn't matter *who*, at this stage. Just assume that somebody *did* have the power. How would it be done?'

'I really don't ... okay *without* wishing? Time travel perhaps, but even gods can't do that. Or the Djinn either.'

'So, who can?'

'Nobody! That's what I'm telling you.'

'Okay, so what else, how else could it have been done, some sort of spell?'

'Well, technically I suppose, but no witch or sorcerer has that kind of power. It would have to be a hell of a big spell, complicated too. It's a powerful magic that could mess about with people's fates like that. I've never heard of anything like that being done, or anyone who could do it.'

'But technically it *is* possible.' Tamar said. 'Wait, go back a bit.' She thumped the table. 'What did you just say before?'

'What?'

'You mentioned The Fates,'

'I meant ...'

'Yes, I know, but what about it? The Three Fates, are they ... do they ...?'

Cindy looked blank. 'I'm not sure what ...'

'The FATES!' Tamar was getting exasperated. 'Clotho, Lachesis and Atropos. The Maiden, the Mother and the Crone. The weavers of the tapestry of life.'

'Oh, *them*!' said Cindy in some relief. 'They wouldn't do it, I mean I suppose they could, but they *wouldn't*! Definitely, definitely not, no.' her voice was becoming uncertain.

Tamar looked intently at her. 'Are you sure?'

'I'm sure!' said Cindy.

'*How* sure?'

'Well, not all that sure, actually,'

* * *

The house was not locked up. This made Stiles a little uneasy, but it did not seem as if the lock had been broken. Perhaps the people who had lived here had left in a hurry. He was by now absolutely certain that the house had been abandoned. Nobody left their doors unlocked around here anymore – if they ever had – too many soldiers about. That was what was worrying him now. That someone may have got here before him with the same idea and an unwillingness to share.

He opened the door cautiously and sniffed the air. Stale and dusty, no sign there that the place was occupied. He listened next, and heard not a sound. He wandered through the rooms; there was nobody here. Perhaps someone had been here and moved on. In the living room, he tried the light switch; the room blazed with a sudden light, and then went dark again with a popping sound. 'Bulb gone,' he thought, but at least the place still had electricity. He moved to the window and closed the curtains before trying a lamp. Now the room was filled with a soft yellow glow, which made it look almost homely.

He found the controls for the gas fire and set it merrily blazing away. He had not been so warm and comfortable in months. Once he had warmed up a little he decided to explore the house. It seemed pretty ordinary, if rather large and posh by Stiles's usual standards. Wide hallway with coat rack and telephone table and a huge staircase. Nice, if somewhat old fashioned, furniture in the living and dining rooms. Old fashioned diamond pattern bay windows, the real kind that twinkled as you walked past them, because of the separate panes. The kitchen was fitted out with all mod cons cleverly hidden to make it look like an old Victorian kitchen with a genuine old-fashioned top of the range electric Range oven. Stiles laughed (as people do at the pretensions of others). There was also a library and a room with a snooker table in it. Upstairs the bedroom doors ran along one side of the long landing; at the end, the bathroom door stood open, so he went in. This was set up in the same way as the kitchen; modern conveniences cleverly disguised as old-fashioned inconveniences, and a bathtub so large he could have taken a swim in it. Pity there would not be any hot water. What he would not give for a hot bath.

He decided to go downstairs and put the boiler on, since the gas was obviously still on, as testified to by the fire in the living room. He would find some food and have a bath in about an hour, and then he would find a bed and get some sleep.

He felt like Goldilocks. First looking for food and then poking his head into the bedrooms to see which one he fancied. He just hoped that the Three Bears did not come home.

And he was almost certain that he was not going mad at all, not insane in any way, nor was he completely bonkers, no. Just because he had gone AWOL on the word of a dream or vision of a beautiful woman who he was certain he knew from somewhere (although he was sure he had never seen her before in his life). Just because he was suffering from delusions and *déjà vu* at the same time. And just because he was bivouacking in a large house in the middle of Nowhere (a little known village in South Western China, spelled, he believed 'No'Wer') and now appeared to be thinking in fairy tales. And all this without having a single drink. That did not mean he was going mad. He was absolutely certain of that – not all that certain actually – little bit worried about that one perhaps – maybe slightly bonkers – completely round the twist? – Absolutely certain! Not mad at all – I think.

While his bath was running, he wandered down to the library to grab a book. One caught his eye almost immediately – "The Adventures of Sherlock Holmes". Something to sneer at. It was almost as if somebody had known. He was not altogether surprised when, as he slid the book out, the entire bookcase panel creaked around on its axis revealing the almost mandatory secret passage. Now this would be too much for the curiosity of a normal person – who would at least have probably remembered to go and turn the bathwater off first –

but Stiles was a policeman. It was practically his job to be curious, and not at all out of his tiny mind – no not a bit.

The passageway was delightfully ghoulish; the most hardened gothic investigator would not have been disappointed. It was lit with flaming torches that flickered eerily and lit up eldritch shapes in the shadows. The walls were cold and damp and gave off a greenish glow. Cobwebs fluttered in an unearthly breeze, insects scuttled under his feet, and there was a funny smell. Stiles gave a shiver of delicious fear; this was fun. At the end of the passage was a lighted archway, and through that, he found a large hall, more like a gigantic cavern really, but it was all marble and gilt. All around the edges were more archways, lit, as it were, from within. The hall itself was not lit, but it could be seen quite clearly by the lights from these alcoves, for that is what they were. In each one, Stiles noticed, was a plinth as if for a statue. Some of the plinths were still adorned by statues, but most of them had nothing on them but a pile of dust.

Stiles moved forward curiously and peered at the stone plinth below a pile of greyish dust which lay atop a broken off marble foot. It read APOLLO. He moved to the next one. The plinth again was empty apart from the pile of dust. This one read ARTEMIS. He looked around for a plinth with a statue on it, perhaps there might be some clue there as to what all this meant. He was attracted to a very elegant statue of a tall woman. The name on the plinth read HECATÉ. And beside her was another empty plinth, which proclaimed that the previous tenant had been called HADES. On the other side of him, was the deserted plinth of ZEUS, a huge one this, more than twice the size of the others and in the side of the plinth, there seemed to be a small doorway or hatch. By now Stiles was getting the idea. These were the ancient gods. As he wandered around, he saw plinths for HERA and APHRODITE, ARES and DIONYSUS and ATHENE. On the other side of the hall, he found THOR and LOKI, ODIN and FREYA. And in the middle, RA and ANUBIS and ISIS and OSIRIS. But why were they all destroyed? Well, almost all of them.

PSYCHE still stood gracefully on her plinth, as did the Muses – Calliope, Clio, Erato, Euterpe, Melpomene, Polyhymnia, Terpsichore, Thalia and Urania, all together on one large plinth in a dancing circle – and the Fates and also POSEIDON, and of course HECATÉ. He was drawn back to this particular statue to take a closer look. He had a feeling that he had seen it before.

It was nearly a minute before he recognized her, and when he did, he almost fell over from the shock. He felt like he needed a drink.

~ Chapter Fifteen ~

TALBOT HAD WONDERED if perhaps Zeus had set the box among the stars. It had been a habit of his to do this with things – and even people – that he did not know what else to do with.

'A bad habit,' said Crispin, but it was an inspired thought, he said. Until it turned out that it was wrong, whereupon it magically became: 'A bloody stupid idea that only an idiot like you would come up with. Almost as daft as that other idea you had, "a metaphorical box, my modem."

Talbot had expanded this idea into quite an intricate theory that came under the heading of, as Crispin pointed out, "clutching at straws".

'It's a *real* box, Talbot, get that into your thick head, and we might just be getting somewhere'

The situation was grave. The Apocalypse was now seriously behind schedule, if it were not sorted out soon, then heads were going to roll. It would be Bloody Ragnoroc all over again. The Twilight of the gods had gone completely wrong the first time, and had had to be staged all over again, thanks to young Whatisname, sticking his oar in. – Bloody heroes. And even then, they had not got all of them in the end. There were still a few of them hanging around. And this was far more important than the demise of a few mouldy old gods.

It was rumoured that up on thirteenth, a young programmer had ventured the opinion: 'Sod the box, why don't we just chuck a great big asteroid at them?' but Crispin did not know if it was true. If it was, it was a mark of how desperate things were getting up there. They would never do it, though. They were the sorts who would always do everything "by the book" as the saying goes.

'Pity,' thought Crispin, 'it wasn't a bad idea.' It would certainly solve *his* problem anyway.

* * *

'What's the big deal with that thing anyway?' Jamie was curious about Denny's apparent obsession with what looked to him like an old dagger. It was a curiosity, he supposed, but not really worth the minute attention that his companion was paying to it, surely? He had woken that morning to discover Denny sat in a patch of melted snow just looking at it. He was still looking at it now, several hours later.

Denny reluctantly tore his gaze from his treasure. 'I wish I knew,' he said.

He said this while holding the Athame and so, quite suddenly, he did know. At least he knew what it was, and what it was for and the powers it possessed. But it did not help him in the least to access any memories that he might have had regarding his ownership of it. He still could not find out what his connection with it was. He did not need to, he decided. It was enough to understand that the connection was there, and now he knew …

He stood up. 'Time to go,' he said.

* * *

Stiles never remembered afterwards how he had stumbled and slipped in a daze back to the library. Nor did he remember falling asleep in a large armchair in the library. It was late morning when he was awakened by the sun streaming through the window, casting pretty patterns on the wall behind him, and, had he known it, on his own unshaven face. He had been completely incapable of any kind of constructive thought the night before. But now he felt – what? Almost normal? He opened his eyes and looked around the room, and he was almost certain that he was not insane at all. He was slowly reaching that point of self-delusion that says: 'It was all a dream'

That was it. He had fallen asleep in this chair, and had a very vivid dream. He could not possibly have seen what he thought he saw. Because things like that did not happen. He must have imagined the whole thing.

He had now talked himself into a state of complete reassurance. Which was abruptly shattered when he opened the door and found himself in … well, he wasn't in No' Wer, anymore.

* * *

Denny was concentrating on Tamar – with one hand on Jamie's shoulder – in order to teleport to her, when he heard a sound behind him. It was a large sound, not a loud sound, but a large sound, which is quite different. It went "Whump!" It was the sound of quite a lot of air being displaced. He looked round. There, behind him in the clearing, was a house. And Denny was quite certain that it had not been there before.

Denny walked all around the house looking at the ground.

Jamie was puzzled. 'What are you doing?' he asked.

'I'm looking for the Wicked Witch of the East,' said Denny balefully.

It should be clarified at this point that Jamie had had magic explained to him by now ('Magic's real, get used to it') in view of what Denny was planning with the Athame, and he was taking it pretty calmly. People usually did: well, in fact, a *person* usually took it well. *People* tended to get panicky and do stupid things, like tell the newspapers.

'Not really?' said Jamie, he was getting the hang of Denny's sarcasm too, which was much harder to adjust to. Denny never used a sarcastic tone when employing sarcasm, but always sounded absolutely sincere. It was the only really nasty aspect to his character.

While Denny was around the back of the house, Stiles came warily out of the front, blinking in the bright sunshine. He wondered where he was. He appeared to be in a large field, not dissimilar to the one the house had stood in before, but definitely not the same, unless he really was going mad. When he saw Denny coming round the side of the house with his head bent to the ground and an enemy soldier in tow, he descended into an icy calm certainty. He had indeed lost his mind – seeing things was definite proof. He seemed to remember reading that somewhere. So, he was definitely insane. Good, that was that cleared up then. He probably was not in a field at all; no doubt, he was in a nice hospital somewhere, with kind nurses and doctors and little blue pills every day to stop him trying to jump off the roof. Perhaps the war had turned his mind, some horrible atrocity that he had witnessed … or maybe there had not been a war, maybe it was all a part of his madness. Maybe he had never been a policeman. Maybe he was not Jack Stiles at all. There was a kind of tranquility in the idea, which was rudely shattered when Denny spotted him.

'Jack?' he said, in shocked tones. Then: 'Oh sorry Captain, I don't know why I said that.'

'It's all right,' said Stiles. 'I'm not a Captain any more anyway. I must say, you're a very convincing sort of delusion,' he added. 'I didn't know delusions could talk to you. What am I saying? Of course, you can. You did before, didn't you? And she did. Oh boy did *she* talk. You know who I mean, of course you do. You're all of you in my head together, so you must know each other.'

'Izzee all right?' asked Jamie in concern.

'He's fine,' said Denny wryly. 'He's just clutching at straws. Aren't you Cap … Jack?'

'Oh bugger,' was Stiles elegant response. 'I nearly had myself convinced there.'

'Worth a try,' said Denny, and added: 'I know how you feel. I think I'd rather be nuts at times.'

'So,' Stiles nodded to Jamie, 'who's this?'

'Later,' said Denny. 'Watch this.' He vanished and reappeared. 'Cool, hey?'

Stiles snorted his contempt. 'That's nothing! I made an entire house move from China to … where are we anyway?'

'Cambridgeshire. Are you sure, it was you?'

'No,' Stiles admitted. 'I think it was her.'

'Who?'

'Hecaté, I found out her name in …'

Jamie interrupted them. 'You guys are crazy,' he said, looking nervously from one to the other, as if calculating his chances of getting away. They were not good.

Denny and Stiles looked at each other and laughed.

'Ah,' said Stiles, 'wouldn't it be nice.'

Denny got his face straight and turned to Jamie. 'I think we've established that that is definitely *not* the case.'

'Be easier if it was,' said Stiles. He shrugged. 'Oh well, what's next?'

Denny grinned. 'Want to meet my wife?'

* * *

Tamar's problems were increasing. Now she was having memories of the future.

'Not premonitions,' she tried to explain to Cindy. 'They feel just like ordinary memories, I think a premonition would be more – vague. More like a possibility, these feel like they've already happened.'

'But you can't remember the future,' said Cindy reasonably. 'It hasn't happened yet.'

'How do *you* know? I tell you, I'm not certain of *anything* anymore.'

'Maybe I should summon Hecaté again,' said Cindy, she was feeling as if she were in over her head.

'How's that going to help?' said Tamar shortly. 'She said she wasn't going to tell me any more than she already has.'

'It might make *me* feel better,' said Cindy stubbornly.

'I am here,' said Hecaté from behind them. They looked round and saw …

'Denny!' squealed Tamar rushing at him.

Stiles looked around the assorted group. His gaze rested on Cindy, who he had not seen before – as far as he knew. She patted her hair. His gaze shifted to Hecaté and stayed there for a while.

'Well,' he said, as Tamar released Denny, 'it looks like the gang's all here'

PART TWO

And the great dragon was cast out, that old serpent called the Devil and Satan, which deceiveth the whole world: he was cast out into the earth and his angels were cast out with him.

REV XII. 9

An idol-maker does not worship the gods: he knows what stuff they are made of.

Traditional Chinese Proverb.

~ Chapter Sixteen ~

A year earlier...

ASKPHRIT SURVEYED his new surroundings with a certain satisfaction, okay so it certainly was not the Ritz, but he had been in worse places. His time in prison had been infinitely worse. Here, at least he had his own room and hot and cold running devils – mostly hot. No, he decided, it was not too bad at all.

And Satan seemed an okay sort of creature. A little lax perhaps. He seemed inclined to treat Askphrit more as a sort of favourite than anything.

He was jaded, Askphrit decided. He had been in this job too long. He did not seem to get any pleasure out of it any more. Security was lax and the torments done by rote, a mere matter of form, with little enthusiasm. Some of the devils, Askphrit had discovered, resented this, and the fact that there was no chance any longer, for promotion for the inventive and enthusiastic devil. There had been no promotions in Hell for an eternity, he was told.

He moved among the employees and inmates of Hell alike. Like a campaigning politician. And he found out more about Hell than Satan ever knew.

He also employed a fiercely resentful Pierce as an extra pair of eyes and ears.

Askphrit had not been surprised to see Pierce arrive shortly after himself.

'Thought they would get you, without me to keep an eye on you.' Was the extent of what he had to say about it? He did not bother to ask how it had happened. And he did not tell Peirce what had happened to him. That was the past, and the thing to do now, was assess the future.

It was Askphrit's nature to look at every place from the point of view of its strategic usefulness. This place, he decided, had possibilities.

* * *

Askphrit assessed his troops. They were a fine bunch of … troops. He had already had the vampire vote of course, being their god. And, naturally, hell was lousy with vampires; it had been a good start. These he had sent out campaigning on his behalf and soon at least half the devils had been behind him. And the inmates were mostly behind him too, since he had promised to abolish story time in favour of more traditional punishments. Which they would be allowed to administer to each other – in certain circumstances – he had vowed that under his rule, the old promotion scheme would be reinstated, which meant that some of the inmates, those who showed promise, would be elevated to imp status and from there, they would have their hooves on the promotion ladder. Considering the type of person, you often found in Hell, this was a popular move. Up the revolution! And up yours Satan, His time was nearly over.

And now it *was* time. The present government had no idea what had been going on, behind their backs, and now Askphrit was ready to make his move.

He made ready to give his stirring speech.

'Okay lads,' he began, then he thought, 'oh forget it, this bunch of bloodthirsty bastards know what to do.'

He raised a large sabre. 'Let's get 'em boys.' This seemed to have the desired effect. It got a rousing cheer at any rate.

To be fair to Askphrit, he did actually intend to honour most of his promises. How else was he going to persuade them that their next move should be to help him take over the world?

It would be easy with troops like these. They would not have to do very much, just be terrifying, and they were *good* at that. And then he would finally have all the power that he had always wanted. It was with these pleasant thoughts in his head that Askphrit triumphantly ascended Satan's throne.

As he looked down at Satan, (who was bound hand and foot, kneeling – there being no other position possible in his current condition) he imagined that it was another face in front of him, one that had tormented him for many years, even when she had not been around. What he would not give to have *her* under his boot heel.

The minions were waiting.

Askphrit gave the order. 'Throw him out.'

And the minions responded with glee. They raised Satan above their heads and passed him from claw to claw along the top of the crowd like a triumphant basketball player. Except that triumphant basketball, players are not often poked in sensitive areas with pitchforks as they make their progress.

The demons were jubilant, but Askphrit's mood had been spoiled by his untimely reminder of his nemesis. In his secret heart, he was forced to acknowledge that, if anyone could spoil his plans, it would be her! Tamar Black – stupid name. She had stopped him before. Even in the face of the seemingly impossible odds that he had been very careful to stack up against her, she always found a way. Well not his time, he decided. This time he was finally in a position to make sure that she would not get the chance. But it would never do to be overconfident. This time he would not underestimate her. And just to be safe, he would fix that sidekick of hers as well, and those other lackeys who hung around with her.

Askphrit did not think in terms of people having friends – people who would do things for you without having to be intimidated into it, people who would do you a favour, as opposed to taking orders. If anyone had tried to explain this concept to him, he probably would not have been able to understand it. Nor did he understand the concept of teamwork. This was probably why he always failed when he went up against Tamar. He did not realise that he was one against six – even with all his minions. They did not count; they only did what he told them to, and it would never have occurred to him to ask them for their advice.

When Peirce came and reported to him that Satan was now ejected Askphrit gave a satisfied sigh. He had done it – stage one complete. He laughed. 'Good, good,' he said. 'Let him "walk the Earth" for a while, the rest will do him good.'

He left the celebrations in full swing, and stalked into the palace, taking Peirce with him. It would, he thought, need extensive renovations to make it fitting for his new status as the ruler of the world. But he must not get ahead of himself. First, there were things to take care of.

He turned to Peirce. 'Send for the Fates,' he said settling into what was now, after all, *his* throne. 'And bring me a cup of tea.'

* * *

Up on the thirteenth floor, the news was out. Satan had been overthrown, now was the time that had been foreseen from the beginning (they had been overseeing the human world for so long now that they were even beginning to talk like them). The time was at hand (see what I mean?) Anyway, it was the first step. It was time for the program to begin its final run. Time to set up the Apocalypse program.

'What *already*?' said Matlus who had been promoted recently – well about thirteen hundred years ago.

'Yes,' said a senior programmer, name of Dylosius. ''Tis a bit sooner than we expected, but these things are not always quantifiable, not when you are dealing with – *people*.' He gave this word all the contempt he was capable of, and that was a lot. 'Anyway, it's right enough. I expect the program just ran a bit faster in places than we expected. Besides, you have to remember, we did edit out a large chunk of the mythological age.'

'I suppose,' said Matlus doubtfully. 'That shouldn't have made a difference to the time up here,' he thought. But he decided it would be wiser to say nothing. After all, he was new. And these guys ought to know what they were doing.

That had been a year ago – in human terms – and still no Apocalypse. Matlus was smug. He had been right, in some indefinable way, it was too soon. (He was, by the way, dead wrong about this) He wondered if he ought to mention his doubts about the wisdom of their editing of the mythological age, in the face of what had happened to the box. (He may have had a point about this) but he refrained from making this observation on the basis that in this job, as in so many others, "he who points out the problem, invariably get the blame". But the possibility remained that the box itself, being a part of the mythological age, may well have been lost somewhere in the deleted files of mythology.

~ Chapter Seventeen ~

CINDY WATCHED STILES and Hecaté. There was a definite "vibe" (as it was sometimes called) that said to her "married" – with a dash of confusion on his part. But there are many married men who appear confused about how they ended up that way.

Cindy turned her attention to Jamie, giving him an inviting smile; she was rewarded with a confused grin.

The "gang" had split up. Hecaté had left unobtrusively and Tamar, Denny and Stiles had formed the nuclei of the group, leaving Cindy and Jamie on the fringes, listening. They were talking intently together, explaining everything that had happened to them.

Denny told them about the Athame and Tamar told of the underground vampires. Stiles told them about the house and the Hall of Idols.

'Well,' said Tamar eventually, 'at least we can all agree that we probably all know each other. We just don't know that we know each other.' She tried this sentence in her head. 'Well, you know what I mean,' she added.

'Except me,' interrupted Jamie. 'I'm damn sure that I don't know *any* of you. I'm not a part of this.'

'You're a part of it now,' Denny told him.

'Yes but,' said Cindy, 'a part of what? Does anybody have the least idea about what's going on?'

'Where's Hecaté?' asked Tamar.

'She's not going to tell us any more,' said Cindy.

'I didn't mean that,' lied Tamar, reluctantly realising that this was true.

'I think we're stuck, personally,' said Stiles. 'I mean look, we can't remember who we are until the world changes back, and we won't know how to change the world back until we remember who we are.'

'I can remember *some* things,' said Denny.

'Me too,' said Tamar.

'And so can I,' said Stiles, but it's not enough. 'Take Tamar, was she a Djinn or not? Was it because of her that the world has been changed? Or was it because of one of the other of us? Or *all* of us? If it was someone else, do we *know* who did this, but we just can't remember? Surely, whoever this was aimed at can't have made such a powerful enemy without knowing it. I think we probably all know who did this, or we would if we could just remember it. And we probably have a good idea why, too. Or we should.'

'We thought it might have been the Fates,' said Tamar, who was impressed at Stiles' neat summary of their situation.

'Okay,' said Stiles, 'but does any of us know how we can find out? Can any of us say how we can go and ask them?'

'*Ask* them?' gasped Cindy.

'Sure, it's called interrogating the suspect, or suspects as the case may be.'

'I wouldn't know where to begin,' said Tamar gloomily.

'Exactly,' said Stiles.

'Maybe the answer is in one of those books of yours,' said Tamar to Denny.

'What books?'

'Ah.'

'The Fates are part of the Underworld,' volunteered Cindy. 'But the only way down there is to die.'

'Any volunteers?' said Denny with an evil grin.

'Ah,' said Tamar, who was beginning to catch on to Stiles way of thinking. 'There probably is another way. We just can't remember it.'

'Right,' agreed Stiles. 'Only …'

'What?' they all said in unison. Even Jamie leaned over to listen. 'Well, I'm not good at thinking laterally,' began Stiles, uncertainly, 'except where criminals are concerned. But it seems to me, that maybe we're being a bit too literal, I tend to think in straight lines. A follows B leading to C. But there's nothing straight about all this, is there? We need to think in loops, d'ya see?'

The blank expressions told him that they, did not, in fact, see.

Stiles cleared his throat. 'Okay, I'm not good at this, so bear with me. What if we had already found the Fates in the Underworld or wherever, how would we have done that?'

'By dying,' said Jamie. There was laughter.

'Okay,' said Stiles carefully when their laughter died away. 'Or?'

There was silence.

'So, we're in the underworld, and we're not dead, how did we get here?'

'Ooh, I know,' said Cindy. 'The river Styx, like Hercules.'

'Oh yes,' said Denny, 'And how did we find *that*?'

'Um.'

'Okay,' said Stiles, realising this line of enquiry was petering out. 'How about this? The Fates, right, how did we bring them to us?'

'We haven't,' said Denny, puzzled.

'Shut up,' said Tamar. 'I see what he means. He means if we *had*, how would we have done that? But go back a bit. How did we discover that the Fates were responsible for this mess?'

'Now you're getting it,' Stiles nodded approvingly.

'By a process of elimination,' said Tamar. 'And now … if we're sure that it *was* them, how do we …? Wait, I lost it.'

There was a collective groan from everyone except Stiles. 'Just keep following your thought through,' he said encouragingly.

'No, it's all wrong,' she said. 'It's like, okay, we keep saying that we're not who we think we are, but we are. This world is just as real as the other one. They're both real now. Running side by side maybe, I don't know. But we know that the other world is still there, because we can remember bits of it. And I even think I saw it once.'

'I did too,' said Denny excitedly.

'Right. And sometimes I feel – different. So, if the other world is still there, how do we get to it?'

'Through the back of a wardrobe?' said Denny.

'Very funny.'

'Look,' said Cindy, wearily. 'It's a spell. There aren't *two* worlds, just two versions of the *same* world, in our heads. The Fates will have changed history at some crucial point and then altered our memories to fit in with it, so that our lives were totally different from that point on. Why, only the gods know, and they're not telling. And we have no idea when it happened either, not that it matters. But the problem is in our *heads*. Tamar was right about one thing. This is the real world. We can't change that. But our memories, I don't know, maybe we can get them back somehow.'

'How?' said Tamar.

Cindy shrugged. 'Break the spell,' she said.

Tamar thought of what Stiles had told them about the Hall of Idols. 'What would happen, do you think, if the Fates no longer existed?' she asked.

~ Chapter Eighteen ~

THERE WAS A FEELING of timelessness in the hall, which was not altogether surprising, since it was one of those places where time does not exist. Tamar had had this thought in the back of her mind ever since Stiles had described it to them.

'It felt like it had been there forever.' He had said. 'But it also felt like it had only just sprung into existence when I walked in. Like it had been waiting, just for me to arrive, before it became real.'

Tamar had already got her head around the idea of there being no time on the astral plane, as Cindy had explained it to her. And she had theorised in her head that this was, no doubt, how the house had moved continents apparently overnight, because it existed on the astral plane, or at least, the inside of it did. This had seemed important to her at the time, but she had not known why.'

Now, as they stood in the hall, courtesy of Denny and the Athame, she realised why.

From here the gods had been destroyed – deleted might be a better word – so that they had never existed at all. This was entirely possible in a place, which existed at all times and at none.

The gods never really existed – everybody agrees on that. The stories about the gods still exist, but the gods themselves were never real. At least not anymore.

A god, or any anthropomorphic personification can only exist as a product of belief, and it needs to be seen, if only in people's minds, to be believed. Therefore, every deity and other unreal form of life needs an image. For that is all they really are – an image. And the Hall of Idols is where the image is held. A place without time or space, except the space in people's heads. The gods that had been reduced to dust, had now, never existed at all. It was Stiles, who had first put this idea into her head.

He had said: 'I knew that Zeus and all that lot weren't real, but I knew that Hecaté *was* because I'd *seen* her. But why had their statues been hammered to bits?'

Who knew which way round it had happened? Had the belief faded and the images crumbled because of that? Or had the images been destroyed first? Cause and effect – effect and cause. In this place, Tamar did not think it actually mattered.

'Because,' as she finished explaining, 'it works either way. Without their images, they will never have existed. And all the things they have done will never have happened.'

She turned to Stiles. 'Where is the statue of the Fates?' she asked.

As it turned out, destroying the statue was not as easy as just hitting it with a hammer. They even tried explosives, which Denny had "popped out", as it were, to get. But the statue remained intact. Only Jamie, who had not quite followed all of Tamar's reasoning, was uneasy about the situation, saying that it was either property damage or murder they were committing, and he was not happy about either.

'*Attempting* to commit,' corrected Tamar grumpily. It just wasn't fair. She had reasoned it all out so beautifully and now, they couldn't do anything about it. The damn thing did not have so much as a scratch.

'Maybe it only works the other way around after all,' said Denny, taking out the Athame and dangling it idly from his fingers.

Tamar's eyes followed the gleaming blade, back and forth, back and forth. Denny looked down at his hand and then at Tamar. Their eyes met; Denny nodded and flung the Athame – a blade so sharp it can cut through dimensional space – straight at the heart of the middle Fate. There was a thin, high scream from somewhere, and the statue crumbled.

'One down.' This was Tamar.

As the last high-pitched wail died away, the world rocked on its axis and then began to fall away from them.

Only Jamie was unaffected. He watched in bewilderment as they all fell onto their knees. To them, everything was spinning. They had all been having this feeling recently, but in smaller doses, one memory at a time as it were. Now they were under deluge.

Then, just as suddenly, the world returned to normal and stood still like a good world should. Feeling sick and dizzy, they stumbled to their feet and met each other's eyes and knew.

Tamar looked at Denny. 'Askphrit,' she said. Her fists were clenched, her face white with rage.

Denny nodded. 'He's gone too far this time,' he said.

'He *always* goes too far,' said Stiles. 'Remember when he killed me?'

'I remember everything,' said Tamar grimly. 'And I do mean everything.'

They all did.

'Which memories are real?' said Cindy.

Tamar manifested a spoon. 'Everyone's except mine,' she said. 'I'm the only one whose memory was actually tampered with. Because it had to be. I see it now. The rest of you just led different lives from the point history was changed. But, before that point, my memory *had* to be changed, because I've been around for so long. I became a Djinn over 5000 years ago. But I wasn't able to remember that.'

'Why not just change your past right back then?'

'Ha, Askphrit's consistent you have to give him that. He was protecting his own back there.'

'He couldn't afford to risk tampering with his and Tamar's shared past,' explained Denny. 'Otherwise, he might change his *own* destiny.'

'It's the same mistake he made before,' said Tamar. 'He couldn't prevent my becoming a Djinn, because that would have meant that he never tricked me into freeing him. If he had, he might have won; I'd have lived and died centuries ago. Although, he'd also have lost.'

'Actually, I meant which set of memories are real?' said Cindy.

'Both,' said Tamar. 'They both happened.

'But,' she continued, we are now back in the reality where the Fates never changed our destinies, because they never existed. But we can still remember that other reality that they created because, as far as we're concerned, that happened too.

'It only took one event to change all our lives,' she mused. 'I can see it now. It was about ten years ago. I was freed by one of my former masters, before I ever met Denny, and I can tell you, that couldn't have been easy to arrange. I took on another life and other memories and forgot all about who I really was. I even had a new family, although I suppose they're not really my family. It was all part of the wish. You were right about that Cindy. I *did* do this, in a way. At least it was *my* magic that did it.'

'Ten years?' said Stiles, something was bothering him. 'But that can't be right, because I remember meeting you two years ago,'

'Right, in *this* reality. Who knows when Askphrit set this up, it may have only been last week for all we know, it can't have been long ago anyway.'

'What makes you say that?'

'Because he must have set it up from the Underworld, that's where the Fates are – were –*weren't* ... bah, whatever! Anyway, we only sent him to Hell about a year ago. Besides, now I think about it, I have only one set of memories for the last year. That must have been when he actually did it.'

'So, round about the time that the war started then,' said Stiles.

There was quite a long silence after this.

Eventually Denny said. 'Let's go home.'

'Where's home?' said Tamar. 'Correct me if I'm wrong, but isn't our house currently full of American soldiers?'

They looked at Jamie. 'I guess it is,' said Denny. '*He's* still here.'

'Of course he is,'

~ Chapter Nineteen ~

THEY ALL TROOPED back to the library. It not being possible to teleport from within the hall. They had decided that the best thing to do would be to go back to Denny and Tamar's flat in London. There being nowhere else they could think of, at the moment, that they *could* go.

'It's a nice place, isn't it?' said Cindy as they made their way into the living room.

'Thank you,' said a voice from the high backed armchair that was facing the fireplace. 'I try, although I think it might be a little old fashioned nowadays.' The chair turned to face them, and the body in the chair rose up from the seat like a pantomime demon.

'Clive!' Tamar exclaimed.

'*That's* Clive?' said Stiles, who had never seen him, only heard about him.

Denny nodded. He was not all that surprised to see him. The little tit was always interfering.

'Yes, of course,' Clive answered. 'So, nice to meet you Mr. Stiles.' And Stiles could have sworn there was a very slight emphasis on the Mister.

'And you my dear,' he turned to Cindy. 'Charmed.' He gave a slight bow. Cindy just looked at him with her mouth open. 'So nice of you to admire my humble home,' he said to her, ignoring her uncouth stance. 'Too kind indeed.'

'*Your* house?' said Tamar. 'This is *your* house?'

Clive gave a little shrug.

'You live on Earth?' said Denny.

'No, no, not exactly, this place is – wherever I want it to be. So handy for getting to work in the morning, and always on time too.'

'What about ...? Stiles pointed vaguely back toward the library.

'The Hall of Idols?' said Clive. 'Ah, that's just a file that I opened. Not for you – that was just a coincidence. I was actually looking for – er something else. I usually use that tunnel for getting to work, but I thought, well, you kids seemed to need some help.' He turned to Tamar. 'I knew you would work it out eventually,' he said. 'You just needed a little push.'

Denny groaned. 'Now I *know* we're back,' he said.

Clive smiled nervously; Denny had always made him a little edgy. Denny made everyone (except Tamar) edgy. You never knew what he might take it into his head to do next.

'What were you looking for?' asked Tamar.

'All in good time,' said Clive. He looked around them expansively. 'I *am* glad that you are all back to normal,' he told them.

'Why,' said Denny. 'What do you want us to do?'

Clive scowled at Denny. He was too quick with his tongue, that one. 'Oh, nothing much,' he said airily. 'Just stop the Apocalypse.'

'About a year ago,' Clive told them. 'Satan was overthrown.'

'Askphrit?' said Tamar – who always caught on fast.

'Quite,' agreed Clive. 'Anyway that was the signal for the Apocalypse to begin. The Horsemen are ready and, as you know, the world is at war.'

'I *knew* there was something funny about this war,' interrupted Denny.

'Indeed. Contrary to evidence, this war was *not* begun by humanity. I needn't go into specifics. You know how this sort of thing works. Anyway, they've made a mistake up there. Par for the course, quite frankly, but in this case ...' he shrugged expressively. 'You see, it's like this, they've lost Pandora's Box.'

Denny winced. He had been there when the box had been opened, and it was not something he was ever likely to forget – at least not again.

'Quite,' said Clive. 'But it now contains only one thing, the hope of mankind. It's an integral part of the Apocalypse you see. As long as the box remains closed, hope remains for humanity and as long as they have hope, they will never destroy the world. So, we have a chance. If we, and by that of course, I mean *you*, find it first ...' he looked expectantly at them.

'Okay, I'll buy it,' said Denny. He sighed. 'I don't suppose we have much choice do we?'

'Of course you do,' said Clive, 'You could let them find it and open it.'

'What makes you think *we* can find it first?' asked Tamar.

'They don't know how to look.' He smiled at them. 'I have every faith in you.'

'Why do you care so much whether we stop the Apocalypse or not?' said Denny.

Clive spread his hands theatrically. 'I'm hurt,' he said. 'Really hurt, that you could even ask me a question like that.'

Which was not an answer of course, but Denny recognised a brick wall when he saw one. It was the only answer he was going to get.

'Please consider my house as yours for the duration. I am sure you will find its – *features* an advantage.' said Clive. 'I have a small '*pied a terre*' in the outer rings that will do me very well in the meantime.'

Cindy bobbed forward. 'Um please Mr. – er – Clive, I was just wondering, um where is Eugene, you know ...'

'Ah,' Clive looked evasive. 'Well, I can't really tell you that.'

'Why not?' Denny swooped on him.

'Well, it's just that ...'

'Is he all right, at least?' said Cindy plaintively.

'Oh, yes, he's fine, absolutely fine, nothing to worry about. But I can't tell you where he is. You'll probably find out soon enough anyway.'

'So, why can't you tell us then?' Denny persisted.

'Because – oh all right then, because he asked me not to! There, satisfied? Now you've made her cry.'

'I'm not crying,' protested Cindy in the face of the evidence, which everyone tactfully ignored.

Denny did not know what to say, he felt as if he had somehow been put in the wrong, and he was not quite sure how.

It was Stiles who brought the conversation back to business. 'What can you tell us about this box then?' he asked.

* * *

Before he left Clive filled them in on the history of Pandora's Box and the details of the search that had already been made for it. What was known for certain was that Zeus had reclaimed the box after Pandora had opened it, and then later both Zeus and box had disappeared. They had tried backtracking through the historical files to no effect.

Tamar snorted when she heard this. 'Whose stupid idea was that?' she scoffed.

'Exactly what I thought, but I'm afraid that's how these people think,' Clive had said. 'I knew you were the right people for the job. But they might get lucky. You never know. Although,' he had laughed here, 'they actually re-opened the mythology files and went to ask Zeus where he might hide an important box, if he should have such a thing. I think they thought they were being cunning.'

'What did Zeus say?' asked Tamar, laughing herself.

'He said, he said, oh dear, forgive me.' He wiped his eyes. 'He said, "I wouldn't tell you where I was going to hide it, otherwise what would be the point of hiding it?" You should have seen their faces when they reported back. I had to go outside'

'And these are the idiots we've got to beat to the punch?' said Tamar. 'No problem.'

But later, after Clive had gone, it seemed that Tamar had other things on her mind.

Askphrit.

She was sitting alone in the corner of the room while the others discussed the box situation, each coming up with ever more ridiculous ideas about where it might be found.

These ranged from: 'I 'spect the US government has it in a secret underground bunker somewhere.' From Stiles, the conspiracy theorist and all round suspicious bastard, to: 'It's probably on top of somebody's wardrobe.' (Clive really didn't give himself enough credit sometimes for the humanity of his thought processes) This one from Denny – the pragmatist. And all this was right, of course. You always had to go through every wrong answer before you came to the right one, and Tamar did not intend to interfere.

But as far as she was concerned, the box could wait. The clowns that Clive had described to them would never find it in a million years. There was a far more immediate problem to be dealt with.

It was Denny naturally who noticed her preoccupation. He wandered over to her.

'Wotcher thinking about?' he said.

'Hell.' She looked him in the eye. 'Remember the vampires under the sewers?'

'Yes,'

'And all the demons?'

'Of course.'

'Remember what we found down there?'

Denny smacked his head. 'Oh Christ,' he said. 'How the hell could I have forgotten?'

'I only remembered it because I went down there again recently,' she said.

'You did?'

'Only I couldn't remember then what was so important about it, I know now.'

'Hey guys,' Denny called over. 'You remember what we found in the sewers right?'

'Crap?' said Jamie. Who naturally did not know anything about the vampires, and was, in any case, convinced that he was trapped inside a very persistent nightmare.

'We found that under the sewers were caverns, which are full of what we thought were feral vampires and demons,' explained Tamar. 'And we noticed that the more we got rid of, the more seemed to come. And we wondered where they were all coming from. Then we found out.' She looked at Stiles to see if he remembered.

'A doorway from Hell,' he supplied on cue.

'That's right. Those are not ordinary feral vampires. They're coming from hell – the demons too. And who's in charge down there now?'

Stiles put his head in his hands. 'Oh shit!' he groaned.

'He must have opened it up from below. It's probably always been a weak spot. There have always been vampires down there anyway, attracted to the evil no doubt.' said Tamar. 'It leaks through in certain places,' she explained. 'There's a weak spot under the Houses of Parliament. It must have been Askphrit who broke through. He's trying to take over the world again, he probably doesn't even know about the Apocalypse.'

'That's probably why he got the Fates to interfere,' said Denny, 'when he realised we'd found the doorway. I mean it was only a matter of time before we figured it out. We knew he was down there, and the vampires, of course, were a big clue.'

'Well, we have to stop him,' said Tamar. 'He could send an army through there. Legions of demons and vampires *and* all the damned. And there may be other doorways too. The men upstairs would get their Apocalypse then, all right.'

Jamie was listening to all this with increasing horror. 'You guys are all crazy,' he said. 'I'm outta here, and anyone who tries to stop me – well, just don't try to stop me okay!' He got up and backed nervously toward the door, his eyes darting apprehensively from one to the other of them. He reached the door and scrambled behind him with one hand to find the doorknob. 'Okay, I'm going now,' he said shakily. 'Don't worry about me, I'll be all right, and I won't tell anyone about you, ha, ha, I mean, who the hell would believe me, right?' Denny made to rise from his seat, but Tamar stopped him. This was the crisis that she had been expecting.

Jamie swallowed once or twice. 'This is a trick, right?' he said. 'A trap, I mean you're never just going to let me outta here, are you?'

'If you want to go,' said Tamar. 'We won't stop you. – Make your mind up time,' she added softly under, her breath.

'What's that supposed to mean?' snapped Jamie. 'Oh hoh no, I'm not falling for *that* one. Don't think you can get rid of me that easily. I reckon that's what you want. Well, it ain't going to work, see? I'm staying right here. Vampires my ass!'

And with that, he sat back down on the rug in front of the fire and affected an air of indifference to the whole proceeding. The others continued their discussion as if nothing had happened. But now, Jamie was one of them, like it or not. And gradually, as if he had never had any doubts about them at all, he joined the conversation.

'Well, I say we go back down there and do a little recon,' said Stiles. 'See what we're up against.'

'That sounds sensible,' agreed Denny. 'That's probably what *he's* doing. Otherwise he'd have struck by now.'

'He's not been in any hurry – yet,' said Tamar. 'But he must know by now, that we'll be on to him. We can't assume anything. It may have already started. We have to be ready.'

'It may be that I speak as a fool,' said Jamie, tentatively, 'but why can't you all just do that Star Trek thing straight into Hell and finish this guy off?'

'It doesn't work like that,' explained Tamar. 'For one thing, you can't teleport into Hell. It's not a part of the world. And anyway, it's too late for that now. He's already opened the doorway. The damned will be coming through regardless. Askphrit doesn't know it, but this is a part of something bigger than him and all his schemes. Six months ago we might have tried it, but now, all we can do is fight.'

'Fight how?' said Jamie. 'I thought you said there'd be legions of them – against five?'

'Six,' corrected Stiles. 'Hecaté will be with us.'

'Okay six, big deal. Look, I ain't trying to ruin your party. I just want to know, what's the plan?'

~ Chapter Twenty ~

THE "MEN UPSTAIRS" as Tamar had referred to them were, as all such men are, completely unaware that they were only on the first level of the top floor. They thought that they were at the very top, the movers and shakers, but in this, they were, of course, deceived. They were very much the moved and shaken. Such men are useful. The buck stops with them, and they give the underlings someone to be in awe of. The real men in charge are always the sort of people that underlings are never in awe of, being merely more intelligent and powerful, not to mention more devious, than other people. These people do not have shiny offices with a nice view of the outer rings. They meet in shadowy rooms and wear shabby clothes. Many of them take a day job of such staggering mundanity that you might wonder, if you ever noticed them at all, how they managed to get from day to day. They make decisions, as opposed to making excuses. And they always know whatever there is to know.

* * *

Tamar went outside for some air. The house felt curiously stuffy, as if it had not been used by people for a long, long time. But she knew the real reason. She was feeling nervous, it was too quiet, even for the middle of the countryside. Outside was better. At least out here, there was the sound of the occasional owl, quiet scuffling noises, probably foxes, even the breeze made a noise, whisper, whisper, whisper. Tamar drew in a deep breath. Now she was ready.

Jamie was right, though, six against untold legions was bad odds even with her powers, Denny's Athame and heroic tendencies, Stiles's dogged determination, Cindy's magic and a goddess plus a trained soldier. What they needed was an army.

* * *

Askphrit had bellowed like a wounded boar when he heard the news. Demons had dived left and right for cover, and Peirce had hit the ground running. The whole of Hell had shaken to the sound of his roaring voice.

'WHAT DO YOU MEAN, THE FATES ARE GONE? DO YOU KNOW WHAT THIS MEANS? WELL *DO* YOU?' His voice hit new decibel levels '**THAT BLOODY WOMAN!!! I'LL KILL HER, THIS TIME I'LL BLOODY WELL KILL! HER. I'LL KILL THE WHOLE BLOODY LOT OF THEM. HOW DID SHE DO IT, EH? ANSWER ME THAT!**' for once, Askphrit had lost his suavity.

'My lord?' whispered Peirce from the shadows in the voice of one who does not really want to be heard. Unfortunately for him, Hell has excellent acoustics.

'WHAT?' Askphrit calmed down a little. 'What?'

'Well sir, what *does* it mean?' Peirce covered his ears and, therefore, almost missed hearing the answer that Askphrit gave, in unexpectedly moderate tones.

'It means, you useless little twerp, that the Fates never existed and, therefore, never could have interfered in anybody's destiny.'

Peirce got the point immediately. 'So they know?' he said, preparing to dive under some furniture.

'Yes, they know. Are the troops ready?'

'Yes sir.' Pierce would have said this no matter what the truth of the situation. Like all Captains, he understood that, when dealing with Generals (or mad overlords of Hell – and some people have trouble telling the difference) whatever the facts are, you must eliminate the impossible, and whatever you can dodge up, however improbable, *will* be the truth. Besides, they were the damned, they were *always* ready. It was not as if they were going to get any more damned.

'Good,' said Askphrit. His mood was improving. 'We must move immediately. Perhaps there is still time. After all, we have at least delayed them for almost a year. And they don't know about ...' he coughed. 'In any case, they have had no time to prepare, and they haven't the manpower to deal with an assault of the magnitude that I am preparing to launch. Ha, they'd need an army.'

* * *

The streets were deserted. This, in itself, would have been suspicious if it were not for the curfew. Civilians were to be indoors by eight p.m. or be carted off to prison. And it was now a quarter to eleven. Armed patrols would swing by at random intervals; the idea was to catch curfew breakers off guard. It was a curfew in the original sense of the word. The idea being to keep people in their homes after dark to prevent plotting. For this reason the curfew was augmented by an enforced complete blackout. This being the origin of the curfew, an anglicised version of the French *'Couvre Feu'*. A law first instigated by William the Conqueror that all fires were to be doused at sunset, to prevent people staying up and plotting. With no fire for heat and light, in those dark old days, people tended to go to bed. At least that was the idea. What the great Conqueror failed to realise, and also his later imitators, was that plotters tend to be devious people who take risks and are quite prepared to break the law to do so.

And if you do not have magic, a good strong pair of heavily lined curtains will do the trick.

The invisibility spell was hardly necessary. The streets were pitch black, and, in any case, everyone knew that the patrol men were notoriously easy to bribe, should they run into any. It was the other things that they might run into that they were worried about. But so far, there had been nothing. The streets were as deserted as they appeared to be.

After about an hour, Tamar said. 'Okay guys let's see what's going on down there.'

'Okay,' said Denny. 'All those without magic of their own catch hands with someone who has.' This of course referred to Stiles and Jamie. Only Jamie disregarded this order, but Tamar grabbed hold of his elbow. 'Believe me,' she said. 'You'll be a lot safer with us.'

He looked at her sourly. 'You've got to be kidding me.'

* * *

Down in the caverns beneath the sewers the curfew was, unsurprisingly, not being observed. Thus it was, ironically, far lighter down here than it had been up on the street. On the minus side, the patrols that they were likely to encounter down here were far more deadly and less open to bribery than the ones above their heads.

Tamar found herself explaining, once again, to Jamie this time, about the homeless people who lived down here.

'That's how we first came across this place,' she said, defending these people against the evil that lurks down here. God, I sound like a bad sermon.'

The sewers were ominously deserted, apart from the few white faced human inhabitants that could be seen scurrying here and there in the dim light.

'Are you sure we're in the right sewer?' asked Jamie after a while, his voice echoing weirdly along the empty tunnels.

Denny was worried about Tamar. She had not even said 'Damn'.

She was looking about her, warily, occasionally sniffing the fetid air. After a while, she visibly relaxed.

'Wherever they are,' she said. 'They're not here. I reckon they ...'

*

They emerged from the sewers, bloody, bruised and battered. Not to mention stinking to High Heaven.

'It was a good fight, though, wasn't it?' said Jamie enthusiastically. Last of the great sceptics. His opinions were revolving faster than a politician's in an election year.

'They ambushed us,' wailed Tamar. 'I don't understand it, I couldn't sense a thing, not even a sniff, and those buggers stink worse than Vikings.'

Denny put an arm around her, which she shook of pettishly. She had been fooled, and she was not in a good mood. Denny raised his eyebrows. As far as he was concerned, they had all survived, and that counted as a win.

It had happened so suddenly, which is the point of an ambush, I suppose. From out of nowhere, apparently, but really from Hell (which was why Tamar had not been able to sense them) about a hundred feral vampires had suddenly appeared. They had set about them with the old divide and conquer, and they seemed to know exactly what they were about. They divided Stiles and Jamie from the others, knowing no doubt, that those two could not escape on their own and that the others would not leave them behind. Unfortunately for them, Tamar was infuriated by this move. The battle was bloody and swift and soon, what passed for the air down there was choked with flying dust and it was raining limbs, for Tamar had manifested a couple of broadswords and made her progress like a demented windmill. Cutting off whatever came within her reach. If not a head, then an arm or leg would do just as well, she really was not fussy.

'Come on,' said Denny now, 'Let's get out of here, we need to regroup, they'll be after us in a minute.'

'I doubt it,' said Tamar. 'That was just a feint. I think we're supposed to think we've won and just go away with a sense of victory. But he made it too easy. I'm not falling for *that*!'

'Of course not,' said Denny. 'That couldn't have been more than a fraction of what he's got down there. That's why I said, "regroup" and not "celebrate". I'm not a complete idiot you know?'

'*Easy*?' said Jamie. 'You call that easy? My Lord!'

'Sorry,' said Tamar, ignoring Jamie. 'I'm just a bit pissed off. I should have seen it coming.'

Stiles who, by his reaction to the ambush, clearly *had* seen it coming – and it was just as bloody well (his most potent weapon was his permanent state of mistrust) – tactfully said nothing.

They headed for home in silence.

Jamie wiped the blood off his neck.

It was a long time until dawn, but, up ahead of them, there were bright lights glowing. They had decided to double-check the streets before going home. This was Stiles's idea, which everyone agreed was a good one.

This seemed like it might be something worth checking out. As they drew closer, they heard the sounds of what seemed to be a riot.

'It's the prison,' said Jamie. 'Look they're on the roof.'

They were indeed. Distant shapes, silhouetted against the glow of the searchlights, were dancing and gibbering, brandishing long pieces of wood and iron bars, and shouting defiance. There were a few small fires.

'Sign of the times,' said Stiles. 'It's the bloody overcrowding. It's got a lot worse of course, since the curfew.'

Jamie had the grace to hang his head.

'Just look at them,' said Cindy. 'Like animals, disgraceful! They ought to be locked up.'

They all turned to look at her. Even those of them who were used to this sort of thing from Cindy stared.

'Locked up you say?' said Denny, trying to keep a straight face.

Then they burst out laughing.

'What?' said Cindy. 'What? What have I said now?'

'Nothing, darling,' said Denny. 'Oh Cind.' He draped an arm over her shoulder. 'Don't ever change.'

Cindy pouted. 'I don't see what's so funny.'

* * *

'It all went exactly as you planned sir,' said Peirce, the dutiful captain.

Askphrit frowned. 'They only *just* got away, you're sure? It wasn't too easy?'

'Oh no sir, I sent at least a hundred …' he faltered at Askphrit's expression. 'Wasn't that right?'

Askphrit rose glowering from his throne. 'A hundred?' he said. '*One* hundred, that's *all*?'

'Sir?'

'Oh God. Chimps, I am working with chimps!' he groaned. 'One hundred, I don't believe it.'

'Sir, I assure you …'

Askphrit grabbed Peirce by the collar. 'And I assure *you*,' he snarled. 'She won't fall for that. She'll be back.'

~ Chapter Twenty One ~

THEY DECIDED TO stop off at their old flat (they would probably never get back to Clive's house tonight, at this rate, and that suited most of them just fine) and give Jamie a crash course in monster fighting using the training weapons that Denny had used. Not that he was not a good fighter, he was a trained soldier after all, but vampires require a special skill that is not, as a rule, taught at West Point.

The problem was that Jamie was exhausted to the point of collapse. As soon as they arrived at the flat he dropped like a stone where he stood on the living room rug, and could not be woken.

Stiles and Denny heaved him on to the sofa and left him there, where he went off into deep reverberating snore.

Tamar shrugged and idly pulled at a drawer behind her. It fell out, spilling the contents all over the floor. As she bent down to pick them up, she gave a cry of shock.

The floor was covered in old photographs of – her! Her family, her childhood – surely an impossible thing.

'What the hell …?' she stared in utter bewilderment. 'B-but these things were not real.' she said. She picked up a photo of herself aged about three, with a big shaggy nondescript dog. 'My mother took this,' she said in a shaky voice. 'That's me and Flopsie.' She started to cry. 'Oh God.' Denny darted forward to comfort her, while Stiles hung back awkwardly. Cindy was in the kitchen.

'What does this mean?' sobbed Tamar. 'Was it real or not, how can there be pictures? I don't understand it.'

Denny shook his head helplessly. He knew, beyond a shadow of doubt, that Tamar had never had this family, never had a dog called Flopsie. (It sounded like the sort of name they would come up with in Hell; there were just too many Beatrix Potter books floating around down there) had not been a human child within the last 5000 years. And yet, the pictures were here. Her parents, her best friend, her eighth birthday party. He knew that, nowhere in the world was there a mother waiting at home for a phone call from Tamar. He *knew* it. On the other hand, he was not sure.

Tamar was not sure anymore either.

Within a few minutes, the whole world had fallen apart in a welter of confusion. Of course, if you were Stiles, you might wonder, in a cynical part of your brain (which was the part that he used the most) whether, from somebody's point of view at least, that was not the point.

He gathered up the photos and unceremoniously dumped them back in the box. Neither Tamar nor Denny attempted to stop him. Tamar was still crying.

Stiles then took his life in his hands and hauled Tamar up by the shoulders and stood her up facing him, he looked her right in the eye and told her straight. 'They may or may not be real, but for right now, it doesn't matter. Do you hear me? We've got more – well not more important maybe, but certainly more immediate problems. Don't you agree?'

Tamar nodded.

'And it's worth keeping in mind who is responsible for all of this confusion in the first place,' he added.

Tamar's face darkened. 'Askphrit.'

'If it helps, think of it like this. It's like you told us. It *was* real, all of it. It's not anymore.'

'Tamar nodded. 'I guess,' she said.

* * *

It was almost dawn, and most of the group had fallen asleep. Denny had tried, but Tamar was restless and he kept on waking up, to see her pacing the room. She said that she was thinking about Askphrit and what his next move might be and what they could do to counter it. And she may have been too, but Denny thought. 'Well we *know* what his next move will be, what is there to think about?'

Around ten, he could stand it no longer. 'Look, what's up really?' he said, quite kindly, leaning up on one elbow.

'An army,' she muttered. 'Hmm.'

She snapped her fingers at the puzzled Denny. 'I've got it,' she said. 'I'll be back later,' she vanished. Her face reappeared briefly – just her face, hanging in mid-air like the Cheshire cat, she was grinning like him too. 'Don't start the fun without me,' she said.

'We won't,' Denny assured her, with a fixed smile.

Tamar nodded, without her neck, this was a peculiar sight.

'Askphrit might, though,' Denny muttered to himself after she had gone.

He waited all day. The others woke variously at two, five thirty and nine pm. The last to wake was Jamie. Stiles was first up. At around seven, Hecaté appeared.

They sat, they ate, Stiles smoked, and Denny drank beer and they talked about trivia. No one mentioned the coming night, or tried to speculate on what Tamar might be doing, although all of them were separately thinking about it.

At ten, every light in the street went out; this was customary these days under the blackout law. But tonight, it was like a signal. Everyone tensed. Denny clenched and unclenched his fists. Where the hell was Tamar?

Then they heard the screaming. It was cut off abruptly as only a vampire knows how to do. But only to make way for some more screaming, which had been queuing politely, waiting its turn. Then all such good manners were forgotten, and all Hell was let loose.

When people use the term "All Hell was let loose", let me assure you now, they do not know what they are talking about. This expression can be used for anything from a Saturday night at the Two Goats and a Bucket to a political incursion. They are referring to a riot, perhaps at a football ground or at a political rally that has got out of hand. Where the police turn up in riot gear and make everything worse. Then arrest the recumbent when it's all over.

They may say it of the overthrowing of governments or dictators. Almost every country has seen this at some point. And, although all Hell has not, in fact, been let loose on these occasions, perhaps from a certain point of view, it is hard to tell the difference. Until now.

At the last official count, done by a bishop in the later days of the sixteenth century, there were officially estimated to be over fourteen million devils in hell (only lazy people refer to 'The Devil') and that's just the ordinary devils, not even counting the minor imps and demonic entities – including vampires, or the Lords and Princes of Hell. And that count was a long time ago. Askphrit had been doing a lot of promoting since then. I invite you, therefore, to reconsider the words "all Hell was let loose."

'Marie Antoinette said. 'Let them eat cake.' And the people threw stale bread at her. Vampires tend to have a more direct – go for the throat – type of approach. Devils, of course, just frighten you to death.

However this may be, on the London Streets, a Saturday night quite often looked like Hell – from a certain angle – for instance, face down in a gutter full of vomit, not necessarily your own, with both knees broken.

Quite a few people, certainly more than was usual, were experiencing this exact view of the city tonight. And there was worse than this going on.

The term "Bloodbath" is also one that is often used, and, without going into another diatribe about it, I invite you to really think about this one too. Of course, this has been, on occasion, a pretty accurate description of human behaviour. –

The massacre of St Bartholomew's Eve in 1572, when the Seine actually ran red with the blood of the Huguenots, comes to mind, well to my mind anyway, I am sure you can think of your own examples. But nothing on this scale had been seen before, or rather nothing this concentrated.

Because of course, the carnage that was going on was at this time, confined to a handful of streets and a mere forty thousand vampires and devils. But it was spreading. More were coming. This was only the beginning.

* * *

'Well,' said Denny eventually, 'I suppose, we'd better ...'

Stiles shrugged. Between them was the unspoken assumption that they would go and they would fight, even though there was no hope of them winning or even surviving for more than a few minutes – if they were lucky.

Even if Tamar had come back, they would have no chance; it was obvious to them now. They were several streets away from the centre of it. But even from here, the noise and the smell of brimstone and blood was indescribable.

They all grabbed what weapons they could carry and just stood looking at each other for a moment. They did not say "Lock and Load" or "Let's kick some arse". This was not the time. They were headed out to an unheralded, useless, pointless inglorious, tasteless and probably rather greasy certain death. There did not seem to be anything to say, or any point in saying it. No valiant last stand, this. It was more like suicide. No one would see them fight and die. No one would care or remember them. They would save no lives. But they were going to do it anyway. Because, in the end, what else was there to do? This was what it was all about in the end. This is why soldiers go over the top. It's not for glory, it's because there's nothing else they *can* do. Because, some things are worth fighting for. Even if you are already beaten before you start, that's no reason not to try.

'It is better to be a broken jade,' muttered Denny. Part of an old Chinese proverb, which runs: "It is better to be broken jade, than a rude, whole clay pot."

'Death before dishonour,' translated Cindy surprisingly.

He smiled at her; she was loaded up with a crossbow, an axe, a sword and a backpack full of wooden stakes. It was clear that she intended to go down fighting. That was if she could even walk under all that weight. At least she was not going to run away. She would not be able to.

* * *

The devils etc. were making themselves at home. The streets actually looked quite a lot like Hell, as Denny remembered it from his brief visit. Every house for miles was on fire. This was an effective way of driving people out into the streets. Although, Denny thought, had they realised what was waiting for them outside, most people would have preferred to burn. They were going to anyway.

Stiles was in the lead for some reason. He would have said, had he been able to articulate his motives, that it was for reasons of seniority. But, since Hecaté was with them, this argument, on its own, would have fallen down. Just as he did, as soon as he entered the seething crowd of frenzied vampires and devils.

Denny followed him. Abruptly, like walking through the back of an enchanted wardrobe, he was in a different world. A blood red world punctuated by indistinct black shapes dancing against the flames, hazy in the heat and smoke. He felt as if he was moving in slow motion. Up ahead of him, he saw the figure of Stiles; he seemed to be moving quite fast. He watched him swing a large battle-axe at a vampire and remove its head in a shower of dust.

Suddenly he was running. 'I've got your back,' he yelled. He surged forward unhampered dragging Cindy in his wake, who dragged Jamie in hers. Hecaté was ahead of him.

They formed a circle facing out, while the vampires moved in on them menacingly.

Vampires traditionally do not play well with others, but these seemed to have learned a level of cooperation, or at least, the basic tenets of ganging up on a common enemy.

As paleontologists have extrapolated that the velociraptors may have done, but which Tamar said was nonsense, they all leapt at once. As they had done the night before, they employed the "divide and conquer" method. Jamie was the first to be dragged away. Denny did not see any more. It took twenty vampires to bring him down. But there was no shortage let's face it.

Stiles was next; Cindy saw him being hoisted up and passed along the top of the screeching crowd, before she herself was grabbed from behind by her hair. The claws passed within millimetres of her head, slicing off a large chunk of her shining, blonde crowning glory.

Cindy was furious. 'That was my *hair*, you bastard,' she screeched, turning on the unfortunate devil with a ferocity that was rarely seen, even in Hell. The devil was soon in tiny pieces, if it had been on its own, Cindy would have been laughing. As it was, there was nothing funny about fifteen enraged devils bearing down on you and banging your head against the pavement.

It was Hecaté who had the best view of what happened next. She was in the centre of a phalanx of circling vampires, none of whom seemed too keen to get near to her, the reason being, she was on fire. Or at least, she *appeared* to be on fire, which is nearly the same thing. The vampires suddenly stopped moving.

Denny was on the ground waiting for fanged death, when he realised that everything had gone quiet. The vampire that had him by the throat was frozen in an attitude of vicious ferocity that now looked faintly absurd. Denny leapt to his feet and looked around him. The shrieking world around him was now silent. The grotesque dancing figures, a ghastly frieze. Time had stopped.

Only one person was capable of that, that he knew of. This was confirmed when a loud familiar voice was heard echoing around the silent streets. 'I thought I told you not to start without me.'

Then another sound could be heard. The sound of many thousands of marching feet. Behind him, he heard Hecaté gasp.

The marching stopped. A cold wind blew suddenly through the streets, clearing the smoke away and revealing, by the light of the frozen flames, Tamar standing triumphantly at the head of an army of … of …

'Oh the clever, clever girl,' said Hecaté.

'I don't believe it,' said Denny.

'Do not say that,' warned Hecaté. 'Half the magic is in the belief.' She smiled abstractedly 'You needed an army. She has made you one.'

'How?'

'They're golems.'

'What are *they*?' hissed Denny.

'Oh the clever, clever girl,' said Hecaté. 'And look behind you.'

Behind them was another army, just the same. And, in fact, all around them the streets that the hordes of hell had occupied were now blocked off on every side by Tamar's multitudes.

'But,' persisted Denny. 'What the hell are they?'

'They're golems,' Hecaté repeated.

Denny's brow furrowed 'Gollums, what're they?'

'Go – lems,' corrected Hecaté. 'They are … well, any inanimate three dimensional representation of a human being, like for instance, a statue can be … well, not brought to life exactly, but …'

'Okay, I get the idea,' said Denny. 'Sort of like robots – artificial intelligence?'

'Yes,' said Hecaté dubiously. 'That is not a bad interpretation of it. They are not alive, as we understand it. They have the accoutrements of life, but not the living spark.'

'You mean that they can walk and talk but there's nothing going on inside, a bit like Civil Servants?'

But Hecaté had never heard of Civil Servants. However, she assented to the general thrust of this statement.

Statues eh?' he continued. He looked more closely at the ranks of warriors ahead. They did indeed, now he looked at them, seem to be statues of some sort, although they were a rather unattractive shade of reddish brown.

'I think that the first few ranks of each – battalion?' said Hecaté. 'Would that be the term?'

'It'll do,' said Denny, wondering where she was going with this.

'Yes, the first ranks of each are made up of the Emperor Qin Shi Huang-di's army of Terracotta Warriors, which guard his grave. But look behind them.'

'Terracotta warriors?' said Denny. 'Like flowerpots are made of?'

Then, in response to Hecaté's urging, he looked beyond them. And saw ...

Every possible representation of the human form that mankind had ever come up with. Thousands upon thousands, rank upon rank of ... Statues, shop dummies, scarecrows, some of these, were no more than a few farm implements covered in old potato sacks with a face painted on the topmost sack, but they stood to attention in the eerie light and gave an impression of alertness. Denny was horrified by them.

On his right, he saw several hundred Michelin men bobbing importantly like overfed businessmen. And on his left, among the sartorial elegance of the department store mannequins he could just pick out the odd Ronald McDonald. The bright red heads nodding ridiculously above the crowd.

'I think I'm having a seizure,' said Denny.

Tamar's voice was heard again, from the front lines. 'Get the civilians out,' she ordered. 'I'm going to start up time again.'

'Why not just leave them like this?' said Denny gesturing to the frozen hordes.

'No, it has to end here,' said Hecaté.

'First wave,' shouted Tamar. 'Attack.'

The Terracotta Warriors of China's first Emperor surged forward.

'They take orders?' said Denny.

'They wouldn't be much use to us if they didn't,' observed Stiles. He had been far less astounded than Denny had been by the golems. To Stiles, it was all equally incredible, whereas Denny worked on different levels of incredulity. The sight of five thousand of these "flowerpot men" as he thought of them, marching forward with slow deliberation stamping out the fires of Hell and ripping up lampposts like daffodils as they went, was somewhere right at the top. In an abstracted way, he could see why Tamar had put them at the front. They were terrifying.

The dammed thought so too. Most of them did not stay to fight, which Denny thought was very sensible of them. The problem that they had, was that there was nowhere for them to run. Tamar, with a military prowess that Denny felt he should have expected of her (she certainly ran his life with terrifying precision) had blocked off all possible exits. Suddenly the thought struck Denny, which had possibly already occurred to you. They were going to win. And why not? Their army was far bigger than Askphrit's and was entirely composed of beings, which, by virtue of not being alive in the first place, could not die. Of course, technically the dammed were not alive either. But they were merely un-dead.

'What we have here,' he thought, 'are the *un-alive*!' He was beginning to enjoy himself.

He was now facing away from what he had thought of as the front lines, because that was where Tamar was, but, in fact, there was a front line in every direction. It was the lesser known, "Box 'em in and slaughter 'em" movement *

From behind him, he heard Tamar's voice ringing out. 'Second wave – ATTACK.'

The golems, of all types, had this in common. They all commenced hostilities in absolute silence, which made their attack all the more unnerving. The only sounds were the thin despairing wails of the damned as the tables were turned on them. Now, as the ranks of mannequins and statues ran them

---

* The difference between this manoeuvre and other typical military manoeuvres, is that this one works

---

down in eerie silence, their retreat became a rout. On his left, Stiles was startled to hear another sound rupture the night air. The sound of war whoops. He turned, startled, and nudged Denny. Behind them, breaking ranks was, what was, by comparison to the other battalions, a mere raiding party of Cigar Store Indians firing wooden arrows with unerring accuracy into the welter of vampires in the streets.

Now it may have occurred to the more astute among you that vampires can fly. At least some of them can. Vampires have different talents, just as humans do. Golems do not ordinarily fly, because humans do not ordinarily fly. But there are exceptions. As one or two of them managed to escape the turmoil in the street and rose into the air, the sound of a cock-crow could be heard above the streets. Every head automatically turned upwards. And there, circling gracefully, firing rapid arrows at the horrified vampires, was the statue of Peter Pan that is usually to be found, standing charmingly on its plinth (and behaving itself far better than the original could ever have done) in front of the house that inspired his existence. Tamar had thought of everything.

'Oh, isn't he lovely,' cooed Cindy predictably. And he really was too.

'More to the point,' said Stiles, isn't he vicious?' and this was also true.

'Still, I'd say he could use a hand,' said Denny, it was true, there were more vampires trying the vertical escape route and Peter was running out of arrows.

Denny manifested a bow and arrow and rose up into the air to join him. Thus becoming the unconscious object of envy of small boys everywhere, even in these cynical times.

When he saw Denny, the statue of Peter Pan let out a delighted 'Cock a doodle doo.' And flipped a somersault in mid-air. Denny mimicked this sound and his "crowing" was unerringly accurate too – one of the lesser known advantages of having perfect pitch.

Stiles could not help laughing.

From this vantage, Denny could see the ranks of golems stretching out below him for what seemed like miles in every direction. Over the horizon, he was quite certain that the neon figure lounging nonchalantly against the skyline was L.A.'s infamous Marlboro Man. But he "hadn't seen nothin' yet."

Down on the ground, Stiles was astounded to see coming up behind the mannequins and scarecrows, a rather *smaller* army. 'Jesus,' he thought, 'Tamar must have raided every toyshop in the western world.'

It was like "Small Soldiers" meets "Bride of Chucky" and some of those "Tiny Tears" dolls, really did have preternaturally ferocious expressions.

Jamie, at Tamar's side, was watching the carnage with an unusually abstracted expression, as if he were watching, from very far away, events that did not really matter very much. Tamar was rather too busy to notice his strange behaviour at the moment.

After a while, he turned abruptly and disappeared into the shadows.

Tamar never noticed him go.

At this point, the vampires, who had been running and shrieking for some time, now appeared to redouble this activity. Denny found himself in the absolute thick of a veritable swarm of panicking bloodsuckers who had all risen suddenly, as if by command. The devils on the ground now had more room to manoeuvre, and they also began to try even more desperately than before, to escape.

Denny, higher up than the others, was first to notice a weird light in the East. A gentle glow that seemed to be spreading. He shook his head stupidly. Then all activity ceased abruptly, as every head was turned to follow his gaze. The dammed shrieked in despair as Tamar and the others let out a cheer, both weary and triumphant. And Denny suddenly realised what he was seeing.

It was the dawn.

~ Chapter Twenty Two ~

ASKPHRIT SAT DRUMMING his fingers impatiently. Why had no one come to bring him news of his victory? The lack of discipline down here was appalling. Well, there would be a day of reckoning all right. If they thought they could get away with this they could … he would light a fire under them all right, just as soon as … and then they would all be … Once he ruled the world there would be no more of this slack behaviour. He would see to that. It would all be … Aha, yes, he would be the Despot that he had always wanted to be, and then… and then … oh yes – then there would be some … and everybody would be sorry. Then they would see what he … mmm.

Askphrit often thought like this, in a kind of shorthand. He would talk this way too, leaving people to guess the ends of his sentences, which even for an imp, was not too difficult. There are only so many ways the sentence. 'I'm not happy, and when I'm not happy…' can end, and none of them are good, at least not out of certain mouths.

He was just making his mind up to stir himself and head up to the surface to find out for himself what was going on, when Peirce appeared in the room. Askphrit scowled at him and Pierce very unwisely backed away nervously. This only served to irritate Askphrit. He glared at Peirce who, he noticed now, did not look at all happy and suddenly Askphrit had a premonition.

'What's happened?' he snapped.

* * *

The vampires crumbled to dust. The demons all turned to stone where they stood, providing, as Tamar said, a lot of interestingly ugly statues, which did nothing to enhance the ambience of the neighbourhood.

In the chill dawn light, the streets now looked, if possible, even more eerie than they had done during the night, particularly with the ranks of the golems now standing perfectly still and silent. The vampires were not a problem anymore, but the demons were. Come the night, Askphrit would be able to resurrect them in much the same way as Tamar had created the golems. They would not be the same as they had been, but perhaps, from Askphrit's point of view, that would not necessarily be a bad thing. As golems, the demons would be more – suggestible, than they had previously been.

Well Tamar had an answer for that. She gave the order. 'Smash them all,' she told the golems.

From deep in the earth they all heard the groan. It rose to a roar that made the ground shake. Tamar grinned at Denny who returned the look. It was Askphrit.

* * *

It looked like Tokyo after a visit from Godzilla. No mere earthquake could have caused this amount of devastation. Even Tamar did not think she could fix this mess.

'Never mind,' said Denny. 'We won, that's the main thing.'

'This round anyway,' said Tamar. But she was smiling.

The golems, without being asked, had started to clean up the rubble in the streets.

'Handy aren't they?' said Stiles.

'You are a genius,' said Hecaté appearing behind them. 'I never would have thought of this.'

Tamar inclined her head modestly. 'Sometimes they just come to me,' she said. 'I knew there was an answer, I just …

well, the truth is, I was culpably slow in reaching it. I should have thought of it a lot sooner.'

'Well, the point is, that it worked,' said Stiles. 'Bloody amazing.' He stopped and looked around him, frowning 'Where's Jamie gone?' he asked.

They had no time to ponder this question, and, in fact, it was generally assumed that it had all been too much for him, and he had run away. No one blamed him; even by their standards, it had been a full night. Some people never have a night like it in their whole lives. Most people actually – but surprisingly, not *no* people. You would be surprised what some people can get up to. Well, not people as such, not human people anyway. Stiles, on the other hand, did not think that Jamie had run away out of fear, at least not the fear of the hordes of the damned anyway. For one thing, he had been the only person to observe Jamie's strange behaviour during the night and for another thing, suspicion was by way of being the ground state of Stiles's personality. But he did not say so – for one thing, he did not have time.

To the absolute horror of them all, there was a loud rumbling noise as the ground shook violently, knocking them all off their feet. Then a huge fissure opened up in the ground causing everyone to back away hastily, on their hands and knees. Tamar felt the indignity of her position, and stood up shakily. The ground was still shuddering under their feet. From within the fissure a billowing black cloud was rising slowly and deliberately. A venomous, viscous, swirling murkiness that could not have come from anywhere but Hell, the spiritual home of pollution. Despite seeming to move slowly it soon filled the sky, seeming to curdle the very air as it made contact with it and turned it an almost impenetrable black. Within minutes, you literally could not see your hand in front of your face. From the fissure itself, there was now visible a dull red light, and a hot blast of sulphurous gas was emitted every now and again.

'What the hell is it?' came Stiles's voice from somewhere in the now almost solid darkness. It sounded muffled, as if he had a sock stuffed in his mouth.

'It must be Askphrit,' said Denny from somewhere, in the same deadened tone. 'Tamar?'

'He's come back quicker than I expected,' she confirmed. 'Look in the pit,' she pointed, but of course, they could not see her.

They all looked anyway. By the light of a dim red glow, they could see thousands of dark shapes climbing up the sides of the fissure, which was getting wider.

'Goddammit,' blasphemed Tamar from somewhere within the oily living darkness. 'Blast, blast, blast!' This utterance was met with a questioning silence. To which she answered. 'I didn't expect him to get his act together this quickly. I don't know what to do. I mean you can't fight what you can't see.'

'Can't we at least relight some of the fires?' Tamar judged this to be Stiles' voice.

'In this murk?' said – Denny? 'I don't think we'd be able to see them. This isn't ordinary darkness.'

This was true, it seemed not to be a shadow cast by light, which even the dark of night ultimately is, but to be a living thing that swallowed light.

'I think … urrrgh.' His voice was cut off abruptly by a choking gurgle.

'Denny?' From the depths of the darkness came the muffled sounds of a struggle.

'Denny!' Tamar sounded frantic. There was a long ominous silence and then. 'Everyone okay?' It was Denny's voice – unmistakably.

There were all round sighs of relief and confirmations of presence and correctness.

Then all Hell was let loose – again.

* * *

This time it was rather different. For one thing, it was deadly cold and as black as pitch, and all of them were now exhausted, even Tamar.

The golems, of course, were not tired. But much of their advantage was gone in the darkness. It is difficult to inspire terror in an enemy that cannot see you. And this time, it seemed as if they were outnumbered. Askphrit had really let loose this time. And worse, this time, there was no hope of a reprieve at dawn. There would be no dawn. Askphrit would simply carry on emptying Hell until the golem army was destroyed. It was this sense of hopelessness, as well as the exhaustion, that seeped through the defenders. In a few swift moments, it seemed that their victory had been turned into certain defeat. But then, they never had had much hope really, and they certainly had not expected to survive even this long, and it was not in their nature – even Cindy's – to give up.

'Death before dishonour,' she muttered and, behind her, she heard a cackle. 'That can be arranged'.

She swung round and stabbed at the empty air (called so by courtesy) there was nothing there.

Then she heard Stiles' voice. 'Gotcha.'

She smiled to herself in the darkness. At least they would take some of the enemy with them. It was all the satisfaction they could hope for.

Hecaté was trying desperately to disperse the darkness using various spells to no effect. Tamar was nearly sobbing with frustration. Suddenly, though she became calm. She closed her eyes where she stood and clenched her fists. 'Dear God,' she whispered. 'If you ever loved us at all, help us now.' This was ridiculous. It was not that she did not believe in God. On the contrary, Tamar knew perfectly well that "God" was a computer program in mainframe. She had even talked to it. And then again, God in the abstract, resided in the hearts and minds of humanity and …

This train of thought was derailed by a sudden cry of triumph from Hecaté as a shaft of light suddenly penetrated the darkness. A shaft of the purest light ever seen, straight from the heavens, Accompanied by a loud musical chord, such as a computer makes when an email is received, but far louder and longer and on a purer note. It was not sunlight; it was far brighter and the colour of pure gold. The defenders had to shield their eyes, but the effect on the dammed was far more dramatic. Those standing in the pool of light fell on their faces wailing. Tamar looked at Hecaté who shook her head. 'It is not I who is doing it,' she said. Then another shaft of light broke through a few yards away, and another and another. The darkness was spectacularly dispersed, and the sky shimmered. The music increased in volume, and it *was* music by this time. The sound of many voices singing, in fact.

'Well, I'll be damned,' said Tamar.

The shimmering light shook and parted and revealed that the sky was, in fact, swarming with angels.

'I don't believe it,' said Tamar to no one in particular.

The angels descended regally to the earth, still singing, and literally mopped up the remains of the army of the damned, who had dissolved into craven puddles of acquiescence.

Tamar just stared in stupefaction.

She was finally, after 5000 years of seeing, as she thought, everything, flabbergasted into utter speechlessness.

Then the angels descended into Hell and dragged Askphrit out into the light and threw him on his face before Tamar.

There was an expectant silence Tamar was evidently expected to say something, but she could not, for the life of her, think of a single thing to say. There was a rustling of wings, and a tall, blonde, muscular angel pushed his way forward to face Tamar. He looked her in the eyes, with a faintly amused look on his face. Tamar took in his face for a moment then stepped backwards in shock.

'Tamar Black,' said the angel. 'Do you know me?'

Tamar nodded. 'You're … you … but you can't be …' she blinked and finally made up her mind to go for broke. 'Eugene?'

There was a cry from Cindy, who made as if to dart forward. Denny stopped her, but the angel merely smiled at Cindy.

'That was my name,' he confirmed. 'On Earth, the name that you gave to me. It is uncannily similar to my real name actually. But how could you have known?' He smiled again. 'One of the many things you gave to me, thank you.'

'What *is* your real name?' asked Cindy in a choked voice.

'Erasmus.'

'That's not similar to Eugene,' muttered Stiles. 'Not really.' He could not have stopped himself for all the cheap whisky in Mexico. 'Same initial, I suppose, but that's all.' Hecaté smiled indulgently at him.

'Similar in meaning, I meant,' said Erasmus. He turned his attention back to Tamar. 'You trust me then?' he asked.

'I – I suppose.'

'Wait a minute,' interrupted Cindy. 'What about me? How come you never told me you were an angel?'

Erasmus had the grace to look slightly awkward. He exchanged an embarrassed glance with Tamar that Cindy did not fail to notice.

She rounded on Tamar. 'You,' she said, infuriated. 'You *knew* about this?'

Tamar shrugged. 'Not exactly. I mean I did know. Then I forgot about it somehow.' She shot a questioning look at Erasmus who nodded.

'That's right, I too forgot who I really was, while on earth, until they took me back.'

He looked at Cindy remorsefully. 'I am sorry,' he said. 'The worst of it is, that when this is over, you will all forget again. I can do nothing about that. I have been received back into Heaven because I have atoned for my sin,' he glanced at Tamar. 'You know how,' he said.

She nodded. She remembered his sacrifice in Hell

'When the world changed, it was deemed that the time was ripe for me to re-enter Heaven.'

'Then this is what Clive was talking about,' said Denny suddenly. 'He knew about this.'

Erasmus frowned. 'Clive?'

'Yes, you remember Clive. The clerk – from mainframe.'

'I remember,' said Erasmus. 'But no mere clerk could have access to this information. I should say that this Clive is more than he is telling you. I should be wary of him if I were you. People who conceal their true nature are also likely to be concealing their true motives.'

Denny narrowed his eyes at this news; but said nothing.

A tall, swarthy angel came forward impatiently at this point. 'Can we get on with it?' he said, indicating Askphrit.

'Get on with what?' asked Tamar.

'It is for you to pass judgment on him,' Erasmus told her. 'He is *your* enemy, is he not?'

At this point, Askphrit let out a howl of indignation, which was largely ignored.

Tamar closed her eyes. This was awful. Finally, the moment had come to destroy him forever, and she just could not do it. Not in cold blood. Her eyes went imploringly to Denny, who smiled understandingly.

He nodded to her. 'It's all right,' he said. 'Just do what you think is right.'

Tamar looked at Erasmus. 'Okay,' she said. 'What are my options here? Can we just banish him or imprison him or something like that?'

The angels went into a kind of huddle and discussed this with much frantic gesturing and a certain panicked urgency in their voices. It was clear that they had not expected this. It was not how things were done in heaven.

'You can send him back to Hell in chains,' said Erasmus eventually.

'And ...?' said Stiles.

'Er.'

'He means,' said Denny. 'What guarantee do we have that he won't try to pull this same stunt again?'

'Oh, er yes. He won't be able to. Hell will be sealed up forthwith. We will see to that. We were going to do so anyway as part of the Apocalypse you know.'

'The Apocalypse?' said Tamar in a stunned tone. She had forgotten all about that. They all had. They all stood and stared at Erasmus, feeling like so many fools.

'Yes, this world is ending now,' Erasmus said in a gentle tone, sensing their shock.

Tamar gave him an inscrutable look. 'We'll see,' she told him.

~ Chapter Twenty Three ~

'IT DOESN'T REALLY matter what he wants it for,' Tamar was saying, 'even supposing he is up to something, which I just bet he is. As long as we find it first, we don't have to give it to him if we don't want to.'

This was inarguable. They were, of course talking about Clive and his request that they find Pandora's Box before it was too late. They had returned to Clive's house to, as Tamar put it, "make use of the facilities". Nearly everyone had the idea that, at some point, they would probably have to either go into mainframe or use the house's teleportation facility.

'The thing is,' said Denny, who seemed to have been infected lately with Stiles's perpetual mistrust. 'How do we even know that the box is as important as Clive says it is? Or even that it exists at all for that matter. How do we know that he's not just distracting us from something else?'

This was a difficult one, and Tamar solved it by ignoring it. The truth was that she had misgivings of her own in this area. The seeds of doubt and suspicion had been sown by Erasmus's words, which she still remembered quite clearly despite what he had told them. They all did. Denny had surmised that they had not lost the memory because it was not over yet. This was not an entirely encouraging thought.

'Well,' she said now. 'It's all we've got at the moment. So, any ideas anyone?' She was looking in particular at Stiles as she said this, as the one who had the most natural talent in this area.

Stiles shrugged. 'Homicide,' he said laconically, referring to his former career. 'Not lost property.'

'Private investigator,' countered Tamar, referring to his present career, since Scotland Yard had "let him go". 'Besides, we have to assume that the damn thing has been stolen and as for homicide. I think that opening that box constitutes mass homicide in the largest sense of the words. The Holocaust was nothing compared to what ...'

Stiles held his hands up in resignation. 'Okay, okay, you've made your point,' he said. 'So, who, apart from us, has a reason to want the box?'

'And Clive,' pointed out Denny. 'He wants it too.'

'I think we can eliminate him from our investigations,' said Tamar. (Stiles's police jargon was catching. Tamar had already hypothesised that the disappearance of the box could have been an "inside job".).

'I don't see why,' said Denny, just because he asked us to find it for him. Maybe that was just to distract us from finding out that he's already got it.'

'But we wouldn't even be looking for it in the first place, if it wasn't for him,' supplied Stiles. 'I really think we can forget that idea – for now anyway.'

Denny shrugged, as if he was not really convinced.

'What about a finding spell?' asked Cindy.

'Clive said that they'd already tried that,' Tamar told her. 'Although I suppose it wouldn't hurt to try.'

'As long as we back it up with a proper investigation,' said Stiles.

Tamar smiled.

'What a pity none of us is clairvoyant,' mused Cindy. 'We'd find it then all right I expect.'

Nobody bothered to answer this.

'Those Fates,' she continued. 'I bet they could have found it. They probably already knew where it was actually. It's a shame we couldn't have asked them.'

At the conclusion of this observation, Stiles leapt to his feet as if galvanised. 'Say that again,' he ordered Cindy.

Cindy obligingly repeated what she had said.

'Hmmm.' Stiles was thoughtful. The others maintained a respectful silence as he paced the room. Evidently some train of thought had been started by Cindy's remarks that they did not wish to interrupt.

Eventually he stopped. 'Okay,' he said. 'So, who else has a reason for wanting that box?' he did not wait for an answer to this question but answered it himself. 'Askphrit, that's who. No wait, think about it,' he held up his hands against their protestations. 'He also would want to keep it out of the hands of those who would open it. After all, if there's no world, then there's no world to conquer. We already know that he was in contact with the Fates, and they would know about the Apocalypse, naturally. And, like Cindy said, they would also know the fate of the box. All he would have to do is ask. He has it. I'll bet my life on it.'

'Oh My God,' said Tamar. 'I think you're right.'

'Denny looked worried. 'How soon can we get down there?'

'There's no hurry surely?' said Cindy, 'if he's not going to open it either.'

'I think there is,' said Denny. 'I think that the moment he gets a chance, Askphrit *will* open that box, now that he's been defeated. He's the sort of bastard who wouldn't mind losing quite so much, if he thought there was a chance of taking everyone else down with him.'

Without saying a word, Tamar picked up an axe and headed for the library. This being their easiest access into mainframe, and from there, Hell.

'Of course, now that the angels have sealed Hell up,' observed Denny. 'We may not be able to get out again like we did before.'

Tamar stopped. 'Hmm, maybe we shouldn't all go. Just in case we're wrong about this.'

Denny shrugged. He knew what was coming. 'You're the most powerful after me,' she said. 'You should stay behind with the others.'

Stiles picked up an axe, 'I'm going too,' he announced. 'Anyway, I'm not wrong about this.'

Tamar nodded. 'Okay, you and me then.' Tamar believed in letting people go with their instincts – as she always did. Up to a point anyway. She glanced at Denny, who gave her a smile to reassure her that he did not mind.

Stiles and Tamar hefted their axes onto their shoulders (why axes is anybody's guess) and Stiles began to sing (very flat and slightly nasally) 'Hi Ho, Hi Ho, It's off to Hell we go. With a bucket and spade and a nice, sharp blade. Hi Ho, Hi Ho, Hi Ho. Hi HO-O-O!' Until Tamar made him stop.

* * *

After they had gone Denny took charge. There was no dissent about this, although neither Cindy nor Hecaté were women who were naturally subservient in any way.

'Okay,' he said. 'We have two things we have to do. No, three actually. I suppose that's one each.'

They waited expectantly. It was at times like this, when Denny became masterful, that Cindy's intermittent crush on Denny resurfaced. Most of the time, she hardly registered him, which was the way Denny, who was naturally self-effacing and quiet, usually preferred it, and not just with regard to Cindy. And then suddenly he would go all commanding on her, out of nowhere, and make her notice him again. Denny was well aware of the effect his authoritative behaviour had on Cindy, and was not above using it to get things done in an emergency, which was the only time he behaved this way in any case.

Hecaté, being a goddess, was not affected in the same way, but she did see the sense in Denny being in charge. She had, in any case, the utmost respect for Denny, which was not dependent on his being domineering. He had, despite his comparatively tender years, as compared with her own millennia, seen a lot more danger than she herself had and survived with his sanity more or less intact. She also had a deeper vision than Cindy and was always aware, as opposed to only on those rare occasions when he took command, of Denny's inner strength. The only person she respected more than Denny, apart from Stiles, whom she also loved, was Tamar.

'Okay,' said Denny. 'First then, we need to see if we can't find a definite way out of Hell, for Tamar and Jack, just in case. Hecaté, I think you'd be best at that, okay?'

Hecaté nodded.

'Cindy.'

Cindy fluttered slightly, although she tried to suppress this.

'I want you to try and find Jamie. God knows where he's got to, or what he must be feeling. Can you manage a finding spell or something like that?'

'I can try,' said Cindy.

'Okay good.' Denny winked at her, causing Hecaté to smile and mutter 'Wicked boy,' under her breath.

'I'm going to explore alternative explanations for the disappearance of Pandora's Box,' he told them, 'just in case, Jack's wrong. Although I don't think, he is. But we can't afford to assume anything.'

Denny had been on the computer for an hour, searching the Aethernet for "Box" (he doubted that it would be found under "Pandora's Box" now, so what he was looking for was references to other mysterious boxes throughout history that might possibly be it) when Cindy timidly tapped him on the shoulder.

He swung round. 'Yep?' then, he caught sight of her expression. He frowned 'What's wrong?' he snapped.

Cindy blanched.

'It's okay. I won't bite.'

'Well, I found Jamie.'

'Well?' asked Denny, knowing that this was not all of it.

'He's – well the thing is he appears to be – well he's coming up as …'

'Dead?' finished Denny flatly.

'Yes, only, the thing is – he's still moving about.'

Denny narrowed his eyes. 'Could somebody else be moving him?'

'No,' replied Cindy confidently. 'Definitely not! There's nobody else with him.' She paused. 'Look you'd better come and see.'

* * *

'It's a bit quiet down here,' observed Stiles as they picked their way through the dark streets of Hell. They had both been here before, and it *was* unusually quiet.

'Not that I'm complaining,' he added. Stiles had pounded the streets for years in uniform and never said fool things like: 'I don't like it, it's too quiet.' As far as he was concerned, there was no such thing as *too* quiet. Quiet was always better. It meant that the criminal element were somewhere else, hopefully not doing things that would lead to paperwork. Tamar had made the same observations herself although on a rather different scale. But now she was worried. What Stiles had failed to realise, was that these were not the same streets that he was used to; the silence down here was decidedly ominous. It reeked of unseen enemies just waiting to jump out on them.

Up ahead, there was a torn banner above the palace bearing the legend "UNDER NEW MANAGEMENT" it did not flutter in the breeze as one might expect in this forlorn and desolate landscape, because there was no breeze. There was no movement at all. This was not the bustling metropolis that Tamar remembered, a fire in every window, a lava pit on every corner and hot and cold running devils everywhere. This place was uniformly grey – even the shadows were grey and all the fires were out.

They headed for the palace. It too, was deserted. 'We couldn't have got them *all*,' said Stiles.

'We didn't,' said Tamar uncertainly. 'I wish I knew what was going on.'

'They're just lying low,' Stiles assured her. 'It's always like this when the Kingpin is taken down. Secret power struggles going on behind closed doors and everybody else hiding in case they get caught in the crossfire when it all kicks off. Let's knock on a few doors.'

'What for?'

'Information. We want to know where Askphrit is, don't we?'

They tried this, in the absence of any other ideas, but it seemed that no one was home although, in some dwellings, there was definitely some movement behind the doors which was roughly analogous to curtain twitching, except that these people did not have curtains.

As they turned out of an alleyway, Stiles suddenly gave a shout; he had seen something.

A shadow darted across the road and Stiles was after it in a second. 'Hey you, STOP!'

Whatever it was, it did not obey this instruction, but instead redoubled its speed. It was no match for Stiles, however, who caught it easily and slammed it up against a wall.

'All right, all right,' said Stiles trying to hold his captive still. 'Nobody's going to hurt you; we just want to ask you some questions.'

'Don' know nuthin',' said the squirming figure predictably, and Stiles dealt him a heavy blow across the face.

'Why are you lying to me?' he asked in a sorrowful tone. Then he paused. 'I know that voice,' he muttered. He struck a match, which he cupped inside his hand out of sheer habit, despite the lack of breeze, and shone the light in his captive's face. Then he let out a yell of shock. '*Porky?*'

Tamar had watched so far with equanimity. Stiles was usually a calm, balanced and even a gentle sort of man and Tamar had seen him show considerable kindness to the victims of criminal behaviour. But Tamar had seen him like this before; criminals themselves were a different matter. Suspicious characters did not count as people in Stiles's personal lexicon. Thus, she had so far, watched his behaviour without surprise, but now she was inclined to raise an eyebrow.

'You know this – person?' she asked.

Stiles ignored this question, while at the same time answering it. 'Well, well, well,' he addressed the shivering individual. 'If it isn't Paulie "Porkchop" Shinewell, I'd know those shifty, piggy little eyes anywhere. Though the horns are new, eh Porky?'

The putative Paulie "Porkchop" Shinewell now stopped struggling. 'Mr. Stiles?' he said in a shocked tone.

'That's right,' Stiles grinned evilly and, against all probability, his teeth glinted in the total absence of a light.

"Porkchop" shied away from him. 'I ain't dun nuthin',' he protested.'

'Oh yes?' said Stiles, like a cross examining attorney. 'How is it then, that you are in, fact, in Hell?'

'Dunno,' said "Porkchop" sulkily. 'Mix up, lawyer screwed me, 'r summink.'

Tamar raised both eyebrows at this. 'He's a criminal then I take it?' she said.

Stiles turned to her. 'Who, Porky Shinewell? No, he's not a criminal, not really, he doesn't have the guts. He's an informer I used to use. Porky always knows whatever there is to know, don't you Porky?'

'Don' know nuthin',' reiterated "Porkchop" automatically.

'For the right price, naturally,' finished Stiles smoothly.

'Ha,' said "Porkchop". 'There ain't nuthin' down 'ere worth 'avin'. Even if yer was real, which you ain't. Every day I sees yer, all the time. Well I ain't believin' it no more see? I knows now. It ain't real! Cruel and unusual that's what it is. That's all, but I knows now, if'n I ignores yer, yer can't 'urt me.'

Stiles was quite naturally flabbergasted, not to mention nonplussed, by this extraordinary statement.

Tamar, however, burst out laughing. 'How do you like that?' she said. '*You're* his personal Hell.'

'What?'

'Isn't it obvious,' she said, still laughing. 'You have the dubious honour of being this man's everlasting punishment. Being interrogated by you, day after day for the rest of eternity, is his personal idea of Hell. It's quite flattering really, I suppose.'

Stiles groaned. 'Am I really that bad?' Then he thought about it. 'Yes, I suppose I am.'

'Only to a certain type of person,' said Tamar. 'I, for example, quite like you really.'

Stiles cheered up at this. 'Yep,' he said. 'I suppose I can live with being the bane of criminals' lives.'

'It does pose a problem here, though,' said Tamar, thoughtfully. 'I mean, how are we ever going to convince your informant to inform, if he doesn't believe that you're real?'

'Hmmm.'

In the intervening silence, Tamar posed a question that had been bugging her ever since she had been informally introduced to "Porkchop" Shinewell. 'Why is he called "Porkchop"?' she wanted to know. 'I've seen more meat on a butcher's knife.'

This was a fact. The purported "Porkchop" was a small skinny scrap of humanity, even in his demonic form.

'I don't know really,' said Stiles. 'It could be ironic I suppose. Or it could be because of his piggy eyes.'

Tamar took a closer look at the face of the trembling man – he did not seem to be having much success at pretending that none of this was happening – his eyes were indeed of an unusual type small and red rimmed, and with watery irises that seemed almost pink. He blinked rapidly at her and rubbed his eyelids making them even redder. If he had been wearing glasses, he would almost certainly have removed them at this point and started cleaning them. He was, in fact, continually fidgeting and making nervous faces. He tapped his feet and clicked his fingers, pulled at his nose and rubbed his hands up and down his trouser legs. And his face seemed to go through series of anxious tics and grimaces. Occasionally he would blow out a large putrid smelling breath right up his own nose. Tamar found this behaviour extremely annoying and distracting. Stiles did not seem to notice.

'Well Porky,' said Stiles eventually. 'We seem to have a problem don't we?'

Porky feigned deafness at this.

Stiles sighed and looked helplessly at Tamar.

'Let me try,' she said. 'Er, Mr. "Porchop"?' she began. 'You don't know me, do you?' she asked. "Porkchop" gave her a hunted look and eventually conceded that this might perhaps be the case.

'Okay,' she said carefully. 'My name is Tamar.'

This seemed a relatively un-inflammatory statement, but "Porkchop's" reaction to it was spectacular. He gibbered and stammered and pointed at her. 'You – you … Tamar Black?'

'You've heard of me?'

"Porkchop" did not answer right away; he seemed to be pondering whether to admit to what was patently obvious. He seemed to treat everything everybody said to him as a possible trick question. Eventually he decided it was safe enough to say: 'Yes.'

'How?'

'Okay,' interrupted Stiles, 'I've had enough of this. Where's Askphrit? If you tell us, maybe we can get you out of here. Good enough?' he looked at Tamar for confirmation. She nodded.

"Porkchop" swung his head round sharply toward Stiles, his eyes bright. 'Out,' he echoed, 'of 'ere?' he was incredulous. Then he sank his head into his hunched shoulders so that he appeared to have no neck at all. 'No one gets out of 'ere,' he said miserably.

'We did,' Tamar told him.

'Oh yes, *you* did. That's different, you ain't dead neither anyhow. I know all about that. But what about I?' His eyes darted between them, filled with a strange mixture of suspicion and hope. ''Ow am I to get out of 'ere?'

'We'll take you with us, when we leave,' she said. 'We just want Askphrit, that's all. You tell us where he is, and we'll get you out of here I promise.'

'Come on Porky,' wheedled Stiles. 'You know me, I keep my word. Is it a deal?'

'You ain't given me yer word,' "Porkchop" pointed out. 'Only *she* 'as. An' I don' know 'er from Adam.'

'No flies on him then,' said Tamar, more or less to herself.

'I'll vouch for 'er, I mean her,' said Stiles. 'But if it makes you happy, I give you my word too, okay?'

'You always was a good fella Mr. Stiles,' said "Porkchop" ruminatively. 'You always kep' yer word to ole Porky, didn' you eh?' He appeared to deliberate for a while then he announced. 'Okay deal,' and spat on his hand and held it out to Stiles who reluctantly took it. He then did the same to Tamar, who shrank back. 'I think we'll consider the deal sealed without the usual formalities,' she said frigidly.

'High and mighty,' muttered "Porkchop", but without rancour. He scuttled off down the dark street. 'Come on then,' he beckoned. 'It's this way.' He turned back suddenly toward them and narrowed his eyes 'Remember,' he said. 'You promised.'

* * *

Denny blinked once or twice, apart from the fact that the water in Cindy's improvised scrying pool (an old washing up bowl) would not stop moving, he simply could not believe what he was seeing.

Eventually he cleared his throat and spoke. 'That's never him,' he averred in the face of the evidence.

Make that the *apparent* evidence, Cindy's spells did have a habit of going arse upwards at times, and this was clearly no time to be taking things at face value in any case. What with the Apocalypse and Clive and everything not being what it seemed to be, Denny's paranoia was threatening to spiral out of control. He even suspected Cindy's vapid, vacant face of concealing dark designs.

He got hold of himself. If Cindy was plotting against them, then the entire universe as he knew it was turned upside down and inside out. Not least because Cindy simply did not have the acumen for espionage.

She looked affronted now. 'Of *course* it's him,' she protested. 'Look.'

Denny did not obey this instruction. He looked at Cindy impatiently. 'I know it's him,' he said. 'I just meant ... oh never mind. What the hell is he doing?'

Cindy shrugged. 'He's eating rats,' she said.

Denny's patience was threatening to give out. 'I know he's eating rats,' he snapped. 'I'm not blind. *Why* is he eating rats?'

Cindy shrugged again. 'Because he doesn't want to eat people?' she suggested.

'Hmm,' Denny frowned. 'Go and get Hecaté,' he instructed. 'This wants investigating.'

Cindy scurried away to fetch Hecaté from her explorations of mainframe and Denny continued to stare into the basin. 'That's weird,' he muttered to himself. 'A vampire with a conscience? I don't believe it.'

* * *

'We shouldn't have promised to get him out of here,' whispered Tamar to Stiles as they followed the little rat-like man through the intricate alleys and back streets of the worst neighbourhood in the universe, not even excepting Los Angeles, which is apparently thronging with vampire and demon activity. 'I mean,' she continued, still *sotto voce*. 'We don't even know if *we* can get out of here.'

'We only said, we'd take him with us, *if* we left,' said Stiles. 'I was very careful about that.'

Tamar sighed at this evidence of Stiles's sophistry. She was beginning to worry that she was having a bad influence on him.

It was as if he divined her thoughts. 'It's the way I always work with these types,' he assured her. 'You never know when you might have to back out of your word at the last moment. My superiors used to take a dim view sometimes, of my more nefarious connections. Besides, he'd have done the same to us, given half a chance. You can't trust him an inch.'

'Oh well, if you say so.'

'Anyway, we'll get him out of here if we can,' Stiles continued. 'We are the good guys after all.'

'I sometimes wonder,' returned Tamar mournfully. 'We do seem to spend a lot of time in Hell, for good guys.'

'On business,' said Stiles. 'Only on business. I used to spend a lot of time in criminal haunts, but it didn't make me a criminal.'

'Mmmm, okay.' Tamar sounded unconvinced.

'Here,' announced "Porkchop" suddenly. They had arrived at a large building which both Tamar and Stiles recognised as being some sort of jail.

'Ha!' said Stiles. 'I might have known.'

'How the mighty have fallen,' said Tamar.

'Not a bit of it,' said Stiles. 'He's up to his old tricks see. This place is deserted, look around. No guards, no other prisoners. This place has been abandoned for ages. Right Porky?'

'Right you are Mr. Stiles.' nodded Porky.

'So where is he?' asked Tamar.

'Ah visitors,' came the silky tones of Askphrit himself from somewhere within the depths of the darkened doorway. 'I have been expecting you, of course. Indeed, I waited for you to find me before my final dénouement. I never had any doubt that you would work out that I had the box. I have always had the utmost respect for you as an adversary my dear.' And so saying, he walked out to greet them, resplendent in red velvet and a large crown balanced on his horns. He was smirking and carrying a metallic box, about the size of a box of mansize tissues, under his arm.

He gave Porky a cursory glance. 'Traitor,' he commented mildly enough. Porky trembled. He had been in Hell long enough to know, that Askphrit was at his most dangerous when he was apparently as mild as milk. 'I shall deal with you later, clear off.' Porky cleared.

Askphrit held up the silvery box. 'Curious thing isn't it?' he said. 'I haven't been able to positively identify the element that it is constructed of, only that it is only found elsewhere in the heart of stars.'

'Funny,' Tamar observed. 'It was bigger than that, the last time I saw it.'

'It had a lot more in it back then,' Askphrit told her.

Tamar nodded, not taking her eyes off the box. She was white to the lips – her fists clenched.

'Why would that make a difference to the size of the box?' asked Stiles, literal to the end.

'If that sidekick of yours was here, he could answer that better than any of us, couldn't he?' said Askphrit to Tamar. He was referring to Denny's unfortunate encounter with the previous opening of the box. Tamar had no idea how he knew so much (he had shown no surprise when she had said that she had seen the box before) but she was careful not to show this. As it happened it was a wasted effort, Askphrit knew perfectly well how she was feeling.

'This must be killing you,' he observed sardonically. 'And I'm not going to tell you how I found out either.'

'I'm surprised that boy isn't with you,' he went on. 'I thought you two were joined at the hips, or the groin or whatever.' He smirked. 'Pity, I would have liked to see him again. One last time you know.'

Tamar went on clenching and unclenching her fists.

'So, are you going to tell us where you found the box then?' interposed Stiles smoothly.

'Ah, the interrogator,' said Askphrit equally smoothly, turning his attention to Stiles for the first time. 'I realise, of course, that you are merely stalling for time, but since you have no chance of stopping me, I see no harm in indulging your curiosity. Except I don't see why I should.'

'He didn't find it,' said Tamar. 'It found him.'

Askphrit deigned to look impressed. 'Very good, my dear. Did you just work that out?' He waved a dismissive hand. 'Who cares? You are right of course. The Fates intervened on my behalf. So much easier than all that running about *looking* for the dammed thing.'

'I thought that everything the Fates did, had been undone,' said Stiles.

Tamar trod on his foot. Too late.

'Oh you did, did you?' said Askphrit. 'I can see by her expression that she thought so too. Well, you're both wrong.'

'Not down here eh?' said Tamar.

'That's right, I am outside of the world here, outside of time, normal rules do not apply.'

'Normal?' said Stiles.

'It's a relative term,' conceded Askphrit. 'However, I assure you, this is the genuine article. But you know that, don't you? Whatever else I am, I am no charlatan. There's no fun in it, if it's a lie. No drama.'

'So,' said Tamar after a long pause.

'Indeed,' said Askphrit. 'Bit of an anticlimax after all, isn't it?'

Tamar did not think so. In fact, she recognised a crisis when she saw it. 'Stop him!' she yelled and darted forward as Askphrit delicately and with ironic reverence opened the box.

'No!' she and Stiles cried out together.

As the lid opened, the box vanished in a silvery spiral of glittering smoke. Then it was gone.

'Poof!' said Askphrit.

'You can talk,' muttered Stiles.

~ Chapter Twenty Four ~

IT WAS SO SUDDEN, so final, so irrevocable. Tamar was hit hard, stunned by the flat finality of it. The box was – gone. It was over. And they – she – had lost.

Askphrit exhibited his typical evil nemesis or "villain's" laughter. That is the special kind, which has an independent existence from its owner and remains behind on its own for a little while after the owner has vanished.

Tamar could have also done this, but she had never though it worth her while.

'Well, that's him gone at any rate,' said Stiles, trying to look on the bright side. 'Thank god for small mercies, eh?'

Tamar was just standing there, looking decidedly punchy. Stiles was concerned about this – he would work his way up to worry later, if the situation warranted it. For now, he was just concerned.

He took Tamar gently by the shoulders. 'Come on then,' he encouraged, 'got to find a way out of here.

Tamar swayed slightly in front of him and gazed blankly at him.

'Never say die eh, never give up. Don't let the bastards grind you down?' he tried this one as a last resort.

Tamar switched her unfocussed gaze to Stiles. 'Bastards' she murmured vaguely. She looked as if she was very, very far away. Completely gone, in fact, somewhere deep inside of her own head.

Stiles jumped straight over worry and went directly to panic.

He shook her hard; his grasp of psychology was weak at best. '*Tamar*!'

She did not so much ignore him as seem to be entirely unaware of him.

'Oh shit!' he wondered if he should slap her.

This was beyond him, he decided. She seemed to have withdrawn completely into herself. Probably the shock, he thought. He felt a little like this himself, but within his nature was the unspoken feeling always, that there was always *something* that could be done. Tamar, on the other hand seemed to have given up. Stiles, who had known Tamar for quite a long time, was frightened by this. If Tamar thought it was over, it probably was. If only because, if she gave up, who else could take over for her? He would have to get her back to Denny; he was probably the only one who could snap her out of this.

He put his arm around her shoulders and gently steered her away from the jail. His main problem was that he had not the faintest idea where he was supposed to be going. He kept up a steady stream of reassuring commentary. 'Come in then, off we go.'

'Go,' muttered Tamar.

'Yep, have to get going now. Find a way out of here. Denny will be worried about you, you know.'

'Denny?' She seemed, marginally, to be coming back from wherever she had been.

'That's right. You remember Denny.'

'Of course I remember Denny,' she snapped. She was right back with him now all right. 'What's the matter with you?' she glanced around her. 'This is the wrong way,' she told him.

Stiles flung his arms around her, thus highly embarrassing both of them.

'What *has* got into you?' asked Tamar. 'I was just thinking.'

'Well, you looked,' Stiles informed her, 'like you were Joan of Arc or something, having visions or hearing voices. Thinking about what?'

'I was,' said Tamar simply. 'And I was thinking about what to do next.'

Stiles relief was immeasurable at hearing this. 'Thank God,' he said. 'And what should we do next?'

'Got to get out of here first, obviously.'

'Obviously.'

'And then,' she told him firmly, as if expecting some kind of argument. 'We've got to find that damn box.'

* * *

Stiles did not even pretend to understand it.

Tamar proposed to find the box before Askphrit had. But she did not intend, she said, to use the historical files to do so.

'Takes too bloody long,' she said. 'Too complicated.' She intended to use quantum. But when she tried to explain how this worked, Stiles felt his mind skidding away from the thoughts. Tamar said this was not surprising. All magic was based on quantum, she said, it was essentially a different set of physical laws from the ones that humans regularly used. This was why although humans knew about quantum physics, they did not understand it. Just as previously, humans had known about magic, but had been unable to duplicate it. Stiles could just about follow this part, but his brain was beginning to hurt, so he did not want to encourage this line of conversation further.

He was saved from saying so by the unmistakable sounds of digging below their feet. This sound was accompanied by the sounds of voices arguing.

Against all probability, someone was digging *up*.

'I tell you, we've come the wrong way again.' said one voice.

'Go on,' said another. 'You couldn't find your way out of a one doored room, with a map.'

'I resent that,' came the first voice.

'Yah, you can say what you like,' said yet another voice. 'You're drunk again anyway.'

'Well? Ain't we all drunk?'

'I'm not,' came a fourth voice.

'Well, anyway, you're as stupid as a bleedin' troll,' came the first voice. 'No wonder we're lost.'

'We're not lost.'

Tamar and Stiles listened, fascinated. Stiles looked at Tamar, who shrugged.

Then a large pickaxe burst through the ground just in front of them. And, within seconds, the hole was enlarged by the emergence of a large crowd of small bearded men.

'Dwarfs!' said Tamar, unable to keep the shock out of her voice. 'What the hell …?'

The Dwarfs had not noticed them; they were arguing again. 'There I told you,' said one. 'This isn't right.'

'How would you know, troll brains,' said another. 'We don't know what it looks like, do we?' He bounced the handle of his axe off the other dwarfs head. It made a loud clang as it rebounded of his iron helmet.

'Oi!' said the first dwarf. 'What do you think you are you doing?' his diction was deadly.

'I ham 'itting hyou on the 'ead,' parried the other dwarf. 'Hand hwhat hare hyou a goin' to do habout hit?'

'Why you rotten little bugger,' roared the first dwarf and he ran towards the other dwarf his axe flailing in his hand.

'Time to break this up I think,' murmured Tamar.

She strolled over to the scuffling dwarfs. 'Excuse me …' she began, she got no further. The two fighting dwarfs stopped their *fracas* and the others their shouted encouragements and they all stared at her uneasily.

The first dwarf opened his mouth. 'Snow White, sw'elp us,' he yelled. 'Leg it, lads.' Each and every dwarf made to obey this instruction with alacrity. But Tamar picked up the two fighting dwarfs by their helmets and dangled them a few feet from the ground.

Tamar, it should be pointed out, looked not a bit like Snow White, apart from the obvious similarities of colouring, i.e. skin as white as snow, hair as black as ebony etc. Snow White, at least the Snow White that I read about, never wore a long black leather trench coat nor an expression of extreme ferocity, not even when the dwarfs forgot to put the toilet seat down.

'Stop,' yelled the first dwarf. 'She's got me.' The crowd of dwarfs halted and headed back towards Tamar reluctantly, swinging their axes nevertheless in a determined fashion.

It turned out that the dwarfs did not really think that Tamar was actually Snow White, except in a sort of generic, beautiful but bossy human female, way. It emerged during the conversation that followed that all dwarfs are brought up hearing the story of Snow White as a cautionary tale, much as humans tell the story of Hansel and Gretel to their children. Thus the dwarf who had yelled 'Snow White sw'elp us,' had done so, in much the same spirit as a human might cry out 'Dragon!'

But once they had ascertained to their satisfaction that she had no desire to set them up in a nice little cottage somewhere and force them to clean behind their ears and comb the rats nests out of their beards, they were quite amiable.

'This is Droopy,' said the dwarf who had yelled "stop!", and who had obviously been appointed spokesdwarf. 'And this is Mufti, Tufty and Lofty, 'cause he's the smallest. Rusty, Dusty and Crusty. And over there, that's Dinky, Stinky, Minky and Manky. They're brothers. And Giblet and Dribbler '

Tamar nodded in a bemused fashion.

'And over here, we have Stroppy, Loopy, Itchy, Sleazy, Toerag, Dozy and Sid.

'Sid?' said Stiles.

Sid hung his head.

'We don't talk about it said the spokesdwarf confidentially. 'Poor chap; it's not his fault. His mother was a bit strange. 'Tis true tis not a proper name for a dwarf, but he's a good lad all the same.' He leaned forward, 'that's not the worst of it,' he whispered. 'His brother is called Graham.'

Tamar tried to look suitably shocked and commiserate.

'And what's your name?' said Tamar, keeping an admirably straight face, Stiles thought. He himself was dying to stuff his fists into his mouth, to keep from laughing.

The spokesdwarf drew himself up to his full height. (4'3") and puffed his chest out with considerable pride. 'I am Florid Underdrawers,' he declared. He looked expectantly at them. 'Oh well,' he said to their uncomprehending faces, as he deflated a little. 'Such is fame, I suppose.'

'So what are you all doing here?' asked Stiles.

'Well, we were digging up from Heaven ...' began Florid.

'*Up* from Heaven?' interrupted Stiles.

Tamar dug him in the ribs: 'To dwarfs, Heaven is below,' she told him.

'Yeah,' said Florid. 'Where are we anyway?'

'Hell,' Stiles told him.

'There,' said Florid crossly. 'Didn't I tell you, we'd come the wrong way.'

'Well, you couldn't have done any better,' snapped the dwarf that Stiles recognized as Stroppy.

'I could indeed,' argued Florid. 'Anybody could, I don't know! I thought dwarfs were supposed to have a good sense of direction, especially underground.'

'Are you impugning me?' demanded Stroppy.

Florid hesitated, he was not sure, Stiles thought, what this meant. But he said "Yes" eventually, apparently on the basis, that it was some kind of insult, and an insult, during a row, is seldom out of place.

'Do you even know what impugning means?' said Stroppy. Who had not failed to notice Florid's hesitation.

'Of course I do,' screamed Florid. 'It means – to impugn, ha.

'Our great leader, gentlemen,' said Stroppy sarcastically.

The two dwarfs were bristling and weighing their axes ominously. There was every sign that the fight was about to get underway again, when Stiles interposed smoothly to save Florid's face.

'What *does* it mean?' he asked Stroppy. He was taking a gamble here, but not much of one really. Some words are difficult to define, even though you may know what they mean. He was rewarded by a baffled look coming over Stroppy's countenance as he struggled with this unexpected development. 'It means er ...well obviously it means...'

'Okay, said Stiles, forestalling Florid from expressing an untimely display of tactless glee. 'You never did get around to telling us where you were trying to get to.'

'Earth, obviously,' said Florid. 'Where else?'

Tamar and Stiles looked at each other. 'We want to get there too,' said Tamar.

The dwarfs now exchanged glances, which clearly said. 'Well of course you do, doesn't everybody?'

'We have a map,' said the dwarf previously introduced as Mufti, helpfully.

'Just don't let Stroppy have it,' muttered Florid under his breath, 'and we should be okay.'

'I heard that,' said Stroppy, threatening to take right off again.

'Why don't you give me the map?' said Tamar, sparking off a series of mutterings in which the words 'Bloomin' Snow White' were clearly heard once or twice. Evidently, the dwarfs were not entirely convinced after all, about her lack of proclivities in this area.

'It was only a suggestion,' said Tamar hurriedly. She was not nearly as accomplished as Stiles at pouring oil on troubled waters, her usual method being to bang the heads together of the opposing parties until they saw sense – or passed out. Her attempt, therefore, at diverting the dwarfs from their ongoing argument only worked in that it diverted their animosity towards herself, which, while effective in its way, was not quite what she had had in mind.

'What about it lads?' said Stiles. 'Shall we put our heads together?'

The dwarfs huddled together and began muttering.

'Will we have to take a bath?' said Grotty, looking particularly hard at Tamar.

'Not if you don't want to,' she said.

'Wash behind our ears? Clean out our fingernails.' He gulped. 'Brush our teeth?'

'No, you can be as mucky as you like,' said Tamar. 'I honestly don't care.'

The dwarfs convened again. 'Can you cook?' said Toerag. 'Gooseberry pie, that kind of thing?'

'No.'

There was a sigh of relief. 'Okay then, you can come with us,' said Florid. 'Let's go.'

'Just a minute,' said Tamar. She turned to Stiles. 'We did promise him,' she said.

Stiles sighed. 'We did, didn't we?'

* * *

They had only been in the dwarfs' tunnel for a few moments when they heard, from behind them, an eager voice. 'Oh there you are,' it said. It was not the gruff voice of a dwarf. 'I thought I'd lost you.'

Everybody turned. Even Porky, who had so far made the journey in dazed silence, as if he thought the whole thing a dream. They had found him not far away from the jail where he was just hanging around to see what he could pick up in information.

Making its way up the passage on silent feet was a very strange looking creature. Smaller, even than the dwarfs, and without the beard you could hide a chicken in, it had very large ears, longish curly hair on its head and also on its oversized feet. 'I've been looking everywhere for you,' it whined.

'Blast,' said Florid. 'It's that damn Grabbit again. They're terrible thieves,' he said in an aside to Tamar. 'Push off Hobo,' he said to the Grabbit

'But I want to come with you on your adventure,' whined the Grabbit. 'I want to see the dragon. Dragons have a lot of treasure,' he added, his eyes gleaming.

'How many times do I have to tell you, there is no dragon,' said Florid. 'Now piss off you little bastard or else you'll be sorry.'

'But I'm your good luck,' protested the Grabbit. 'Lucky sevens. And you'll need me when you find the dragon, who else can steal the treasure for you?'

'All right, that's it,' said Florid. 'Get him lads.' The dwarfs roared fearsomely and charged.

Stiles was horrified, but Tamar seemed unperturbed, she smiled at Stiles and winked. Stiles took this to mean that she knew something that he did not and he relaxed.

'Nobody knows where they come from,' Florid told them, as they watched the scuffle. 'They mostly work in the cracker factories, making up riddles, you know, for the inside of the crackers. But you can't trust 'em an inch, and they're all crazy. This one's been following us around for months. Got it into its head that we're looking for a dragon, well you heard it.'

'What did he mean, lucky sevens?' asked Tamar, her eyes dancing with suppressed laughter.

'Oh, they believe that luck goes in sevens, so he thinks he's our lucky number twenty one, crazy I tell you.'

There was an outraged cry from the dwarfs. 'It's gone again, vanished into thin air,' said Dozy.

'Not again?' said Florid. 'We don't know how he does it,' he told Tamar. 'It's not as if they have any magic.'

Tamar stifled a grin.

'All right lads,' he said. 'As long as it's gone, let's get going.'

'Well, that was …' said Stiles.

'I know,' agreed Tamar.

* * *

'What do you make of it?' Denny asked Hecaté.

They had teleported to Jamie's location, after Hecaté had looked in the scrying washing up bowl and declared that she would need a closer look at him. They were now watching him from round a corner. Jamie was crouched like a frightened animal behind some bins at the back entrance to a restaurant.

'Oh, I hardly like to say,' said Hecaté evasively. 'It is so –
so much a cliché, no not a cliché more of a – how would you
say it? A storybook fantasy. Besides, it is so unlikely. And yet
…'

'Just tell us,' said Denny impatiently.

'I think that he still has his soul,' admitted Hecaté
reluctantly and waited for the scorn.

'I think so too,' said Denny unexpectedly. 'Isn't it
ludicrous?'

'A likely story,' agreed Cindy. 'I don't believe it. Surely no
writer would attempt to make a plot turn on such a
contingency.'

'The only question is,' said Denny, ignoring this
contribution, of which he could make neither head nor tail
anyway, 'is it possible?'

Hecaté was emphatic. 'No,' she said. 'But then again, what
has that got to do with it? We are constantly being faced with
the frankly impossible. It has patently happened anyway and
what are we going to do about it?'

'Find out why it happened,' suggested Denny.

'Oh, it'll turn out to be destiny or some such nonsense,' said
Cindy dismissively. She shared with Tamar an immovable
contempt for the concept of destiny.

'Probably,' said Denny gloomily. He believed in destiny in
much the same way that he believed in death. It happened all
the time. The trick was to see that it did not happen to you.

'We should take him home with us,' said Hecaté.

'What?' said Cindy. 'Put him out of his misery, I should
say.'

'No,' said Denny, reverting to his authoritative stance.
'Hecaté's right. He needs our help. I mean just look at him. He
has no idea what's happened to him poor guy. Besides, there's
no point fighting destiny.' Denny did not know how he
managed to say this with a straight face, except that he knew he
had to; it was the only way to convince Cindy. He had to be
firm with her.

Cindy capitulated immediately, as he had known she would.

Hecaté tutted at him amiably. 'You should be ashamed,' she told him.

Denny pretended not to hear this. 'You go,' he said to Hecaté. 'I think he might listen to you. Besides, you're immortal. Just in case he gets twitchy, you know what I mean?'

'I know. You are, as usual, right.'

Hecaté emerged from the shadows and made for the cowering figure of Jamie. Beside him, Cindy felt Denny tense, ready to spring, as he had said, just in case.

But there was no need. After a few minutes, Hecaté returned leading Jamie docilely behind her.

* * *

Jamie was sleeping while the others discussed him. 'I still think that he poses no danger,' said Hecaté. 'He is still the same person inside, as he was before this happened to him.'

'Okay,' said Denny. 'Did he say anything that might help us figure out *why* he's still the same person inside? I mean he really shouldn't be.'

'He is more confused than any of us,' said Hecaté

'Well, it can probably wait,' said Denny. 'These things usually become clear in their own given time. Can we leave him alone, do you think, while we get on?'

'I don't see why not, as long as he's sleeping.'

'Good. Have you had any luck finding any exits from Hell?'

'Not as yet.'

'Keep trying. Cindy – help her. I'm going to keep looking for the box.'

Hecaté glanced at Jamie tenderly. There was something she had not told the others yet, because she was not sure. As yet, it was just a feeling. A very strong feeling. And it would also explain, perhaps, how he had been able to hold on to his soul even after death. Or rather, the form of death that precedes the transformation from human to vampire.

She evaded Cindy easily (Denny had already left the room) and sat beside Jamie.

She stroked his damp hair away from his forehead. It was a distinctly maternal gesture, Denny thought, watching her from behind the door.

* * *

'Hi Ho, Hi Ho, it's out of Hell we go,'

The dwarfs all turned to stare at Stiles. 'You taking the piss?' said Stroppy.

'Sorry,' said Stiles, 'Don't know what came over me.'

'Right lads,' said Florid, 'according to the map, this ought to be it.' He pointed upwards. 'Get digging.' He looked at Stroppy, as if he was expecting comment, but Stroppy said nothing. He just looked. Not in any particular way, he just looked as hard as he could.

'That means you as well Porky,' said Stiles sternly, giving him a dig in the rear with his boot.

I've got a cousin called Porky,' said Toerag absently.

'I bet you have,' muttered Stiles under his breath. Porky just stared stupidly at the dwarfs.

'Is he all right?' asked Dozy in some concern.

'He's fine,' Stiles told him. 'He's just allergic to hard work.'

Oh, leave him alone,' said Tamar. 'No wonder he's made you his idea of Hell.'

'Lazy is he?' asked Dozy, just as if Tamar had never spoken. All the dwarfs were doing this. It helped them to pretend that she did not exist; there was no doubt that they were still irremediably nervous in her presence.

'Not lazy exactly,' said Stiles. 'He just thinks that it's easier to pray for things, than to work for them.'

Dozy laughed, and even Tamar smiled in a disapproving way.

'Why are you lads trying to get out of Heaven anyway?' asked Stiles, he had, quite naturally been wondering about this.

'You lads,' thought Tamar. Stiles had already achieved a rapport with the dwarfs. There was an air of camaraderie between them that she was not a part of. (Porky did not count; he appeared to be in a kind of trance.) She wondered how he had done it. The dwarfs seemed to her, to be a surly bad mannered bunch. Stiles obviously saw them in a different light.

'We-ell, it's dead boring down here,' said the dwarf called Stinky – or was it Minky? 'And it's full of Grabbits too, little blighters they are.'

'Doesn't sound too Heavenly,' conceded Stiles.

'That's because it's not,' said Tamar. 'It's just an alternate dimension that they got shoved into to get rid of them, and told it was Heaven to keep them quiet.'

'That's terrible,' said Stiles.

Tamar shrugged. 'Happens all the time,' she said. 'Remind me to take you into Chuck's forest sometime to see the unicorns. At least they weren't deleted, like some things were.'

Another argument, begun, predictably, by Stroppy, was getting started in the middle of the dwarfs. 'I can read the map perfectly well thank you,' came the irate voice of Florid. 'This is the spot, all right, keep digging lads,' he instructed the dwarfs, who had downed tools to take sides.

'Yeah,' said Stroppy, stirring things up further. 'If we're lucky, we'll only end up in Tartarus. Remember the time we ended up in Hades?'

'Remember the time we ended up in Valhalla?' said Sid.

All the dwarfs took on a dreamy expression. 'Mmmm.'

'We ended up staying there six months,' said Sleazy.

'Well we thought it *was* Earth.' said Toerag. 'It was full of big stupid drunken humans who were always fighting.'

'Sounds like Earth to me,' muttered Tamar.

'Beer was good though,' said Dozy.

'Mmmm,' all the dwarfs sighed in rapturous memory.

'We should have just stayed there,' said Stroppy. 'Remember where we ended up after that?'

All the dwarfs shuddered.

'Yes, okay, okay,' Florid snapped. 'That's enough of that, see. We are all aware that our quest has not been without incident. But one more word out of you and you'll stay behind, look you.'

Stroppy muttered something under his breath and went on digging mutinously. The digging went on in silence except for Tamar's whistling. It was a few minutes before Stiles realised what the tune was. "Whistle While You Work."

The dwarfs went on digging.

* * *

Denny was not, in fact, looking for Pandora's Box anymore. He had a more interesting investigation on hand. Made all the more difficult by the fact that he had no clear idea what it was he was looking for, only that he would know it when he found it.

* * *

They burst out into bright sunlight. Actually, it was not, in fact, all that bright, it was a grey drizzle, but after the dark of the tunnel, it seemed like neon strobe lighting.

The dwarfs emerged blinking and looked swiftly around at the dreary landscape.

'Well,' said Stroppy. 'Looks like we got it wrong again.'

'No,' said Tamar. 'This is it.'

'What?' said Stroppy, surprised into acknowledging Tamar. 'Where are the mountains?'

'Um.'

'Why isn't there any grass?' said Mufti.

'Trees?' added Tufty.

'I don't think much of these castles either,' said Florid. 'They all look the same, and they're too close together, and they don't defend anything.'

'And why do they all look like stacks of dominoes?' said Stroppy.

'Um, those aren't castles,' Tamar advised them. 'They're skyscrapers. This is a city.' She turned to Stiles. 'What do we think?' she asked. 'New York, Hong Kong?'

'Could be either,'

There was a low droning sound from above and the dwarfs, one and all, hit the deck.' 'Aaaaagh!!!'

'Dragon,' yelled Florid.

'That wasn't a dragon,' said Stroppy.

'Well it wasn't a bloody bird,' said Florid.

'Bloody big bird, if it was,' muttered Crusty.

'It was a plane,' said Stiles.

'A plain what?' asked Dozy.

'An Aeroplane,' said Stiles. 'A kind of large – boat, that flies in the air carrying passengers.'

'Well,' said Florid recovering his equanimity. 'Now I've seen about everything I reckon.'

'I've never seen a boat fly,' said Crusty.

'I've seen a dragon-fly,' offered Loopy.

'I've seen a house-fly,' added Dozy.

'I've seen a greenfly, and I saw a horsefly once,' murmured Stinky falling into the spirit of things.

'Have you?' asked Itchy.

'I've even seen an elephant – fly,' said Crusty wearily. 'But I think I've seen about everything, when I see a boat fly,'

There was a groan. Florid stalked over menacingly to Crusty. How – many – times – have – I – told – you?' he said, punctuating each and every word with a smack on the head. 'No – Disney – references – Ok-ay?'

Crusty rubbed his scalp. 'Okay, okay, I'm sorry – it was just a joke. Jeez.'

'These guys have never seen a city, but they know about Walt Disney?' said Stiles.

Tamar shrugged. 'What you gonna do? That guy just gets everywhere.'

'Apparently.'

'Anyway, they did just come from Hell.'

The dwarfs were now having another conference. Tamar and Stiles heard snatches of the conversation. '... Thought I'd have a stroke,' said Mufti.

And, 'Not what I expected at all,' said Loopy.

'It's not how I remembered it,' said Droopy morosely. 'But then, (sigh) I suppose things never are, when you get to my age.'

'I suppose it could have been a mistake,' said Florid.

'… Wasn't my idea anyway,' said Stroppy.

'… Perhaps we should …'

'I think …'

'Good idea …'

'What do we think?'

'So we're all agreed then?'

The dwarfs broke formation and Florid came up to Tamar and Stiles and gave a nervous little bow. 'Ahem,' he began. 'Ahem, well, we er, yes well, the thing is, the thing actually, well the actual thing is …'

'You're not staying,' supplied Stiles to the embarrassed dwarf. 'I can't say I blame you.'

'Going back to Valhalla, are you?' said Tamar shrewdly.

'Well, we thought we might, er, yes, as a matter of fact, how did you …?'

'Lucky guess.'

'Ah. Well, thank you for all your help and everything.'

'Don't mention it,' said Stiles. 'I'm sure you're doing the right thing.'

The dwarf saluted and turned to go, he turned back briefly to Stiles. 'You wouldn't like to come with us would you?' he asked.

'More than you know,' said Stiles. 'But I really can't, thank you all the same.'

'Ah well,' said Florid amiably, 'just thought I'd ask.'

~ Chapter Twenty Five ~

IT WAS DAWN AGAIN. Traditionally the time when light dawns on a quest – as well as over the tops of all the buildings and trees and things. Actually, dawn is traditionally the time when everyone is still asleep, even the terminally suspicious who have waited up all night with a hammer under their pillow in case of burglars.

However this may be, Denny had waited up all night (for inspiration – not burglars) and all the dawn had brought him was the desire for a strong cup of coffee and someone to hit – hard. At least the Apocalypse had not happened yet. (Tamar and Stiles had arrived back a few hours ago and told them about the opening of the box.) He was sure he would have noticed if it had.

In fact, everything seemed to have just – stopped. Hecaté had gone to wherever it was goddesses go when they're not around. Stiles and Tamar were sleeping, as was Cindy and Jamie was still in a coma.

He played the Athame in his hand absently, spinning it over and around his fingers – which, even with an ordinary knife, is a good way to lose a thumb, but Denny knew that the Athame would not hurt him. He knew that he should get some sleep, but, hah! You get enough sleep when you're dead, right? Which, on current showing, would not be long now. He wondered why Tamar did not seem more worried.

'Because I have a plan, of course,' she put her arms around him from behind.

'Oh, yes?' said Denny sceptically. 'You're going to find the box before he does – did – whatever.'

'That's right.'

'How?'

Tamar did not even hesitate. 'Oh, it'll come to me, I expect,' she said airily.

Denny grinned suddenly. You had to hand it to her really; she could make a house of cards out of thin air, and convince you that it was actually an ivory tower.

'Yes,' he said, unaccountably relieved. 'I expect it will, at that.'

'What about him?' she asked, indicating Jamie lying across an armchair.

'What about him?'

'Well ...'

'Look, I don't know, okay? We'll just have to – play it by ear I suppose.'

Tamar looked dubious. 'I don't like vampires,' she said stubbornly.

'Nobody does, but he's sort of – different, you know.' Denny did not dare talk to Tamar about destiny, especially when she was in this mood.

'A vampire with a soul?' she said. 'Sounds like destiny to me,' she added sourly. And Denny was glad that he had not been the one to bring it up.

'Yes,' he agreed. 'And there's something else I should probably tell you. It's just a feeling, but ... well, I'm sure I'm right. Well, almost sure.'

* * *

Jamie opened an eye to make sure that they had left the room, then, in a disbelieving stupor, he stumbled over to the mirror over the fireplace and stared.

The whole house was roused by the terrible wail that he let out. Tamar reached him first, naturally, closely followed by Denny. They stopped short when they saw him gazing at a reflection that, by the very nature of things, did not contain his face. He turned slowly when he saw them in the mirror behind the nothing that should have been him. His face was white and horrified.

He pointed back at the mirror. 'Where am I?' he croaked.

Tamar wrung her hands helplessly.

Jamie did not wait for an answer. 'You can see me.' It was not a question. 'I thought it was a nightmare,' he gabbled desperately. 'Even when I heard you talking, I thought ... Oh God, what's happened to me?'

'Jamie...' Tamar began.

'And I was ...' he trailed off miserably.

'Get Hecaté,' suggested Denny, in a tone of voice that made it clear that this was anything but a suggestion.

Tamar vanished.

Cindy, who had been watching from the doorway, moved tentatively toward him. Jamie backed away, shrieking hysterically. 'No, No, don't. Don't come near me. I don't want ... mustn't ...'

Cindy stopped awkwardly, her face a mask of pity.

'What's going on?' Stiles had appeared from upstairs. 'Oh!'

Jamie turned. 'You!' he rasped. 'Is it true? Is it? Is it?'

Stiles looked at Denny, completely bewildered. Wha...?

'We don't know yet,' said Denny. He indicated Stiles. He doesn't know anything about it.'

'About what?' said Stiles.

Denny ignored him. 'So you heard everything?' he said to Jamie. 'I'm sorry. We should have been more careful. I should have been more careful. You shouldn't have had to find out like that.'

'Find out what?' said Stiles.

'Dear,' came the soft voice of Hecaté from behind him. 'I think I should deal with this.'

Tamar took Cindy gently by the elbow and led her from the room. Denny followed them. 'We should leave them alone,' said Tamar. 'They have a lot to talk about.'

'Without us?' asked Cindy.

'Yes,' Denny told her firmly. 'This is ... family business?' he glanced at Tamar for confirmation. She gave a small nod.

* * *

Stiles was having difficulty understanding what Hecaté was telling him. 'He's our son?' he asked incredulously. 'But we don't have a son ... do we?'

'Evidently we will have,' said Hecaté calmly.

Stiles was an intelligent man; he would get there eventually. She just had to be patient.

'But he's a grown man.'

'Yes,'

'How...? I don't...'

'Jack!' said Hecaté sharply. 'Now is perhaps not the time for this.' She glanced at Jamie meaningfully. 'Believe me, this is our son, and he needs our help.'

Stiles looked at Jamie who was looking bewilderedly from one to the other of them. He was jerked back to, for want of a better word, reality. 'Right, yes, you're right.'

'He's right, though, isn't he?' said Jamie suddenly. 'It's not possible, is it? I heard them talking before. They said you must've sent me back in time to grow up in the past.' His brow wrinkled. 'Or you will, anyway, when I'm born. Why would you do that though?'

'Only because, I now know, though meeting you here, that I *did* do it, or rather, that I will. Perhaps the reason for it will become clear, in time.' Hecaté told him despairingly.

'You didn't want me,' said Jamie sullenly.

Hecaté suppressed a sob. 'No!' she said vehemently.

'You didn't have to,' he persisted. 'If you hadn't, this wouldn't have happened to me.' He glared at Stiles. 'Was it you, was it your idea?'

'I doubt it,' said Stiles. 'I always wanted a son.'

'You could not have escaped your destiny in any case,' Hecaté told him. 'None of us can. But we will help you as much as we can now.'

Jamie subsided. 'It's too late to change it now, I suppose,' he said.

Stiles and Hecaté looked at each other. Both of them were aware of the elastic nature of time, and the fact that, it was not too late. Technically, it had not happened yet. If they decided right now to keep their son whenever he was born, it would change the present immediately.

Hecaté shook her head. 'No. We do not yet know all the reasons why this has happened,' she told Stiles silently. 'How do we know that we might not make things worse?'

Stiles found it hard to imagine what could be worse than being presented with a grown up son, whose existence he had not even known about and who clearly hated him, and with good reason, he had to admit. And who was, to top it all off, a vampire. What could be worse than that? To have missed out on his son's whole life, and then to have let him down so badly at the last. It was unbearable. He could see that Hecaté felt the same way and yet she could think this way. What else could he do, but back her up?'

'I can see things,' said Jamie, 'in my head. Thoughts and memories that aren't mine. Other ... things like me ... horrors ... atrocities ... murders...' he stared blankly at his newfound mother. 'Please,' he said. 'Make this not have happened.'

* * *

'... Make this not have happened,' said Tamar. She, Denny and Cindy had retreated to the library. 'If we could somehow get to the box before Askphrit ...'

'I know,' said Denny. 'But you still haven't said how.'

'That's because I don't know yet. But the answer's there. In what I just said, I know it is. If we ...'

'Look,' said Denny kindly. 'We're going about this all wrong, as usual. What we need to do is what we always do in the end. Face the situation in front of us.' He sighed. 'The Apocalypse is coming, right?'

'Right,'

'So, what does that mean in practical terms, what can we do about it?'

'Kidnap the American President's daughter and hold her to ransom until he agrees not to bomb us,' said Cindy. 'What? It could work.'

'No, it couldn't,' said Tamar. 'The reason being, that without hope, he's not going to care about his daughter. Or anything else for that matter … what's that?'

Denny looked out of the window. 'Dragon,' he said idly. Then his brain caught up with his ears. 'Um … that's weird,' he added.

'It's in revelations,' said Cindy, 'I guess this means it's started.'

'Revelations!' snorted Denny. 'Like the four Horsemen and all that …' he trailed off, well verbally at least, his thought continued in Tamar's head.

She nodded. 'It's got to be worth a try,' she said.

'What has?' asked Cindy.

'We're going to see if we can stall the Horsemen,' Tamar told her. 'At least until we can think of something better.'

* * *

Jamie was staring fixedly and despairingly into the mirror in an upstairs bedroom, where he had locked himself in, away from the others. As if, if he looked hard enough, he could force his image to appear, through sheer willpower. *Make this not have happened.*

He had tried to kill himself, a stake through the heart, self-immolation, but it did not work, he had the blood of a God, he had been told. It was why he had retained his soul. It was why he was trapped in this torment. And the hunger … *Make this not have happened.*

His head was full of ghastly images that he could not get rid of, thousands of years of terror. Horrors perpetrated, massacres attended, even just sheer petty cruelties, performed for the sake of it. His head rang with them. *Make this not have happened.*

His mother had said that he had acquired a sort of genetic memory from the blood. Blood memory? All the memories of all the other monsters like him. Because he too was now a monster like them. No, no, *not* like them. Never, never, never ... *Make this not have happened.*

And he could see it all, all the way back to the beginning. And he thought... 'Make this not have happened'. And he saw the way.

* * *

'Stall them how?' demanded Cindy.

'We'll just ... play it by ear,' said Denny. 'See what happens.'

'Got to find them first,' muttered Tamar.

'I could scry,' offered Cindy, with just a *soupçon* of sarcasm, which was not like her.

'You've given up hope,' accused Tamar.

'It's not her fault,' said Denny.

'No?' Come on Cindy; are you a witch or a woman? Use your magic, try!'

'What for?' said Cindy hopelessly. 'It's over.'

'It's not over until I *say* it's over,' said Tamar grimly. A thought struck her. 'Oh my God – Jack! If *she's* like this, with a magical buffer, what kind of a state will he be in by now?'

Outside the sky grew darker and the sounds of a heated argument met their ears.

'Naw, this can't be the place! We've come the wrong bloody way again! Give me that map, yer stupid scunner.'

'Scunner is it, yeh great Pillock. Wot do you know about anything anyhow? She won't be in a wee cottage with roses round the door, yeh know. Not *her*.'

'How do you know? Pah, Snow *White*!' Somebody spat on the ground.

Another voice piped up. 'Wot do we want with her anyway?' This was greeted with a loud chorus of agreement. Myriad voices cried things like. 'Yeah, wot do we want her for?' And 'he's right, look you.' And 'bloody Snow White, my arse.'

'SHUT UP THE LOT OF YOU!'

'I know that voice,' said Tamar, leaning out of the window. 'Hello Florid, what are you doing here?'

'Ah, it's yourself all right,' said Florid, looking a little flustered.

'Tole you, it was the right place,' muttered Stroppy sulkily.

'What are you doing here?' repeated Tamar. 'I thought you were all going to Valhalla.'

'Ah, well, we did all right, but ...'

'They didn't throw you out did they?'

'Naw, well, that is to say... Look, can we come in?'

'Of course, if you want to, but ...'

The dwarfs piled through the window, clambering over each other to reach the sill. When they were all inside the library, they stood about, quite at their ease, stamping their feet and making a mess of the carpets. Clive would have been horrified.

'Has you got any food?'

'Beer?'

'Beer!'

'BEER!'

'I wouldn't say no to a small nip of whisky.'

'Ahem!' Florid cleared his throat meaningfully. 'Sorry about the lads,' he said. 'But – well, the fact is we've had a bit of a disappointment see.'

'Why don't you tell me all about it?'

'Do we have time for this? Denny cut in.

Tamar looked at the assembled dwarfs. They were all covered in mud and blood, and their beards seemed even more tangled than they had before, if that were possible. 'Hmm, we may have,' she said.

At this Florid addressed Denny. 'Ah, good day sir,' he intoned pompously, and far more politely than Tamar would have believed of him. 'May I apologise for this sudden intrusion. My name is Florid Underdrawers.'

'Really?' asked Denny, clearly impressed. 'I wish mine was.' This last piece of sarcasm, said in tones of absolute sincerity, as was Denny's custom, went, as it were, right over Florid's head. He bowed.

At this point, Cindy gave an impressive snort and left the room.

'Who was that?' asked Florid

'Wicked witch?' came a voice from deep within the crowd of dwarfs. There was some muffled laughter.

'Who said that?' snapped Florid, straining to see.

'Me sir,' came the voice again, and a tiny dwarf struggled out of the huddle. 'Lofty, sir.'

'Oh my,' said Denny.

'Okay, okay,' said Tamar. 'That was just Cindy. She *is* a witch actually, but not wicked, just not all that bright. You can ignore her for now – she's just in a bad mood. So, you were going to tell us what happened to you. You can start by telling us how you found us.'

'The map of course,' said Florid. He held it out to Tamar. It was the most peculiar thing she had ever seen. A mere piece of shabby parchment marked with a large cross labelled "SNOW WHITE COTTAGE", and a large arrow pointing to it bearing the legend "YOU ARE HERE". There was nothing else on it.

'It's a magical map,' said Stroppy helpfully. 'We stole it from a witch, Oh – years ago. It shows you where you are, and how to get to where you want to go. You just have to ask it, see.'

'I see,' said Tamar thoughtfully.

'Snow White Cottage?' snorted Denny looking over her shoulder.

'Ah, well, we didn't know where you lived see, but the map understands what you mean and well …'

'And why did you want to find me?' said Tamar giving Denny an annoyed dig with her foot. 'What happened in Valhalla?'

'Well, see, we got there all right …' began Florid.

'Eventually,' put in Stroppy. 'If you's'd just listened to me in the first place. I *am* the official map reader you know.'

'Ah, shut up you,' snapped Florid. 'I'm telling the story, look you. And if you interrupts me again, you'll be looking for thy head in the gutter, see?' He turned to Stroppy and pointed his axe at him scoldingly. 'Official map reader, huh! You couldn't find your own arse with both hands you couldn't.'

He turned to Tamar. 'Terrible sense of direction for a dwarf,' he confided.

'Then why is he the map reader?' asked Denny.

Florid hesitated. 'Ah, well …'

'Because I'm the only one who can read,' retorted Stroppy, then he retreated quickly behind Stinky. Or was it Minky?

'We're not big readers us dwarfs,' agreed Florid unperturbed, now that the secret was out.

'Go on with your story,' said Denny, seeing that Tamar's patience was running out – it never had far to run in any case. 'You arrived in Valhalla … and?'

'Ah, well, turns out it was closing up or something, everyone was leaving. Off to Ragnoroc, the final battle, or some such thing they said. Well, we heard something about it being the end of the world anyway, so we decided to come here 'cos we … that is Mufti here says he heard you saying something about that. So we thought you might know what it was all about, see?'

'You could say that,' murmured Denny. The dwarfs were looking at them expectantly.

'Well,' began Tamar eventually. 'It's like this ...'

~ Chapter Twenty Six ~

'HELP ME TO FIND the way back,' Jamie asked his mother. 'I know you know how, you must do, you sent me back once before, didn't you?'

'But I do not know how, I have not yet done it.'

'But you will.'

'It may be that I will learn it from you.'

'That doesn't make any sense. I don't know how to do it.'

'But you can see into the past. I cannot.'

'You can't? But it's easy, I've always been able to … you really can't? Then where did I get it from?'

'You are not speaking of memory, are you?'

'No … not exactly. I mean, I can remember things obviously, things that have happened to me. And now I can remember a lot of things that *never* happened to me. But sometimes, like if I was reading a book about William the Conqueror or something, I could see what had happened, like a movie running through my head, only real. I never understood how it happened, and I thought maybe, now I mean, I thought it must have come from you.'

Hecaté raised an eyebrow. 'Like a movie?'

'Well, sort of, but well, more real, like being there, with it all around me, and the smells and the air and all that stuff.'

'You *were* there.'

'That's not possible.'

'As to that, that is more than I can tell. But what I can tell you is that the gods do not have this facility. It belongs to the imagination, to the ability to put yourself aside and say. "What if…" To go to a place in your head and make it "thus" instead of "thus" which is uniquely human. I think this gift of yours owes more to your father than to me.'

'Humans can't time travel,' objected Jamie, but uncertainly – he was really not sure of anything anymore.

'Neither can you. This is something different.'

'Then I *can't* go back?'

'Hmm, I wonder if I can explain. As a human, you can go to a place in your head that you can imagine, and as a god, you seem to have the ability to take your body with you. Do you understand?'

'I think so,'

'I can take my body to any place that I know of in any realm or dimension, but I cannot go to a place of my imagining, because I cannot make my mind understand this concept. Your father can take his mind to any place that he can imagine, but his body will not follow, because he has not this power.'

'But you can remember the past?'

'Of course, but I cannot see it clearly in my head as you do. For that, you need a human mind.'

'Like mine?'

'Exactly. My son, you can go to any place that you can see clearly in your head. You know this to be so, because you have already done it. Can you see the place you wish to go to?'

'Yes.'

'Then you are already half way there. Your mind is there. Let your body follow. Close your eyes and see it. Now, feel your way there. See the way through. Do not think about it, you are already there.'

Jamie closed his eyes and vanished.

* * *

The dwarfs were arguing again. There were three factions. One wanted to go back to dwarf heaven and to hell with it.

Another group wanted to stay and fight. And the last group wanted to have another drink and decide tomorrow. What had sparked the argument was Tamar's request to borrow the map in order to find the Horsemen and stall the Apocalypse. Many of the dwarfs had been shocked at the suggestion of lending her the precious map, and some had said that it would be all right if they could go with her. But others said that that was all very well, but would they have to do any fighting? To which the second group had retorted, were they dwarfs or not? Dwarfs like fighting, at least real dwarfs do. To which the reply had come back, that dwarfs did indeed like fighting, but only if they weren't drinking. This was indisputable, but led to a long harangue from Florid about duty and honour and so on, which met with a lot of jeering 'Honour be blowed,' 'pass the ale,' etc, etc.

At this point, Cindy came scurrying into the library, pale faced and worried. She plucked at Denny's sleeve.

'What is it?' he asked.

'It's Jack,' she gasped. 'I've never seen him like this. I've never seen *anyone* like this. You've got to come, now! I think he might die.'

The fighting stopped at once. Each and every dwarf turned to look at Denny, concern radiating from every visible feature.

'Where?' said Denny tersely.

'In the wine cellar,' said Cindy, wringing her hands. 'Come on!'

'Oh Christ!' said Tamar. 'I didn't know this place had a wine cellar.'

They found Stiles lying on the floor of the cellar surrounded by dozens of empty bottles singing happily about bears doing things that, had real bears tried them, they would certainly have been thrown out of the animal kingdom.

He looked up fuzzily. 'Dwarfffsss!' he shouted. 'Hi ho – sliver, whatever they may shay, you all look bloody tall to me.'

'That's because you're on the floor,' said Tamar dryly.

Stiles looked surprised. 'Am I? Well, there's a thing. Thingggg, ding, ting a ling ding, whoops.' He tried to get up and fell over again.

'Okay, let's get him upstairs,' said Tamar. 'Come on you.' She hauled him to his feet.

Stiles stared at her. 'Snow White sw'elp me,' he said and went off into a long stream of giggles.

'You'll pay for that later,' muttered Tamar. She threw him over her shoulder and carried him up the cellar steps.

'It's so nice to have a man about the house,' murmured Stiles. Then he threw up all down her back.

*

By the time they got him into the library, Stiles had stopped singing and was reaching that stage of drunkenness known as "almost comatose".

The dwarfs piled in behind them.

'Well,' said Loopy. 'He's drunk all right,'

'Is he all right?' asked Crusty.

'Dunno,' replied Droopy. 'He looks sort of – green. Humans ain't supposed to be green are they?'

'And he's dribbling,' put in Itchy. 'You can see it clear, on account of he hasn't got a proper beard to catch it in.'

'Nothing wrong with a bit of dribble,' said Dribbler.

Tamar sighed. 'You two,' she snapped at Rusty and Dusty, 'sit him up. Denny, you hold his nose.' She manifested a phial of evil looking purple liquid, smoke rose from the top of it.

Denny winced. 'Not that stuff,' he groaned.

'Well?' said Tamar, 'I'm not giving it to *you*, am I? If you've got a better idea …'

'Just don't give him too much.'

'I'm not sure that's possible,' said Tamar, 'even the Vikings were never this drunk.'

'That's true,' said Florid. 'Why did he get so drunk anyway? Everyone knows it isn't any fun after you throw up for the fifth time.'

'He's in despair,' said Tamar, 'we told you about that, about the box. Now help me.'

She poured the liquid down Stiles's throat and held his mouth closed for a moment until he swallowed.

'Okay, you can let him go now.'

The dwarfs scrambled back.

After a moment, Stiles opened his eyes blearily, 'Hullo,' he slurred sleepily. Then he grinned and lurched forward.

Tamar's face fell. 'He's *still* drunk,' she said disbelievingly.

Stiles located her with some difficulty. ''m not drun',' he objected. 'You wouldn' dare call me drun' 'f I was sober.' He grabbed her by the shoulder. 'Wow!' he said, startling her. 'You – are – beautiful.'

Tamar rolled her eyes. 'Oh, God,' she sighed. 'The amorous stage, I hate this bit. Any minute now he'll start singing ...'

'I bet you were a beautiful baby,' warbled Stiles suddenly.

'That!' finished Tamar.

'I bet you were a beautiful chii-ild.'

'He's not *as* drunk,' said Denny. 'At least he's walking and talking again. Maybe you should give him a bit more.'

'I daren't give him any more,' said Tamar. 'He's already had more than the maximum dose for his weight.'

'Good God!' Denny was impressed. 'I'm amazed he was still breathing.'

'He damn well nearly wasn't. Cindy was right about that.'

'All right lads,' said Florid. 'Let's give him some wakeup juice.' He turned to Tamar. 'Old fashioned dwarf remedy,' he explained. 'Works a treat, no problem. You leave him to us, okay.'

'ALL RIGHT JACK,' yelled Giblet. 'COME ON SON, HAVE A TASTE OF THIS HERE, SOON HAVE YOU FEELING BETTER.' He produced a small bottle from his sack and opened it up. The stench that rose from it was mostly indescribable, with just a hint of rotten eggs. Jack took the bottle gingerly and held it up to his face, his nose wrinkled involuntarily, but his brain was lagging somewhat behind and he threw it down as instructed. Then fell over, straight backwards like a falling tree.

'Ah, good,' said Florid. 'I was afraid it might not work on humans. Don't worry. He'll be all right, takes about ten minutes to work.' He frowned. 'Maybe fifteen,' he amended. 'Or twenty. Definitely won't be more than half an hour anyway.'

The Dwarfs were in a huddle in the corner muttering anxiously together, occasionally one of them would make a loud remark or objection only to be shushed vehemently by the others. Tamar and Denny weren't listening anyway; they were worriedly watching Stiles for any signs of life, as yet there were none.

'Well what I say is this ...' began Loopy in a loud voice and was hushed down by the others. 'Well, what I say is this,' he began again in a lower voice. 'Jack is our friend! And I say if we can help him – we must, and there's no arguing with that. So there.'

'He's right,' muttered Stinky. 'There ain't no gittin' out of it, when you puts it that way.'

'So, are we all agreed then?' said Florid.

Slowly every dwarf hand was raised.

'The ayes have it,' said Florid looking relieved. 'Let's go and tell them.'

'What does he mean, the eyes have it?' asked Sid of Dozy.

Dozy shrugged. 'Dunno, what're I's?'

Stiles sat up suddenly and groaned. 'Oh God!' He stared blearily at Tamar, 'What the hell happened?'

Tamar gave him a stern look, and he turned into a lamp stand. 'Whoops,' she said and turned him back.

He shook his head, a procedure that he immediately regretted. 'Aaaaagh,' he yelled clutching his ears.

'Hmm,' said Tamar. 'Got a bit of a headache there, have ya? Serves you right,' she added with the smug censoriousness of the tee totaller.

'Don't' said Denny, who had had his share of hangovers and could only sympathise with how Stiles must be feeling. 'I think he probably feels bad enough.'

'Right!' agreed Stiles fervently still clutching his head. 'Er, why?' he added.

Denny understood. 'I'm afraid you were a little drunk,' he told him.

Tamar snorted. 'A little?'

'Okay – very,' amended Denny.

'Drunk?' said Stiles, aghast. 'But I don't do that anymore. Why would I ...?' he turned his head gingerly at the sound of the approaching dwarfs. 'What are they doing here?'

'You don't remember anything?' said Tamar, ignoring this.

'Don't frown at him,' warned Denny, 'he might turn into a bedspread next.'

'It's okay,' Tamar reassured him. 'I think this might all be for the best after all. If he can't remember what's happened, then he might be able to fight the despair better.' She looked thoughtful. 'It might even have been what he had in mind all along, he's not daft you know.'

'What's the last thing you remember?' Denny asked him.

Stiles frowned in concentration. 'Um, I'm not sure. It's all a bit blurred. I think I remember Hell – bits of it anyway. I remember these guys – I think.' He indicated the dwarfs. 'But ...'

'It's okay,' said Tamar. 'He doesn't remember. And no one is to tell him, okay?' she looked threateningly at the dwarfs.

Stiles threw up *allegro mon troppo*.

'Can't you do something for him?' asked Denny, who unlike Tamar, felt extremely sorry for Stiles's predicament.

'In a minute,' said Tamar impatiently; she sensed the dwarfs had something urgent to communicate.

Denny took her elbow gently but firmly and turned her toward the suffering Stiles. 'No Tamar,' he said with the quiet authority that he rarely employed. 'Now.'

Tamar glanced at him in surprise. He looked angrier than Tamar had ever seen him.

'He's our *friend*, Tamar.' said Denny. 'Help him.'

Tamar had the grace to look ashamed. 'Sorry,' she muttered, gazing at the floor. She waved her hands vaguely over Stiles shuddering body. He gave a little sigh and fell asleep immediately. 'He'll be fine when he wakes up,' she said. 'It's the best I can do.'

Denny smiled.

He turned to the dwarfs. 'Now then fellers,' he said employing that same friendly camaraderie that had endeared the dwarfs to Stiles. 'What's up?'

Florid stepped forward solemnly and handed Tamar the map, glancing at the other dwarfs nervously as he did so. As Tamar opened her mouth to thank him, he waved his hand dismissively. 'Not a word,' he warned her. 'Not one word. Least we can do,' he gestured to the prostrate Stiles. 'Under the circumstances, look you.' Tamar nodded.

Denny slapped Florid on the back and winked. 'Knew you'd come through,' he told them, smiling at the dwarfs who looked pleased.

'Get Cindy,' said Tamar unrolling the map, 'and Hecaté and Jamie too,' she added.

Denny nodded. He glanced at Stiles, 'how long before he wakes up?' he asked.

Tamar smiled. 'Oh not long,'

~Chapter Twenty Seven ~

THE HORSEMEN WERE trekking down a dusty road. They were not so much riding out, thought Tamar, as sauntering out.
'I guess there's no need for them to hurry,' observed Denny. 'It's not as if it can start without them.'

'Where are we anyway?' asked Stiles, now fully recovered and, due to his impaired memory, somewhat puzzled by this mission.

Tamar consulted the map. It had taken them three days to catch up to the Horsemen, who were slowly but surely taking the apocalypse to every corner of the world. 'Um,' she frowned. 'Somewhere in middle America,' she hazarded. 'Wisconsin or one of those places, what does it matter?' she snapped annoyed that she didn't know. Tamar hated to admit that she didn't know everything.

Denny tried unsuccessfully to hide a smile.

'And you can shut up as well,' she told him waspishly.

'So what are we going to do?' asked Cindy nervously. The Horsemen were approaching steadily.

'Fight!' said Tamar bluntly.

'Fight?' gibbered Cindy. 'Fight *them*?' she looked at Stiles and Denny for support, but they were both already un-slinging swords from their backs, the light of battle already in their eyes. 'You're all crazy,' she said.

'Why?' said Tamar, genuinely astonished. 'There's four of them and four of us.'

They had been unable to find Hecaté and Jamie in the house, and Tamar had been unwilling to waste time searching for them.

Florid, behind her, cleared his throat indignantly.

'And all the lads,' Tamar added without missing a beat. 'We've definitely faced worse odds,'

'But they're not human,' objected Cindy.

'Well?' said Tamar. 'Neither are most of us. What's your point?'

Cindy sighed, giving in. 'I suppose they can't be worse than vampires,' she said, without believing a word of it.

'Oh yes they can,' said Tamar grimly.

'Why did you have to say that?' moaned Cindy.

The Horsemen rode nonchalantly toward them, then stopped a few yards ahead of them and looked curiously at them, particularly the dwarfs.

All four protagonists were frozen to the spot. Tamar gazed into the face of Death, unable to look away. She frowned, struggling to remember something that was just on the edge of her memory. Denny seemed equally transfixed by Pestilence and for much the same reason, as it would turn out. He felt he had seen his face before. Of course, technically, we have all looked into the faces of all that the Horsemen represent, but this was different. Stiles and Cindy stopped short and looked nervously from Tamar to Denny's faces and went cold with fear.

It was Denny who broke the silence. He pointed a shaking finger at Pestilence. 'Here?' he said, 'aren't you ...? I know you. You are! You're Lazarus Moult,'

Pestilence broke into a huge smile 'A fan!' he said delightedly.

Death released Tamar from his gaze to turn a stern face on Pestilence. 'You're *who*?' he rumbled.

'Oh, um, just my little joke,' he muttered shamefacedly, even his horse looked embarrassed.

'He's *who*?' repeated Tamar incredulously.

'He's a rock star,' explained Denny, 'sort of anyway. He used to be hugely famous in the sixties. I've got his album.'

'Album? Singular?'

'Well, yes, just the one. It's very good though,' he added, aware that all eyes were now on him.

Tamar rolled her eyes. 'Oh for God's sake,' she groaned. 'Why does this sort of thing keep happening to us?'

War and Famine were sniggering, but Death kept up a stony silence. It was impossible to tell, what with his face being a mere skull, but it seemed that he was looking disapproving.

Pestilence ignored him. He leaned down to Denny, flies buzzed around his head. 'You liked it?' he asked eagerly. 'Really?'

Denny nodded, agitating the flies; he brushed them away from his eyes.

'Oh, sorry about them,' said Pestilence, can't seem to get rid of them.'

'You are a musician, I see,' he added, 'looking into Denny's face earnestly.

Tamar snorted.

'Well,' said Denny. 'I like to play and write songs sometimes, but I'm not particularly good.' He glanced at Tamar, who had nothing to say about this. 'How did you know?'

'I can see it,' said Pestilence. 'And,' he turned to Tamar, 'this is your Muse?'

Tamar laughed, but the laughter died on her lips when Denny answered: 'Yes.'

'B-But ... I'm not a muse,' she said.

Pestilence looked keenly at her. 'No, I see now, that you are not,' he said. 'I was misled by the rather obvious facts that you are not human and are beautiful and of course, the fact that the songs that I see in his head are full of you.'

'S-songs?'

'Yes, many, many wonderful songs. Songs that he has never played. Such a shame, they should be brought to life.'

Denny was scarlet by this time. 'They're nothing really,' he muttered looking at his feet scuffing up dust.

'Indeed they are *not* nothing,' said Pestilence heartily. 'You should play them for us; I should very much like to hear them played. Perhaps we could play them together, eh? What do you say to that?'

Denny's eyes were like saucers. 'Really?' he gasped. 'Play – with *you*?'

Pestilence turned to the Horsemen. 'What do you say boys?' he asked. 'We've got time for a quick number or two, wouldn't you say?'

The Horsemen looked at each other and shrugged.

'Why not?' was the opinion voiced by War. 'It's not as if the apocalypse can start without us.'

Tamar was delighted. The Horsemen were distracted, and they hadn't even had to fight.

'Okay,' said Pestilence. 'Now let's do the thing properly. Where shall we put the stage?'

'What is going on?'

Stiles turned in surprise. Hecaté had arrived.

'Where's Jamie?' he asked.

'I have no idea,' she answered, truthfully enough, but Stiles knew better than that. He had been around magic too long to let an ingenuous statement like that go by him. He narrowed his eyes. 'Okay then,' he said shrewdly. '*When* is Jamie?'

Hecaté laughed. 'There is no getting past you is there?' she said. 'You suspicious old sod. But the truth is, my love, I do not know.'

'But you know something?' He persisted.

Hecaté shrugged elegantly, but there was steel in her tone. 'Let it go,' she told him.

Stiles left it, after all, she wasn't a suspect to be interrogated, and he was sure he would find out more when it all started to go wrong.

'Wembley Stadium,' Pestilence was saying excitedly. 'I always wanted to play Wembley. Or the Garden, yeah!'

'Covent or Madison Square?' asked Famine dryly.

Denny was starting to look nervous. 'Look – guys we don't need …'

'Madison of course,' said Pestilence testily.

'It will not be necessary,' intoned Death sombrely to Denny's relief. 'Here will be fine.'

His relief, however, was to be short lived as Death added. 'People will come.'

'That's true.' said War. 'Remember the Gobi Desert concert of '84? That's 1384,' he added for Denny's benefit. Denny nodded looking bemused, as far as he was concerned, this was getting out of hand.

* * *

The stage was set up, over the muttered objections of Pestilence, in a nearby field.

'Don't see why we couldn't play the Garden,' he moaned. 'Probably the only time ever that it's not booked for something else. Always wanted to play the Garden. Probably be my last chance too.'

Tamar thought she saw an opening here when she overheard this. 'Probably?' she snorted derisively. 'Don't you just know it? After all, after today, there won't be a Garden. There won't be a world even.' To her secret delight, the effect of these words was immediate. His face puckered, and he looked almost as if he was going to cry. 'Not that it matters much,' continued Tamar, pressing her advantage ruthlessly. 'I mean – you won't exist either any more, will you? And even if you did, no more audiences – no more people.'

She decided to leave it there, no point going over the top. Pestilence was looking thoughtful as she walked away.

Denny was looking as if he was going to throw up. Fighting he had been prepared for, but not this! This was far more terrifying. He decided that he would rather have faced a thousand angry vampires – riding dragons – with machine guns – than this.

People were already drifting into the field, just as Death had said they would. They sat on the grass in front of the stage, gazing up at it wonderingly, as if they were uncertain how they had got here, and why. Denny was more afraid of them than he had been of all the devils that Hell could spit out at him. Why the hell, had he agreed to this?

'To save the world,' said Tamar, catching his thought. 'You didn't think it was going to be easy, did you?'

'Huh,' sniffed Denny, 's' all right for you to talk, *you* don't have to get up there.'

'I wouldn't mind if I did,' she retorted, twirling a lock of hair around her fingers.

'No, I don't suppose you would,' said Denny. 'You're a born exhibitionist. I'm not.'

'There's a little bit of the exhibitionist in everyone,' declared Tamar.

'Not me.'

'You'll be okay.' She debated telling him to picture the audience in their underwear, but the presence of several extremely pretty girls in the front rows of the burgeoning audience put her off this idea. Besides, that didn't really work anyway, did it?'

The stage was impressive but not as impressive as the fact that not one of the audience seemed to be in the least surprised that it was there. Pestilence looked out from behind the curtain. 'Hmm,' he frowned. 'Coupla hundred, maybe five or six, not as impressive as usual, I must say.' He turned petulantly to Death. 'If we'd played at the Garden,' he complained. 'We could have been,' he gulped, '*televised.*'

'This is not a large event,' intoned Death. 'It is no more than an informal get together. Be told!'

'It could have been great,' whinged Pestilence. 'Our farewell concert, the last hurrah. And you want to do it in a field in the middle of nowhere. I don't know. Some people have no sense of occasion.'

'I thought we were doing this for *him*,' said War, indicating Denny, who was shivering behind an old packing crate.* 'if this thing gets any bigger I think the poor bugger might have an aneurysm.

'Stage fright,' said Pestilence dismissively. 'It'll go away once he's on stage.'

'Got to get him on stage first,' said Famine dubiously.

'Leave him to me,' said Pestilence confidently. 'They'll love him.'

* * *

The lineup went like this.

On Lead Guitar/vocals – Denny Sanger.

On Rhythm guitar – Pestilence / Lazarus Moult.

On keyboards – Famine.

On the double bass (for some strange reason) – Death / The Grim Reaper

On Drums – War.

Tamar's heart was in her mouth as Denny took the stage. Front and centre, the spotlight shining down on his blond hair, making him look like a skinny rock 'n roll angel.

But Denny himself suddenly relaxed, with the spotlight in his eyes he found that he couldn't see a thing anyway; this was not as bad as he had feared. In any case, it was too late to change his mind now. As the inevitability of the situation dawned on him, he felt a strange calm descend on him. He struck a chord. The band started to play, and Denny opened his mouth, and his heart, and began to sing.

He sang about love, about frustration and longing and thwarted desire. And Tamar recognised the early stages of their relationship, when they had been kept apart by circumstance. Yet this was no sappy "lurve song", it had a rocking beat and it had soul. The audience was transfixed. It was an incredible song and Denny's voice was ardently compelling.

Tamar wept. 'He's singing my heart,' she told Stiles. Although, she was later to deny having said any such sentimental nonsense.

---

* These always turn up behind the scenes on stages. Nobody knows why

Stiles just smiled and said. 'Well of course he is, didn't you know?'

He then sang another song, this time about his dreams of their being together. It was a vivid portrayal of an apparently unattainable fantasy made real in his head.

The audience was rapt as Denny sang next, with the voice of angels, about the fulfillment of his love and the fear of losing it when the world was torn apart. Behind him, War wiped away a surreptitious tear.

'Damn me, he's good,' muttered Pestilence.

Tamar was in bits. 'I never knew,' she said, 'I never knew he had all this inside.'

He was singing about his determination never to be parted from her, not by death or the sweeping away of worlds. He wished her to be strong, he would find her again. He hoped she would be strong enough to survive without him until he did.

'I didn't know he thought like this,' said Stiles.

Nobody was listening to him. Cindy was gazing at the stage in girlish adulation, and the dwarfs were all sniffing into their beards and trying to hide this fact from the other dwarfs. Hecaté was smiling to herself. She had known.

Tamar had not though; Denny had somehow kept this part of himself rigorously hidden from her. She thought she understood why, as the tears fell fast down her face. Hadn't she done the same thing, in her way? 'I mean,' she thought, 'I knew he felt this way, sort of knew anyway. I knew he cared, but I didn't know... I didn't know... about *this*! I didn't know he had thought about it so much, that he could express it this way. No,' she admitted to herself, 'I didn't know about all this, all these feelings, I had no idea that he felt ... felt the same as *me*.'

'And to think,' muttered Stiles. 'I thought all his songs were crap.'

The audience were going wild. Some girls were screaming, not all of them for Denny, it has to be admitted, there are always one or two who prefer the sweaty drummer or the moth eaten rhythm guitarist just to prove their individuality. There was a tentative attempt at underwear throwing, which, fortunately, didn't catch on. If any fool girl had thrown her knickers at Denny at that moment, Tamar would probably have eviscerated her.

Denny sang. He had finally opened his heart, and now it was bleeding all over the stage, it was a relief in a way. Now that he had started, he did not want to stop. Which was okay with the audience, but the Horsemen were getting tired and Tamar did not think she could take much more.

And then, as abruptly as it had begun, it was over. Death waved a bony hand in a gesture of dismissal and there was suddenly a field full bewildered people all wondering what the hell they were doing there when they had jobs to go to, or kids to look after or exams to take etc.

Denny blinked, the field was emptying rapidly. Within a few minutes everyone had gone, except the Horsemen, Tamar, Cindy, Stiles, Hecaté and a crowd of embarrassed looking dwarfs.

'You was crying, I seen you.'

'Was not, you was.'

'Huh, I'd like to see me.'

'Well, you should have been standing where I was then.'

This was Monty Python level satire for a dwarf, and his antagonist was temporarily stumped.

Denny stumbled off the stage which then vanished. 'W-what happened?'

Tamar stared. 'You don't remember?'

'You were singing mate,' said Stiles.

'I know that,' said Denny. 'Why, was sort of what I was getting at.'

The Horsemen bustled towards them.

'Well, that's that,' said Death ponderously.

Pestilence took Denny by the hand before Denny could stop him. 'Wonderful show man, terrific, been a pleasure. Oh sorry about that,' he added, seeing Denny wiping his hand on his trousers, with a look of extreme distaste (And this is Denny, we're talking about, the man who would turn his skin inside out in order to get another day out of it before washing, were the thing feasible. It makes you wonder what Pestilence had on his hands. Probably better not to speculate.)

'That is THAT,' repeated Death ominously. 'We must ride out now.'

The other Horsemen looked at each other uneasily. Pestilence stroked his chin. War stroked his beard. Famine kneaded his doughy cheeks. All looked thoughtful.

It was War who spoke up. 'Well, now,' he began uncertainly. 'What if, and I only say if, sort of as a suggestion you understand? And not as any kind of … Ahem. Well, what I mean is, suppose we, and I'm just throwing this into the air you might say, to see where it lands, and not, as it were …'

'Oh spit it out man!' snapped Pestilence.

'Well, then,' resumed War with an angry look at Pestilence. 'Suppose that we, instead of riding out, suppose we er – didn't.'

Tamar gasped. *Yes*!

'Didn't what?' said Death.

'Um, ride out,' said War in a small voice, then hid himself behind Famine, who could have concealed a killer whale with ease.

'I see,' said Death with what all recognised as a forced calm. 'And do you all feel like this?' he addressed the Horsemen.

'No, No, well, yes, but …'

'Well. The thing is …'

'Um…'

Death held up his hand. 'Am I to understand then,' he said in that sarcastic manner beloved of certain head teachers, 'that my Horsemen have decided, after thousands of years of waiting and preparation, of doing their duty and making ready for the fulfillment of their sacred obligation, that now, on the eve of our finest hour, you have decided *not* to ride out? Is that it?'

The Horsemen quailed.

'Oh God,' thought Tamar, 'they're going to give in, they're afraid of him.'

'Well, yeah,' said Pestilence. 'I suppose that's pretty much it, yeah.' He added this last "yeah" with a certain air of hopeless defiance.

'I see,' said Death again, steepling his fingers threateningly.

Pestilence took up position behind Famine.

There was an ominous silence and then Death asked the one word question that was on everybody's mind. 'Why?'

'Well, see, it's hard to explain,' said War.

'Try,' said Death wryly. 'Humour me.'

'We don't want it all to end,' said Pestilence. 'No more music,' he glanced at Denny who smiled.

'No more food,' added Famine dolefully.

'No more War,'

'No more lovely diseases,' said Pestilence, 'and I was just coming up with a lovely line in blotches and boils too.' He sighed. 'Nothing lethal,' he added hurriedly, seeing Denny's face and realising that this argument was unlikely to win him much support, 'just disfiguring.' This was better, but not much.

'No more Death either, you know,' added War with what he imagined to be great cunning. Death ignored him.

'The fact is,' said Pestilence, 'we like humans and the lad's singing reminded us of that. We never wanted to ride out in the first place, you know. And anyway, without humans, we won't exist anymore either you know. Survival is a natural instinct.'

'For humans,' said Death. 'You are not human.'

'We *look* human,' said War. 'Sort of,' he amended glancing at Pestilence, who was looking more and more like a walking sewage farm every moment. 'And we *feel* human, it's sort of catching, you know.'

'I do not know,' Death assured him.

The other Horsemen shrugged helplessly; there was no good answer to this, and they knew it.

'And do you mean to tell me,' Death continued. 'That these rebellious thoughts have been stirred up to the surface of your feeble minds by music? Mere sounds, beats to a rhythm? Caterwauling?* 'How can this be?

War shrugged again. 'It's hard to explain,' he said again. 'I don't think you can understand. You're dead.'

'Death,' Death corrected him.

'Same difference.'

'Not so,' said Death. 'I have never been alive.'

'Maybe you should try it,' suggested Famine.

'Hmm,' Death appeared to consider this suggestion. 'I think not,' he said. 'It will not be necessary.'

The Horsemen looked downcast.

'I have decided.'

And for a moment, Tamar could have sworn that there was a mischievous twinkle in the lights within his empty sockets as he looked at her. She frowned trying to remember ... something.

'We shall ride out,' there was a groan. 'We shall ride out ...' he paused dramatically. 'With them.' he indicated the bemused assemblage of humans and dwarfs (And one goddess) 'Not against them.'

His empty gaze settled on Tamar. 'You remember now, do you not?'

She nodded dumbly.

Death bowed his skull to her. 'You have won,' he said. 'This round, at least.'

* * *

She had lain close to death, after her struggle with the evil god Ran-Kur, and as she had drifted, she had seen Him.

'Have you come to claim me?'

'No, not yet, this is what they call a "Near Death Experience" the latest thing in popular theology, so they tell me. It's playing merry hell with my schedule I can tell you. But I have to keep up with the times.'

---

* Death naturally has a dead ear.

Tamar had sympathised she remembered. Then Death had offered her a choice, go back to your life as it was, or make a fresh start in a new life. She remembered thinking that this was all wrong; surely, it was the Angel of Destiny who offered that choice. But she had chosen. She had chosen to go back to her old life … hadn't she?

Before she had woken up, Death had given her a letter; it had turned out to be a warning.

In an infinite universe, all things are possible. Choices are but forks in the road. Take heed of the other choice, it may come back to haunt you. Beware your enemy.

We will meet again before the end.

Now she understood.

Askphrit had used that other self –the one who had chosen differently on that fateful night and so dropped into a different destiny, in order to change her life around her. She had become that other Tamar; their different destinies had become the same. Didn't the Fates control all destinies? If it had not been for that choice, that other destiny would never have existed, and she could not have been thrust into it.

'Well, two can play at that game,' she thought.

Tamar now understood what she had to do; she just didn't know how she was going to do it.

Death was watching her appraisingly. Would she figure it out?

'We need to get back into Hell?' she said tentatively.

Death shook his head gently. 'Not yet,' he admonished. 'First, we need to do a little dimension hopping. The Fates are destroyed, remember?'

Tamar stared. 'Of course,' she said slowly. 'I see.'

'I wish I did,' muttered Stiles.

She turned to Denny. 'The Athame?' she asked.

Denny drew it out looking confused. 'Dimension hopping?' he said. 'Where are we going?'

Tamar grinned. 'We're going back to the farm,' she quipped. 'Now that we've seen Paris.'

~Chapter Twenty Eight ~

'WHAT'S THE hold up now?' snapped Crispin.

'The Horsemen appear to have stopped sir.' Replied Talbot

'What? Why?'

'Guess?'

'I am not in the mood for ... Wait – it's her isn't it? Interfering little ...'

'Actually sir, I meant the other thing.'

Crispin narrowed his eyes. 'They're not?' he said disbelievingly. 'At a time like this?'

'Yes sir, I'm afraid so.'

'They're having another bloody concert? At the end of the world?'

'Sorry sir.'

'Oh my God!'

'Sir?'

'Figure of speech lad, just a figure of speech.' Crispin groaned. 'I don't believe this.'

'If it helps sir, she *is* there. I just spotted her.'

'It doesn't.'

'Well, it seems to be winding down sir.'

'Keep an eye on them; I'm going to call upstairs.'

'Um, Sir,'

'Yes?'

'They've gone sir,'

'Gone? What do you mean, gone?'

'Well sir, they've just vanished.'

'Vanished? They can't have vanished,' Crispin's voice was rising hysterically. He thumped the desk. Papers flew in all directions.*.

'Find them,' he hissed menacingly. 'They must be somewhere. Find them now!'

Talbot frowned suddenly. What did he mean, "upstairs"?

* * *

Clive was also watching events with a certain satisfaction. It was not precisely how he had foreseen events panning out. There had definitely been a few unexpected hitches along the way, but this was to be expected, he decided, when dealing with humans. Free will was always a problem, and yet, without it, nothing would ever get done at all. He had not expected Tamar to abandon her efforts to regain the box and go after the Horsemen, but perhaps, after all, it was as well that she had. Destiny was a powerful thing. Despite her disdain for it, she was as subject to its vagaries as everyone else. Perhaps, he mused, that accounted for her attitude. She was more full of pride and arrogance than any person he had ever encountered. However, they were back on track now. That was the main thing.

* * *

Jamie was now facing his destiny*, although he was, as yet, unaware of this. Unaware, in fact, that he even *had* a destiny as such. All he knew was that the hatred that filled his soul had to be appeased somehow, and he believed that he had found the way.†

He was standing in a dark primordial world and not far ahead of him in the shadow of a great tree, lurked his destiny.

* * *

---

* All offices in the universe have random papers lying about even if there's no need for them

† For background on Jamie's destiny, see "Reality Bites".

Denny held up the Athame uncertainly. He glanced at Death. 'Will we remember?' he asked. He had got the point of Tamar's somewhat cryptic remark immediately, and he was not happy about it.

'Yes.'

'Okay, then.' He took a deep breath and sliced the air in front of him, concentrating hard. Stiles and Cindy looked at each other perplexed and then they saw it. As Denny withdrew the Athame, a strange sigil appeared in the air apparently written in fire.

Then the world spun.

'What happened?' asked Stiles.

'We are now in a different destiny,' said Death.

'Huh?'

'He means that we're back where we bloody started from,' said Denny. 'I just hope you know what you're doing.' This last addressed to Tamar.

'And I just hope that you've sent us to the right place,' she retorted.

'Back on the farm,' he said lightly. 'I'm certain,' he added more seriously.

'Okay,' snapped Stiles, now thoroughly fed up. 'Will someone please explain what the hell is going on?'

'Oh, sorry,' said Tamar. 'We're in another dimension ...'

'That much I got,' interrupted Stiles waspishly. 'Why? And what dimension?'

'Basically, one where we didn't destroy the Fates. We're going to need them, you see.'

'So we *are* back where we started from?'

'No, not exactly.' She shot a look at Denny. 'It's more like, where we *would* have been, if we hadn't done it.'

'For every decision you make,' Denny continued, seeing Stiles's confusion, 'two possibilities occur. So, when we decided to destroy the Fates, the possibility existed that we wouldn't destroy them. That we would decide differently. And everything that can happen, does happen – somewhere, see?

This is the world where we didn't destroy the Fates. Why am I explaining this to you, you know this stuff.'

'Yes,' agreed Stiles. 'Sort of, but ... So this isn't the universe that Askphrit mucked about with?'

'Yes, it is, and so is the one we just came from, 'said Denny. 'The difference is, in that one, we fixed it, and in this one, we didn't.'

'They were the same place right up until that point,' supplied Tamar.

'Until we destroyed the Fates?' said Stiles. 'Okay, but why are we here, what do we need them for?'

'Buggered if I know,' said Denny. 'Tamar?'

Tamar winked. 'I'm going to fix Askphrit once and for all,' she said.

'Beware,' said Death, 'that in doing so, you do not destroy your own destiny.'

Tamar rounded on him. 'And what's *that* supposed to mean?' she demanded 'do you know something I don't?'

Death inclined his skull. 'Many things,' he said.

'Well, it doesn't matter anyway,' decided Tamar. 'I'll take that risk if I have to, it'll be worth it. That's the mistake he always made. He always tried to get rid of me without making a mess of his own fate, and he couldn't do it. I'm not even going to try.'

'If this is the universe where we didn't fix the Fates' interference,' said Cindy suddenly. 'Then how come we can remember doing it?'

'That's a good question,' said Denny.

'It is?' Cindy was startled.

'It's not important,' said Tamar. Which meant, to anyone who knew her, that she did not have an answer for it. Denny smiled. And Cindy looked almost relieved. The world was back to normal again.

'Okay,' said Tamar briskly. 'How do we get back into Hell?' she looked around fiercely. 'No one is to suggest dying,' she ordered menacingly. 'We already had that joke.'

'Death is not a joke,' said Death.

'Depends on where you're standing,' said Pestilence languidly, giving Death a wry look.

Death ignored this. 'Ask the Athame,' he told Denny.

'You're kidding!' blurted out Stiles. 'Do you mean to tell me, that we could have been doing that all along, instead of all that messing about?'

'Death does not *make* jokes either,' intoned Pestilence in a fair imitation of Death's usual manner.

'Be quiet,' said Denny 'I'm trying to concentrate.' He squinted ahead of him as if he was trying to make something out. 'Ah, yes,' he said. 'I see it.'

'See what?' hissed Tamar. But Denny did not often have the advantage over Tamar like this, so he just winked and looked mysterious. 'You mean you don't see it?' he asked in mock surprise.'

'Denny!'

He sighed. 'Well, I'll just have to lead the way I suppose. Take my hand and … it might be better if you close your eyes.'

'Why?' she asked, startled.

'It's bright,' he said.

Death nodded.

Tamar had a strange sensation of being dragged by the hair through a long tunnel, she could see the brightness Denny had mentioned through her eyelids and then suddenly it all went dark, and she was falling. She opened her eyes for a moment and then decided to close them again. It was a long way down.

* * *

'Huh,' said Charon huffily. 'You again, I don't suppose you remembered the boat fare this time? Thought not, oh well, s'pose I've got no choice. I ain't messing with you again, in you get. Come on come on, I haven't got all day, who's this?' he poked Denny with a contemptuous finger.

For answer, Denny held up the Athame. 'We've met,' he said dryly.

Charon was not impressed. 'Nice bit of metal work,' he said. 'Looks pretty sharp, done by the same chap who made the scythe for the big chap was it? Looks like his work, or similar anyway. I remember you now. You didn't have the bleedin' fare either. Sodding heroes!'

'Where are the others?' asked Tamar.

'It's just us,' said Denny. 'It was hard enough bringing you with me this way. The tunnel is only supposed to carry one person,'

Tamar was shocked when she realised what this meant. She covered it quickly. 'Where's Death?' she asked to fill the silence.

'Death can't come down here,' said Charon. 'Metaphysical impossibility! You see what I mean?'

Tamar nodded 'I suppose so. So we're on our own?' she turned to Denny.

'Alone at last,' he grinned.

Tamar rolled her eyes. 'Not exactly,' she pointed out, indicating the long queue for the ferry.

'Ah,' said Charon chattily. 'Been very busy lately, what with the Apocalypse and everything. This lot can wait,' he laughed croakily. 'It's not as if they're in any hurry.'

Neither Tamar nor Denny thought this very funny.

* * *

'I said *find* them,' howled Crispin tearing at his head, which was bald (because he thought it made him look dignified).

'I don't want to hear your excuses, I want them found, I … what?'

'I said I've found them sir, all except the girl and her sidekick.'

'All except them?' said Crispin.

'Yes sir, they've dimension hopped sir, but …'

'I don't care,' shouted Crispin, threatening to take right off again. 'Find her. Never mind about the others, and I … wait. Did you say dimension hopping?'

'Yes sir.'

'Hmm,' Crispin calmed down suddenly. 'I wonder if … is it possible. Even she wouldn't do that, would she?'

'Sir?'

'Get me a communicator; we need to tell the top floor about this.'

'Um, sir, we *are* the top floor.'

Crispin gave him a wry look. 'That's what *you* think,' he said.

* * *

The Fates were not easy to find. Tamar, remembering her mythology, knew that they were likely to be well guarded, by a giant spider woman, if memory served. She decided not to impart this particular piece of information to Denny just yet, forgetting that he was considerably better informed on these matters than she was and probably already knew. In fact, it was Denny who found them in the end. A large cave entrance decorated with large cobwebs suggested itself.

Denny inclined his head toward it. 'In there?' he muttered.

Tamar shrugged wryly. She should have known.

'Watch out for Arachne,' said Denny.

'Thank you!' breathed Tamar. 'That's been driving me crazy – *Arachne*!'

'Got any bug-bomb?'

Click, click, click.

'Pardon?'

Click, click! Clickclickclickclickclick!

'Uh oh!'

Tamar turned in exasperation. 'Say "oh shit!" like a normal person will you!'

Clickclickclickclickclick!

'Oh shit! There, happy now?'

'Uh oh.'

It was not exactly a spider. Neither was it a woman, but the term "spider-woman" was not totally accurate either. It was more of a woman-spider-scorpion. Spider body, but with an outrageous sting at the back, woman's head, but, on closer inspection – and only Tamar would have had the nerve at this point to make a closer inspection – the face was kind of spidery. But the main point about her, the thing you really noticed, was that she was absolutely gargantuan.

Denny felt his knees actually knocking together. Nevertheless he whipped out the Athame. 'I'll deal with this,' he said, trying to hold his voice steady. 'You go and find the Fates.'

'Oh?' said Arachne, sarcastically. 'A hero!'

This was almost too much for Denny, if it had not been for his recent training, he would have cut and run. Never, since he had met Tamar, had he felt so much like his old, frightened self.

Arachne sighed. 'I'm getting too old for this,' she said.

'I know what you mean,' said Tamar.

'I mean I'm not a monster, you know,' whined Arachne. 'Just because I look – how I look. Can I help it?' she looked at Denny plaintively.

'Er...no?'

'Right! I mean *you* look like an upended broomstick,' she said unflatteringly. 'S'not your fault though. I don't hold it against you.'

Tamar was starting to laugh. Wasn't it always the way? You enter a scary cave expecting to do battle with a horrible monster and end up holding a counselling session. She filed the broomstick remark away for future use.

'Oh well,' sighed Arachne. 'Better get on with it, I suppose. What's the password?'

This was unexpected. Denny floundered. 'Swordfish?' he hazarded and shut his eyes.

'Probably,' said Arachne surprisingly. 'Sounds right, doesn't it? Sounds like a proper password to me. Okay then that'll do.' She laughed at their stunned faces. 'I can't remember what the password is,' she confided. 'I've been here for a – a – well a very long time anyway. What do they think I am, an elephant? I mean nobody's ever challenged me before, not that I can remember anyway – so ...' she shrugged multiple shoulders expressively.

Tamar and Denny looked at each other in bewilderment.

'So ... we can just go in?' asked Denny. 'And you won't – you won't ...?'

'Won't what?'

'Let's go,' said Tamar firmly, 'before she changes her mind,' she added *sotto voce*. And she dragged Denny past Arachne into the inner cave.

* * *

'Where'd they go?' asked Cindy bewilderedly.

'Into Hell of course,' Death told her.

Stiles narrowed his eyes shrewdly. 'To find the Fates,' he said. 'And you know why, don't you? And you know something they don't too, don't you? Are you going to tell us or what?'

Death looked a little puzzled at Stiles's dictatorial attitude. He had never been subjected to a suspect interrogation before. Stiles only wanted a table to thump intimidatingly to be completely in his element.

'I suppose they've gone to try and change Askphrit's fate, like he did to us,' mused Stiles. 'But it's not that simple is it?' he added challengingly. 'Why? What's going to happen?'

Death shook his head, but it was a gesture of sympathy rather than negation.

Stiles was subtle; he recognised the difference and was alarmed. 'Tell us,' he implored. 'What harm can it do now?'

'They can only move him into another destiny which was already his,' Death explained. 'And by doing so, they will alter their own fate – quite dramatically I'm afraid. I can say no more.'

'But – that can't be right,' objected Stiles. 'He invented a whole new fate for Tamar – didn't he? I mean, that whole thing about her being – normal, and only being twenty odd years old and all that, it's impossible! Unless ...' He stopped. Death was shaking his head.

'I don't get it,' said Stiles. 'It's impossible,' he repeated stubbornly. 'She never could have had that fate.'

'She could, if she chose it,' said Death.

'But she wouldn't choose it,' said Stiles.

'The possibility existed,' said Death.

'How? Who would offer her such a choice?'

'I did,' said Death.

* * *

The Fates greeted Tamar and Denny equably enough. 'We have been expecting you,' said Atropos, the eldest and the one who deals with the future.

'Of course you have,' said Tamar impatiently. 'And I expect you know why I'm here.'

'Of course.'

'You destroyed us,' said Clotho a little resentfully, she deals with the past.

'You're looking well,' said Tamar brusquely.

'I see your point,' said Clotho.

'And now to the present,' said Lachesis. 'You wish us to find that fate where the Djinn Askphrit, did not find Pandora's Box?'

'And combine it with all other of his destinies to make them as one,' said Atropos. 'You wish for the Box to remain lost.'

Denny whistled through his teeth. 'Bloody hell, that's clever,' he muttered. The Fates shared a strange smile between them.

'Can you do it?' asked Tamar.

Again, the Fates shared that strange smile. They were beginning to get on Tamar's nerves. Sooner or later, everybody got on Tamar's nerves.

'Can you?' she reiterated.

'We can, of course,' said Clotho. 'But! You must understand the consequences of your choice, before you make it. Askphrit obtained the Box a long, long time ago.'

'I thought you found it for him,' said Denny.

'That does not change the fact that he has had the Box in his possession for many thousands of years,' said Clotho. We are the Fates. Perhaps you do not understand our power.'

'I understand,' said Tamar. 'This changes things a bit.'

'It does indeed,' agreed Atropos.

'We will show you the destiny that you propose to harness all of his destinies to, and you will see all the ramifications thereof. And then you will make your choice.'

* * *

Tamar was clearly in shock Denny could see that.

'As long as that?' she whispered. 'He's had it all that time?'

'It was the only way for him to secure possession,' said Clotho. 'Before the Box was lost forever you see.'

Tamar nodded miserably. 'I see.' She was avoiding looking at Denny for some reason and this was making him nervous.

'And,' she faltered, 'this is the only way?'

The Fates nodded.

'I see,' she said again, numbly. 'He was clever,' she surmised. 'He was protecting himself against me doing this very thing. How did he know?' She laughed bitterly. Of course,' she said. '*You* told him. Well, he's misjudged me,' she said fiercely. 'If he thought that I wouldn't pull his house down just because I'd have to pull down my own at the same time, he was wrong!'

She looked at the Fates, still avoiding Denny's eye. 'But you knew that too, didn't you?'

The Fates nodded.

'We surmised it, yes,' said Lachesis.

'Okay,' Tamar squared her shoulders. 'What do I have to do?'

'Just pull the thread,' said Atropos.

Tamar grasped the proffered thread in her hand and hesitated for a second.

Now she looked at Denny. 'I'm sorry,' she said and pulled.

* * *

Jamie faced his enemy, who was looking at him with an air of bewilderment.

'What are you?' it asked.

'What you made me,' said Jamie and pulled a dagger from his belt. 'But I can change that,'

'I haven't made anything,' protested the creature.

'Not yet,' said Jamie, 'and I aim to see that you never do.'

'You can't kill me with that.'

'Oh yes I can, one god can kill another you know.'

The creature hesitated. It was the last thing it ever did, as Jamie, with a cold fury in his heart plunged the dagger into its breast, and Ran-Kur died instantly before he ever had a chance to create his race of vampires. Thus did the prophecy made by Askphrit come true, and vampires become nothing more than a story to frighten children – and adults too, if they were of a susceptible nature. Because everything that has ever existed or could possibly exist has to continue to exist somewhere, even if it is only in the mind. And mainframe had another deleted file to clutter up its hard drive.

Two deleted files. Jamie smiled contentedly as he ceased to exist.

~ Chapter Twenty Nine ~

TAMARIA SAT UNDER a tree, slipped off her sandals and dangled her feet in the cool water. 'Ahhh – OUCH!' She jumped up. Something extremely solid and heavy had crashed into her ankle.

'By Zeus!' She cursed and then clapped her hand over her mouth and waited for the thunderbolt. Her mother had warned her about blasphemy, 'You can't be too careful,' she had said, 'seems like there's a god behind every tree these days.'

When nothing happened to her, she said it again. Then she bent over the water. 'Rather like Narcissus,' she thought, although with, she had to admit, little chance of the same result. Her own face having what is charitably called an "unfortunate aspect".

She fished out what turned out to be a large, unusual looking bottle, (unusual to Tamaria that is). In the Far East, where it had come from, it was a perfectly ordinary oil bottle such as you would find a dozen of in every household.

To Tamaria, however, it was an intriguing curiosity. She turned it over a few times, shook it and pulled out the cork.

A piece of parchment slid out as she tipped the bottle up. Curiously Tamaria unrolled it and gasped with surprise as she read the words:

Tamaria of the house of Meneleus, greetings,
Go immediately to the Temple of Artemis. There you will learn what is to your advantage. Bring this bottle with you and come alone, do not be afraid.
A friend.

And that was all.

* * *

There was nothing on the TV, and Denny could not settle. The bottle on the mantelpiece kept drawing his attention. He wondered what was in it. He tried to ignore it, it was just an old bottle, but he kept finding his eyes drawn to it. It was making him fidgety. Eventually he gave up. He switched off the TV with a snarl and flung himself off the bed and grabbed the bottle intending to hurl it into the box it had come from, which he would then take out to the bin. But when he had it in his hand, curiosity overcame him. It was very heavy for such a small bottle. It could not hurt just to have a look inside; maybe there was something valuable in it. Its previous owner had been something of a kook in Denny's opinion. Anything was possible. He pulled out the cork.

He was somewhat disappointed to find only a rolled up piece of paper, somehow he had been expecting – what? He had a vague image in his mind of a lovely girl with a sharp tongue – obviously, he was going mad.

This opinion was confirmed when he unrolled the paper and found that it was addressed to himself.

* * *

Tamaria's curiosity was roused by the cryptic message, and she half suspected anyway, that one of her friends was behind it. She had no notion of being afraid. She was, in fact, aware of a vague hope that the message sprung from a certain young man who had been paying her some attention lately. After considering for only a few minutes, she put on her sandals and hurried off to the temple.

She was slightly disappointed to find only a small and rather old looking man waiting for her there.

He hurried forward. 'Tamaria?' he asked, somewhat doubtfully.

'Yes.'

'My goodness, what a plain mien,' he exclaimed. 'No wonder you ... ahem I apologise. Now to business.'

'What do you want?' asked Tamaria suspiciously. She ignored the remark about her looks; she was used to that. 'Who are you?'

'My name is Clive,' said the man.

'Clive?' said Tamar savouring the curious word. 'What a ridiculous name. And what do you want with me – Clive?' Tamaria had always been rude and she saw no reason to placate the little man, he had not been all that polite to her, after all.

'Have you the bottle?'

Tamaria fished it out of her dress and looked expectantly at him.

'Good, good,' he said. 'Now then, you are going to take a ...' he hesitated, 'a fairly long trip up memory lane. Are you ready?'

Tamaria tried this phrase in her head and frowned. Although it was an unfamiliar saying to her, still she felt that there was something wrong with it.

'Shouldn't that be "a trip *down* memory lane?' she ventured after some thought.

Clive seemed delighted by the question. 'Ah,' he said, happily, 'you always were a sharp one, you. A clever girl no matter what your faults. You don't miss much do you?' he winked at her. 'And you're right, yes. But you see, yours is a rather unusual case,' he said, suddenly serious. 'Your past, you see, lies in the future.'

Tamaria frowned. 'But that doesn't make any sense,' she objected. 'You can't remember the future, it hasn't happened yet.'

'It has to you. You just need to remember it.'

Tamaria gaped. She felt as though she ought to regard this person with suspicion or perhaps pity for his apparent lunacy, but there was something hauntingly familiar about him.

'Ask,' said Clive, shrewdly.

'Er, well, it's just that ... do I know you?'

'You will,' said Clive enigmatically. 'Technically, though, we haven't met yet. Ha, work that one out if you can. Even I have trouble with all this sometimes, and this is supposed to be my job.'

Tamaria looked bewildered.

'Look,' said Clive kindly, 'don't you worry about a thing. You'll remember this meeting someday, although you'll forget about it for a long time, and then all this will make sense I promise. But for now, all you have to do, from your point of view anyway, is get on with your life, it's not as if you have any choice anyway, but this meeting had to happen to avoid perpetuating the paradox, now give me the bottle.'

Tamaria shook her head. 'Not until you explain yourself properly,' she insisted.

Clive sighed. 'You wouldn't understand me if I did,' he told her. 'You must just trust me.' And so saying he snatched the bottle out of her hands.

Tamaria blinked sleepily and opened her eyes. She had, she guessed, after a few moments disorientation, fallen asleep by the river. She picked up the bottle she had found and walked dazedly back into her future – or was it her past?

* * *

Denny, having eventually convinced himself that the note was real, finally came to the sensible conclusion that the note had been placed in the bottle by none other than his supplier, the terrifying Barry. Although why he should feel the need to communicate in such a cloak and dagger fashion was beyond Denny's comprehension when he had a perfectly good telephone that could be used for the same purpose. But Barry was weird sometimes, and Denny did not see why he should have the monopoly on strange behaviour. If Barry wanted to go all X Files on him, who was going to argue? Nobody within reach of those dirty great fists, anyway.

The note said to meet at the old church on Bleak Street ASAP. And, with some slight trepidation on behalf of his kneecaps, Denny set out.

* * *

Tamar turned to Denny. 'I'm sorry,' she said and pulled the thread.

The Fates' cavern faded into shades of grey, which became paler and paler until the whole world went white and empty. Then gradually the colours and features returned. But not the same colours and not the same features.

Tamar was alone now, in a large empty room. The floor was white tiles and the walls were also white, apart from one wall, which was covered in blank monitors.

'Mainframe,' she thought. 'Damn!'

'Clive?' she tried tentatively. 'Hey Clive!' she said, more insistently. Then: 'Clive you little bastard, I know you're behind this, you son of a bitch, what did you do? You'd better show yourself Clive, and you'd better have a damn good explanation for all this.'

'Oh do calm down woman,' said Clive pleasantly, appearing from somewhere behind her. 'I had intended to receive you here, but I was a little late. I apologise.'

Tamar turned and gave him a dirty look; she noticed that he was not alone.

'Ah, some of my colleagues,' he explained airily. 'But we need not concern ourselves with them at the moment. You wanted to know what I had done. And the answer to that is: what I had to.' He smiled at her disconcertingly. 'Remember the temple?' He nodded at her expression of sudden comprehension.

'Your actions in the cave of the Fates caused a temporal paradox of unprecedented proportions. In a single stroke; you messed up over 5000 years.' He looked sternly at her.

For once, she was speechless; she raised her hand to her face in a gesture of horror.

'Indeed,' said Clive grimly. Then his eyes twinkled. 'We could have left you to it, I suppose, but you did it unselfishly, and you did get rid of Askphrit for us, so we felt it only right that we should get you out of the mess you'd got yourself into'

'So, it worked then?' asked Tamar with an effort.

'Oh yes, it worked all right, but you didn't think it through, did you? Always so headstrong.' He sighed and shook his head. 'What did you *think* was going to happen?'

Tamar was uncharacteristically silent.

'Let me explain,' said Clive, almost kindly. 'When you looked into the Fates' tapestry, you saw – what?'

'That there was only one thread of fate in which Askphrit *didn't* find the Box, the one where he didn't meet me, therefore, he never became free. He knew all about that one, of course because he chose that fate himself, or rather, he didn't, but he created the possibility himself when he went into the history files. It was the alternative to killing Denny's grandfather – killing me instead, before we met. Anyway, if he wasn't free, then he couldn't take possession of the Box, because the Djinn are not allowed to own anything. Not allowed possessions of their own,' she added, just to be absolutely clear

'So you decided to sacrifice your own future in order to destroy him. A brave act, but think! If you had never met Askphrit that day, then you wouldn't have been alive 5000 years later in order to change his fate so that you never met him, you see. So, you *had* to meet him that day in order to be able to change his fate so that you never met him. And therein lies the paradox that you created.' He spread his hands.

'So you interfered?' said Tamar, suddenly angry, 'you've changed it back, and it was all for nothing!'

'No, not at all,' said Clive. Askphrit is still trapped in the paradox that you created, and we have no intention of helping *him* out, but you were a different case, we have pulled you out of time. The world goes on, outside of the paradox, just as before, but you are no longer in it.'

'Denny?' Tamar had had a sudden revelation.

'I'm here,'

'We pulled him out too,' Clive told her.

Tamar took a tentative step toward Denny, but faltered, there was a strange look on his face.

Then he smiled at her. 'It's all right,' he said. 'I know all about it. You did the right thing.' He gave a short laugh. 'We almost lost each other there, didn't we?' and he held out his arms to her.

Tamar went to him in relief.

'Very touching,' sneered Clive.

Tamar was nettled. 'So, why did you really take us out of the paradox?' she said. 'I don't believe for a second that it was out of the kindness of your heart. You've left the others there haven't you?'

Clive scowled. 'You're too sharp for your own good you are,' he snapped.

'Yes all right, we needed you, and we thought you'd be much more co-operative if we brought him in too. The fact is, we never expected you to cause such a bloody mess. We thought that you would kill Askphrit and take the Box, which was all you were supposed to do. However, perhaps this way is better after all. We have the Box now, in fact, due to your meddling, we *always* had it. And now ...' he clicked his fingers and a tall robed figure came forward carrying a large box.

'Give her the Box,' said Clive. The figure held it out to her.

'What do you expect me to do with that?' asked Tamar.

'That is up to you,' said Clive. 'The Box is yours, by right of conquest and heredity.'

'Heredity?'

'Yes, you are the direct descendant of Pandora. You always knew it on some level, so you can take that look off your face. The Box comes to you, and now you have to make a choice.'

'I'm not opening it,' declared Tamar.

'You must. It is your destiny.'

'Bollocks! Anyway, I thought you said I had a choice.'

'I meant to say, that only you have the *right* to open it, and lead the world into Tomorrow. A millennium of peace, which you will rule over.'

'What?'

Behind him, Denny was shaking his head. There was no need. Tamar was getting angrier and angrier.

'It is time,' insisted Clive. 'This is what you have been trained for. The free world has run its course, and what a bloody mess it's in too. It's now time for us to intervene, to take over to restore order, restore peace.'

'So, you want me to open this damn Box, cause the Apocalypse and then rule the world in a millennium of peace?' said Tamar scornfully. 'You're saying that I would be like God.'

'Look,' said Clive. 'What you call God, resides in the souls of every human being, all we want is for you to take control.'

'Take God away from them you mean?'

'Well, you would be God, so to speak, in an administrative capacity. You could make the world the way you've always wanted it,' Clive told her. 'No hunger, no war, no suffering.'

'At what cost?' said Tamar?

'What?' Clive was temporarily derailed.

'What you're saying is that you want me to enslave the world for its own good,' said Tamar. 'Well, I won't do it!

'You can have world peace,' she continued, 'or you can have free will, but you can't have both. Being a Djinn taught me that. It also taught me the value of freedom.

'I had some good masters during my enslavement, but the best one was the one who set me free,' she smiled at Denny.

'The world belongs to humanity *now*,' she said. 'And I'm not going to take it away from them.'

There was a stunned silence following this diatribe. Even Denny, who was used to Tamar's speeches, had never heard one quite like this.

Eventually Clive found his voice. 'And that's your final answer is it?' he said.

'Yes!'

Clive bit his lip. 'Well, I can't say that this is completely unexpected. I mean we knew that there was a chance that you would react this way. It's just that, we um, haven't got any plan for this eventuality, as such.'

'Why do you need a plan?' asked Denny. 'Just go with the flow. I promise it won't hurt as much as you think it will.'

Tamar laughed at their shocked faces. 'He's right,' she said. 'You're off the road and travelling without a map now, so … improvise.'

'There's a lot to sort out,' said Clive uncertainly. 'More than you realise. I mean your friends are trapped in a temporal paradox. The son of Stiles has created another Paradox by going back in time, and destroying the race of vampires at their inception, and that paradox occurred within the other, the one caused by you, and both of them resulted in a shift which deleted the fate of Stiles and Hecaté in different ways. We had no plan for this eventuality. We didn't think we would need one. Oh God! I'm getting a migraine.'

Tamar patted him on the back reassuringly. 'I'm sure you can sort it all out,' she said.

'But we have to make certain that the vampires remain erased and that Askphrit remains trapped. We can't just put everything back the way it was.'

'Why you do care?' said Tamar.

'Of course we care,' said Clive pettishly, 'all we have done was intended for the greater good.'

'Perhaps you shouldn't have interfered in the first place,' said Denny somewhat sanctimoniously

'Not the time, Denny,' cautioned Tamar.

'No, no, he's right,' moaned Clive. 'But we meant it for the best.'

'Maybe we can help,' suggested Denny. 'But if we do,' he added warningly, 'you have to promise not to interfere anymore.'

Clive nodded. 'You help us sort out this mess, and I promise. But what can you do?'

'I think I might have an idea,' said Denny. 'Humans are better at this stuff than you lot.'

Clive nodded. He knew it. 'Ain't that the truth,' he said.

'What about our friends?' asked Tamar. 'What's going to happen to them? Can you take them out of time, like you did with us?'

Clive looked perplexed. 'Well, we could, I suppose,' he said. 'Although, it would be a grave misappropriation of our powers. However, we would consider it the least we could do in return for your help. There's just one problem.'

'What?'

'Oh, dear, I had hoped to avoid telling you this. The fact is, we can't find them.'

'What?'

~ Chapter Thirty ~

THE HOODED FIGURE was watching from the rooftop opposite. Hood pulled up, melting into the shadows, invisible as people came out of the building below.

Aha, there he was, not quite what the watcher had been expecting. Older (perhaps mid-forties) and maybe wiser. So strange, how the mind plays tricks. He looked like a good man, but the watcher already knew that he was, and he evidently commanded a certain respect. The watcher was impressed.

The man turned up a side street and the watcher hesitated, was it the right time? Somebody called out to him. 'Goodnight Mr. Stiles.' Ah. The watcher slid silently off the roof and followed him.

In a dark alley, which Stiles had been ill advised to take, the watcher confronted him. She threw back her hood and put out a commanding hand.

Stiles stopped. 'Help you?' he queried wonderingly, his mind elsewhere.

'*I* am going to help *you*,' she told him in a low musical voice, which reverberated in his soul.

'Do I – know you?' he asked uncertainly.

She smiled. 'One day you will,' she said. She frowned 'I am not going to lose you again, my love.'

'I don't understand,' said Stiles.

Hecaté put out a hand and touched his face gently. 'Jack,' she whispered. 'My Jack, it will be all right, you will understand one day. Now, come with me, I need to explain some things, and then you will forget for a time, until it is time for you to remember this meeting. You are not afraid of me?'

'No.' Stiles was mesmerised. He followed her out of the alley and into a nearby church.

* * *

Cindy was doing the magic mirror thing. That is, she was scrying, pausing intermittently to admire her flawless, unlined face and shining blonde hair. She was trying to get a fix on Tamar, although she did not know it exactly, but she had sensed the magic when Tamar had stopped outside her house, and she was curious.

She was startled when a face other than her own appeared in the mirror. It had never worked before. Cindy was not terribly interested in magic that was not about herself. She jumped backwards in surprise, knocking over a vase of roses from one of her many admirers.

The face was that of a young man. He smiled reassuringly at her, and, horror of horrors, he stepped out of the mirror. That was not supposed to happen either – Cindy was certain of that.

The room became filled with a bright light, which seemed to emanate from him and, as he turned, she saw what appeared to be large feathered wings sprouting from his back. No, there was no doubt about it, they *were* wings. An angel!

'Cindy,' he said soothingly, and her eyes opened wide in surprise. Erasmus was faintly amused; he allowed himself the sardonic thought, that it was probably a good thing that she would not remember this meeting for some time; she just was not ready for this yet. Yet there was no doubt that he felt tender toward her. Why else would he be doing this?

* * *

'But she wouldn't choose it,' said Stiles.

'The possibility existed,' said Death.

'How? Who would offer her such a choice?'

'I did,' said Death.

And then the world faded away.

* * *

When it came back, Stiles was in a dark cavern, which he instinctively recognised as part of the Underworld, not Hell, but, he suspected, an annexe. Hecaté's home.

She was lighting candles. 'Remember?' she said.

'Yes, I remember now,' he said. 'But, how did you … know?'

'This place, my home, is a part of the Underworld. There is no time here. This is where I would have been, had we never met, and so this is where I found myself when the world changed. But I remembered, and now, so do you. But you had to take the long way here.' She laughed. 'Down here, there is no time, and we are unaffected by the way the world turns. Here, you will be safe,'

'You remembered?' said Stiles. 'Because you, because you're a …?'

'No, because, from here, things are … different. As I said, there is no time. What happens above is irrelevant down here. I remembered because – it happened!'

'What about the others?'

'Tamar and Denny are safe in mainframe. They too, have been taken out of time.'

'And Cindy?'

Hecaté's expression clouded. 'Alas, I cannot find her.'

* * *

Cindy was sitting, or rather perching, precariously on a cloud. Erasmus was facing her.

'So, you've taken me out of time because I was caught up in a temporal paradox that Tamar caused, is that right?'

Erasmus sighed with relief. It had taken her long enough to get the point.

'Exactly!' he said.

'Wow, thanks!'

Erasmus inclined his head graciously. There was a silence.

Cindy might not have been the sharpest tool in the playpen, but she could sense moods. Erasmus was uneasy.

'Will you get into trouble for this?' she asked with a perspicacity that was not to be expected of her. He did not answer her.

'Eugene?'

He raised an eyebrow.

'I'm sorry, I always think of you as Eugene.'

'With you, I *am* Eugene,' he said 'When I first saw you, I thought you the most beautiful thing I had ever seen.'

Cindy bowed her head. 'You can't think that now,' she said. 'You can see me as I really am, can't you? You can see, that my face, my youth, is just a glamour.'

He smiled tenderly at her. 'You *are* vain,' he said 'But after all, vanity is only a venial sin, and if you are vain, you are also kind hearted and good and patient and you have never strayed from your own honourable ideals.'

Cindy blushed.

'And you were kind to me, and patient with me as Eugene, a task that, I see now, could not have been easy at times. I was so lonely when you crossed my path, and even though you may not have realised it, you pitied me. So, you helped me and took me away from my lonely life. Without you, I should never have regained my wings. I think, for that, this was the least I could do for you.'

'I was lonely too,' she said.

'I know,' he smiled again. 'It will not always be so.'

Cindy looked down at the cloud. 'So, what happens if I rock like this?'

'Don't!'

* * *

'The goddess must have helped them,' said Clive, thoughtfully, 'she alone has that power. I daresay they are safe enough.'

'Hecaté?' cried Tamar.

'Yes, her. They have clearly been taken out of time, as you were. They're probably in the Underworld.'

'You're no ordinary clerk are you?' said Denny.

'No!' said Clive shortly.

Well,' said Tamar, there's one way to find out if you're right.' She folded her arms defiantly, to indicate that this was non-negotiable.

'I *am* right,' said Clive. 'They certainly are not here, and they are not in time. Therefore, they can only be in either the underworld or one of the other afterlife dimensions, Heaven or suchlike.'

But Tamar was insistent, and Clive was forced to co-operate.

When he found out where Cindy was, he was not pleased. But Tamar said that if he punished Erasmus, she personally would see to it that he spent the rest of eternity with his head up his own arse. And Clive was not at all certain that she could not do it.

'Okay,' he said to Denny sourly. 'What's this brilliant idea of yours then?'

~ Chapter Thirty Two ~

TAMAR PEEPED HER nose out from under the mass of bubbles. 'Ahhh, it's nice to finally relax,' she said. Denny was shaving – an almost unheard of activity, but occasionally Tamar insisted. Besides, it gave him a good opportunity to watch her in the bath, an occupation not to be sneezed at.

'Almost two weeks with no trouble at all,' he agreed. He looked pensive for a moment. 'It's just not the same without old Askphrit around stirring up trouble is it?'

'You sound as though you miss him.'

'No-o, I wouldn't say that exactly, but …'

'Bit boring?'

Denny pinched his fingers together. 'Little bit,' he admitted.

Tamar laughed contentedly. 'We deserve a break,' she told him.

The world was almost back to normal now. Some things were different, and Denny and Tamar viewed these minor differences as a sort of private joke they shared with the universe. There were big differences too, of course. The main one being, of course, that the war had never happened, it being Askphrit's *coup d'état* in Hell that had kick-started the whole Apocalypse thing in the first place. And finally, Askphrit had gone for good.

* * *

Denny's idea! It had been so simple in the end. Too simple for the clerks (who had spent millennia concocting multiple, intricate and ludicrous shady plots) to comprehend. He told them just to leave it alone.

'Everything that's happened, *stays* happened,' he had said. 'No more messing about with time or alternate dimensions or people's fates. That's what got us into this mess.'

The Clerks had sent up a stream of noisy protest at this, but Denny continued. 'No, enough is enough already. Askphrit is gone, the vampires are gone, now we have to look to the future, not back.'

Then he had suggested that to keep things tidy, they create a "Paradox file" to shove Askphrit into.

This, it appeared, was more like it. Clerks like things tidy, which Denny had realised, it was the main point of their existence.

'He'll be happy enough,' said Denny. 'He'll never know the difference. It's like putting him back in his bottle – *permanently* this time.' He gave Tamar a wry look.

The Clerks agreed, and Denny was satisfied, it would keep them busy and stop them from interfering which, as far as he was concerned, was the main thing. That it was a totally pointless exercise, was largely irrelevant. Neither Tamar nor Denny felt inclined to point out that Askphrit could never escape from the Paradox in any case, nor would he try, since he would be unaware of it. The Clerks seemed to think it was such a good idea.

* * *

And now they were back home. They had taken up residence in Clive's house, since he would not be needing it anymore, and they had, in this new world order, never lived in Askphrit's old mansion. Cindy had moved into Denny's old flat in London, it being far bigger and better furnished than her own, and Stiles and Hecaté remained, for the most part, in the underworld, although, Stiles still had offices in London, and also Manchester, Liverpool. New York, Hong Kong and Los Angeles. (Teleporting had its advantages).

JACK STILES P.P.I (Private Paranormal Investigator) and business was alarmingly brisk. But he spent most of his time, trying to find out what had happened to his son and if there was any way to bring him back. At this, Hecaté just smiled. She had a secret.

* * *

Tamar lifted a leg lazily out of the water and surveyed it complacently. Denny, however, was not watching. He was thinking.

Piqued, she pouted at him. 'What are you dreaming about?'

'Remember that other world, I mean the one Askphrit created for us?'

Tamar shuddered. 'Yes, I remember, it was terrible. No magic, no ...'

Denny smiled remotely. 'It wasn't *all* bad. At least we were together. And there isn't as much magic around now as there was, I don't think.'

'Oh I don't know,' said Tamar, and she gave the bathmat a stern look, and it turned into a chicken and hopped away.

Denny ignored it. 'At least we were together,' he reiterated. He definitely had something on his mind. 'Married actually,' he said, glancing at her questioningly. 'How come we never got married, do you think?'

Tamar shrugged. 'We never had time, I suppose.'

'We have time now,' he suggested.

Tamar opened her eyes wide. 'Denny! Do you mean it?'

Denny shrugged. 'I guess so.'

'Oh no, no, no. No you don't.' cried Tamar leaping gracefully from the bathtub. 'If you're going to propose, you do it properly! Down on one knee with you, go on!'

'I'll take that as a "yes" shall I?' said Denny laughing.

* * *

Having finally gone down on one knee as instructed, and producing a sparkling diamond (with the aid of the Athame) Denny was now waiting at the altar for his bride. He had never felt so damn nervous in his whole life. He wondered, vaguely, why he was. It seemed as though it was a universal symptom of bridegroomhood. Stiles had said that he had felt exactly the same – both times. It was, undoubtedly, just the vibrations of countless terrified bridegrooms reverberating throughout the universe.

Hecaté was maid of honour, as a married woman, a very married woman. She walked before Tamar with her hands placed protectively over her stomach – she was very large now. Cindy had wondered audibly whether it would be a boy or a girl. But that was just Cindy.

'Today a wedding, tomorrow a christening and next week a funeral,' mused Tamar.

'A funeral?' squawked Cindy, 'whose?'

'Denny's if he doesn't stop looking so hunted,' retorted Tamar tartly.

Hecaté smothered a laugh. 'They all look like that,' she assured her. 'Don't take it personally.'

'At least I talked him out of having the theme from "Star Wars" playing as I walked up the aisle,' said Tamar. 'Men!'

But it was a radiantly happy bride who met her husband-to-be at the altar, and when they looked into each other's eyes and saw the love-light shining there, all doubts were swept away.

No one noticed the large, swirling vortex that had opened up behind the happy couple until it was too late.

Denny yelled in protest as Tamar was sucked backwards into the heart of the vortex. He ran toward her, his hand outstretched to grab at her, but he was just too late.

'What the hell …?' cried Stiles?

Denny was silent, lost for words. Drowning in misery, which would soon turn to fury.

* * *

Tamar was set down in a dusty chamber, which appeared to be filled with statues, glass cases, old musty books and packing crates. It looked like a cross between a library and a museum.

She was seething.

She tried to teleport, which apparently amused the old gent who had appeared from behind a large packing crate. 'I'm afraid your powers are no use to you here,' he said nastily. 'I've got the whole place shielded.

'So, what?' snapped Tamar, 'I can still kick your head in.'

'No, I think not,' he said, waving a hand at her, she froze. 'Shielded against all magic but my own, I should have said.'

'Okay, so you're a wizard,' said Tamar.

'A sorcerer, actually, Thespis is my name, and I should be more polite if I were you'

'If you were me,' snapped Tamar, 'you wouldn't be wearing those god-awful sandals. Now, what do you want with me?'

'Why are you wearing that old fashioned dress?' Thespis retaliated.

'It's my wedding day!' stormed Tamar.

'I see, how unfortunate.' He gestured around the room. 'My collection,' he said. 'Everything in it, one of a kind.' He leered at her. 'Like you,'

Tamar rolled her eyes. 'One of those,' she thought.

She glanced around the room. Yes she could see it now, the arms of the Venus de Milo, (Idly she remembered posing for that statue, and knocking the arms off in a fit of pique, because he had made them too fat.) The frowning version of the "Mona Lisa" (Tamar could not see much difference.) The collection swung from the sublime to the ridiculous. Art treasures (it looked as if he had raided the cellars of the Louvré) were filed side by side with pieces of abhorrent kitsch.

'A garden gnome?' Plenty of those about but, she had to admit, she had never seen one doing *that*!

She wondered if he had had it specially made, but no, that would be cheating! This guy might stoop to kidnap and theft, but never forgery.

And gruesome relics. A dragon skull – she thought she recognised it – giant's bones and the brain of Da Vinci, clearly labelled. (Pretty pointless, that one, it was not as if he was using it anymore, it was now just a lump of gristle – pointless *and* horrible.)

And, to her horror, in a cage languished the Purple Hart. The only other live specimen, besides herself. This thought brought her back to her original question.

'And in what way am I one of a kind?' she asked jeeringly.

'The only Djinn ever to have escaped from slavery with your powers intact,' he told her, 'how can you ask?'

Oh the irony of it. There *had* been another – damn Askphrit! It always came down to him.

She was resigned. She was unable to move, for now. And the sorcerer was busy constructing a glass case for her. But Denny would track her down. She had no doubt. In fact, she could already sense him coming. An indication that the shielding around this place was inadequate. And by God, he was going to be furious when he did.

'I wouldn't give a spit's chance in a hot stove for this guy when he gets here,' she thought.

Well, the quiet life could not last forever. Something like this was bound to happen eventually. Askphrit had not been the only lunatic in the world, after all.

Her last thought as the glass case was put into place around her was. 'Here we go again.'

COMING UP NEXT

Tamar Black – Faerie Tale

"All the world's a Stage"

Tamar's back! (Yes - again)

And this time, she is off the chart and travelling without a map.

There are Faeries in the woods, and they are not the cute little wingéd creatures from the stories your mummy read to you.

Faeries are, at best, con artists and tricksters.

And, at worst, homicidal maniacs.

And these faeries are out to take over the world.

Just for the fun of it.

SCI'ON – The Shadow Worlds

Whenever a decision is taken that is of significance to the world, the world divides and two alternate futures are created.

In the beginning, there was only one world. That world we name SCI 'ON. All other worlds that sprang from it we name the Shadow Worlds.

Some believe SCI 'ON is the only real world and that all others are mere reflections; hence the name. Others believe that all the alternate worlds are equally real and important – however they may have come into being.

Whatever the case, one thing is certain. If SCI 'ON itself – the cradle of creation – were to be destroyed, all other worlds would cease to exist. For SCI 'ON is the mainspring and without it, the shadow worlds would have no point of origin.

*

Johnny Hammond is not your ordinary computer nerd. He has the makings of a hero.

When a mysterious man shows him the way to SCI 'ON Johnny becomes obsessed. And only he can find a way to get there through the myriad of shadow worlds that stand in his way.

But someone does not want him to get there.

From earliest childhood, Ryan and Kai have been best friends. The fact that they come from separate universes is not allowed to stand in their way.

As they grow up, they realise that this ability to travel between the worlds is no mere coincidence, as their ultimate destiny unfolds.

About the Author

Nicola Rhodes often can't remember where she lives so she lives inside her own head most of the time, where even if you do get lost, it's still okay.

She has met many interesting people inside her own head and eventually decided to introduce the rest of the world to them, in the hopes that they would stop bothering her and let her sleep.

She has been doing this for ten years now but they still won't leave her alone.
She wrote this book for fun and does not care if you take away a moral lesson from it or not.

You have her full permission to read whatever you wish into this work of fiction. As she says herself:

"Just because I wrote this book, doesn't mean I know anything about it."